A Long Highway

Michael Embry

A Long Highway

The waitress returned with Cora's order. They sat quietly for a few minutes while she took a few bites from her food. Micah picked the paper up and glanced quickly over the agate page to check on scores and the day's schedule.

"So what are your plans this evening?" he asked.

"I'll probably stay at home. I may rent a video or something."

"No hot date?"

"Not for me," she said. "I'll probably be working until early evening. There's not much of social life for this girl."

Micah looked at his watch and saw that it was 10:15.

"I've got forty-five minutes to get to the ball park and the same for you for the news conference," he said. "I think we'd better hit the road."

"Thanks for sharing the booth with me."

"It was my pleasure. It's nice to have someone to talk to in the morning."

After they paid their checks at the counter, they had to go in separate directions to their cars. They stopped at the midway point in the parking lot.

"I hope you have a nice weekend with your children," she said.

"Thanks," he said. "You have a good weekend, too."

Micah didn't move for a couple of seconds as he watched her walk toward her car. He took in her shapely figure before she suddenly turned her head and glanced back at him. Micah felt his face flush and grinned.

"Bye," he said sheepishly and waved.

Cora smiled and then walked on to her vehicle. Micah shook his head slightly and went on his way.

A Long Highway

Michael Embry

A Wings ePress, Inc.

Mainstream

Wings ePress, Inc.

Edited by: Rosalie Franklin
Copy Edited by: Leslie Hodges
Senior Editor: Leslie Hodges
Managing Editor: Karen Babcock
Executive Editor: Marilyn Kapp
Cover Artist: Trisha FitzGerald-Jung

All rights reserved

Names, characters and incidents depicted in this book are products of the author's imagination or are used fictitiously. Any resemblance to actual events, locales, organizations, or persons, living or dead, is entirely coincidental and beyond the intent of the author or the publisher.

No part of this book may be reproduced or transmitted in any form or by any means, electronic or mechanical, including photocopying, recording, or by any information storage and retrieval system, without permission in writing from the publisher.

Wings ePress Books
http://www.wings-press.com

Copyright © 2009 by Michael Embry
ISBN 978-1-59705-613-7:

Published In the United States Of America

Wings ePress Inc.
3000 N. Rock Road
Newton, KS 67114

Dedication

Mickey and George Hackett

One

A soft, warm breeze filled the pressbox behind home plate at Riverfront Stadium,
  giving some relief from the humidity that was typical of Cincinnati during muggy July evenings. The Ohio River slowly flowed by several hundred yards away while the lights across the river in Covington flickered in the heavy air. A sparse crowd sat throughout the ballpark, drinking beer or sodas to beat the heat. Except for an occasional shout at players or umpires from a few of the diehard fans, most of those in the stands appeared to be sitting in their seats in a dull stupor instead of being involved with what was happening on the field.
  "This is the worst time of the year to watch baseball," Micah Stewart, sports columnist for the *Cincinnati Register*, said while peeking out over the pressbox railing. "The team is already out of contention and you've got to sit here and watch them go through the motions. They're bored. The fans are bored. I'm bored. We're all bored."

"Don't complain to me, buddy," said Frank Smith, the newspaper's beat writer. "I've got to be out here every game. At least you can pick and choose what you want to write about. I'm stuck with them through the end of the season."

Micah laughed lightly and took a swallow from a cola. He wiped off perspiration on his neck and leaned back in his chair.

"You've got a point," Micah said. "At least we're past the All-Star game. It's all downhill now."

"Hell, it's been all downhill from the first week of the season," Frank said while recording a groundout in his scorebook. "They haven't been in contention since losing their first eight games. It's been pitiful. Oh well, maybe next season they'll be better."

"That's right. There's always next season. That's why people keep coming back. There's always that hope that things will be different. Hmm, I believe I've got a column idea," Micah said with a chuckle.

"Haven't you written about that already?"

"I'm sure I have, several times if you wanted to be technical about it. I just regurgitate words and try to put a different spin on it. At least you have a different game to write about each time. The results may be the same most of the time but it's still a different game."

"But you know it's drudgery to have to go to the clubhouse and talk to the players," Frank said with a frown. "They're not in any mood to talk about the game. Especially the veterans. They've been through this before."

"You'd think if they didn't like it that they'd try to do something about it," Micah said. "Like win a few more games."

"Hey, you're being too hard on the boys," Frank said. "They can't help it if they're not very good. Blame management."

"You're right," Micah said. "It's the front office that assembled this group of players."

The Dodgers were leading, 8-3, in the top of the eighth. The Reds would need to stage a big rally to pull out a victory but that was unlikely since they had shown little capability of coming back in games because of the lack of power hitters.

"What are you doing after the game?" Frank asked. "Care to go over to the Dugout for a few beers?"

"I don't think so. I've got to attend my son's game tomorrow morning. I promised him I'd be there."

"Then you'd better be there," Frank said. "You don't get many makeups on games when your children are growing up. Before you know it, they're grown and out the door. Cherish these opportunities."

"Hey, I know what you mean. I've already missed quite a few games in the past couple of years. It didn't seem that important at the time but now I know that it was."

"Don't get a guilt trip over it. Some things can't be helped. We're not the only people who miss activities while kids are growing up. It happens to everyone. You just try to make the events that you can. Kids understand more than you think."

"Yeah, but it still doesn't make things easy. I missed enough activities that it helped bust up my marriage."

"That was probably just part of it, pal."

"I know but it still doesn't justify everything that happened," Micah said. "Sometimes I wish I had never got into this profession."

"It was glamour, friend. Going to the big game, being in the middle of everything that was going on."

"It seemed like a big deal coming out of college," Micah said. "I guess that's why they call journalism a young person's game. That's when you've got the enthusiasm and energy for it."

"Hey, you're getting me depressed," Frank said with a laugh. "I've got this terrible ballclub to watch every day, and now you have to throw this heavy stuff on me."

"Sorry, pal," Micah said, raising his eyebrows in amusement. "Just felt like unloading on someone."

"Thanks," Frank said, rolling his eyes.

The Reds rallied in the bottom of the ninth, scoring three runs, but still fell 8-6. Micah and Frank and the other sportswriters and sportscasters rushed to the respective clubhouses for quick interviews and returned to the pressbox to file their stories and beat evening deadlines. About the only sounds were the pecking on the keys of laptops and the ruffling of paper as reporters flipped through notebooks finding the right quotes for their stories.

Micah finished his column before Frank wrote the game story and waited for him in the rear of the pressbox after packing up his gear.

"This is a helluva life," Micah said as they walked out to the media parking lot. "While most people are at home, here we are just finishing work."

"Boy, you're really down about something," Frank said, shaking his head slowly. "What's bugging you? You going through some burnout or something?"

"Oh, I don't know. I guess I'm just a little tired right now. I could use a vacation and get away from all of this for a week or so. Need to get the batteries recharged."

"You sure there's not more to it than being tired?"

"I'm sure there's more. I know I'm restless. I'll give you a report in a day or so." Micah said with a laugh.

"Sure you don't want to talk about it over a couple beers right now?"

"Thanks, Frank, but I really need to be getting home if I'm going to make it to Ben's ball game."

"Oops! I forgot about that. Well, give me a call if you want to talk about anything."

"Will do," Micah said. "I'll see you later."

Micah got into his Ford Explorer and sped out of the parking lot and onto the deserted streets. The street lights cast an eerie glow in the heavy air as he headed home to Mount Adams. He had lived in a two-bedroom townhouse since splitting with his wife, Alice, more than two years ago. It was an amicable divorce and they still remained friends while raising their children, twelve-year-old Ben and ten-year-old Annie.

The red answering-machine light was blinking as he walked into the living room. He laid down his laptop computer satchel on the couch and touched the replay button.

"Dad, this is Ben. Don't forget my ball game in the morning. The game starts at nine at Treadwheel Park. I'll see you. Bye."

Ben's high-pitched voice brought a smile to Micah's face. He wished the marriage had worked out with Alice because he dearly missed his children. Even though he wasn't around them as often as he wanted to be, it was always comforting to go home and have them in his company. He kept framed photos of them on the top shelf of the walnut book case in the living room.

Micah glanced around the living room, picked up three magazines and stacked them neatly on the coffee table. He took the pillows on the couch and put them on each corner. He smiled to himself. Everything appeared nice and tidy. He always put his dirty clothes in a hamper and tried to keep the bathroom clean. While the apartment didn't have any expensive or eye-catching furnishings, he tried to keep it orderly for when his children visited or friends dropped by unexpectedly.

Micah turned on the television, flipping on ESPN to catch the latest sports news. He could never sleep after getting home from covering an event and usually spent about an hour watching TV or reading the newspaper. He watched the last twenty minutes of SportsCenter and then used the remote to click on CNN for any late-breaking news.

Micah glanced at the clock on the bookcase and saw it was three a.m. He turned off the TV and went to bed, knowing he wouldn't be getting much sleep before going to the park to see Ben's game.

Two

The alarm clock blared at eight a.m. Micah, his eyes heavy from only five hours sleep, reached over and turned it off. He lay in bed for several minutes, trying to get the energy to crawl out. He glanced back at the clock and realized ten minutes had already passed. It was a twenty-five-minute drive to Treadmill Park and he knew he couldn't waste any time now. He got out of bed, quickly pulled the covers over the pillows, took a quick shower and brushed his teeth. He put on a pair of jeans, T-shirt, and tennis shoes and headed out of the door by 8:30.

The air was sticky and humid, and heavy gray clouds filled the sky as he drove to the park. Ben's game would the first of the day. There would be games played until dusk as teams would show for games in assembly-line efficiency.

Ben was already out on the field taking infield warm-ups from his shortstop position when Micah pulled into the parking lot. He glanced over at the playground equipment as he got out of his vehicle and saw Annie on the swings with several other girls.

Walking up to the bleachers, he found Alice on the fourth row behind the third-base dugout, among the throng of parents who dutifully come out for each game to cheer on their kids. She saw him, waved her hand, and smiled brightly. Micah slowly worked his way up to her as several fans scooted over for him to get through.

"I wasn't sure if you were going to make it today," she said as Micah sat down beside her in a spot she held for him with her purse. "I saw your column this morning and realized you had to work late last night. I told Ben coming over that you might not make it this morning. He was confident you'd be here."

"We got out of there late but I was determined to be here," he said. "Frank invited me to go out for a few beers with him but I declined the offer."

"That must have been a first," she said.

"I can't argue with that. I've missed too many games because of those late-night happy hours. But I'm here now."

"And that's all the matters right now," Alice said while pushing her short honey-blonde hair back behind her ears. "I know Ben will be pleased."

Ben's team, the Rookies, finished practice and trotted back to the dugout. Ben looked up to the bleachers and saw Micah and Alice. He flashed a big grin and quickly waved before disappearing into the dugout with his teammates. Micah threw up his hand and smiled back. The Colonels then ran out on to the field for warm-ups.

"That boy has really grown," Micah said, almost to himself. "Where has the time gone?"

"He's becoming a young man." Alice said. "He's really developed a man's appetite. You wouldn't believe how much he eats at supper."

"I've got an idea. I took him to Burger King a couple weeks ago and he had two Whoppers, large fries and a shake," Micah said with a laugh. "Speaking of food, can I get you anything at the concession stand? I think I could use a cup of coffee."

"I'll take a cup of coffee," she said. "Thanks."

Micah waited at the concession area while a fresh pot of coffee was percolating. A minute later, Annie's thin arms were wrapped around his waist. He lifted her up and gave her a kiss on the cheek.

"How's my little sweetheart?" he said as she put her arms around his neck. He patted her long, blonde hair that touched her shoulders.

"I'm doing fine, Daddy," she said. "Did you come to watch Ben play ball?"

"I came to see Ben and you," he said with a wide smile.

Micah lowered Annie to the ground and went over to the concession stand and got the coffee. He remembered to put one packet of creamer and two packets of sugar in Alice's coffee. He emptied two creamer packets in his cup.

"Do you want anything?" he asked Annie. "A soda or something?"

"Can I have some M&Ms?" she asked with pleading eyes.

"Only if you promise not to tell you mother I bought them for you," Micah said. "It's too early in the morning for candy." Micah said.

"Okay, Daddy. It's our secret."

Micah paid the concession worker and handed the pack of candy to Annie.

"The game is due to start in a few minutes," Micah said. "Do you want to sit up in the bleachers with mom and me?"

"Is it okay if I go back to the swings with my friends?"

"That's fine, sweetheart. Just be careful."

Annie scampered back to the playground while Micah went back to the bleachers. The team managers were at home plate, giving the umpires their lineup cards when he reached Alice.

"I saw Annie for a few minutes," he said.

"I know you did," Alice said with a mock-angry face. "I saw you buy her some candy. You're going to spoil that child."

They both laughed.

"How are things with you and the kids?" he asked. "Anything I should know?"

"Everything's been going well. We're planning a trip to my parents' house in a few weeks, after Ben finishes baseball. Other than that, we'll start preparing for another school year."

"I know you'll let me know if you need anything," he said.

"Well, I could use a free weekend if you've got one coming up," she said.

"Sure, just let me know. I'd love to have the kids over."

"Next weekend would be great if you could arrange it. Graham asked me to go with him to the philharmonic concert at the zoo next Saturday night."

"That shouldn't be a problem," Micah said. "I'll mark it on my calendar. Let me know if anything else comes up. I saw Graham last night at the ball park for a few minutes."

"He called before his sports report," Alice said. "He mentioned that you and he had chatted before the game."

"Yeah, he came out and did interviews with a few of the players and had to go back to the station and go over the film for the 11 o'clock news," Micah said.

"Graham was wondering if you'd mind if he came here to see Ben play."

"I don't mind," said Micah, shaking his head in mild amusement. "He should know better than that. I've always liked Graham. I can't believe he always wants my permission on these things. I think it's great that you and he are seeing each other, not that it's any of my business who you date."

"The kids really seem to like him. He doesn't force himself on them."

"That doesn't surprise me. He's always been laid-back. He's a real gentleman. How are things going with him for you?"

"Oh, we're dating pretty steady now. I guess you could say that we're getting to the serious stage," she said as a smile crossed his lips.

"Marriage?"

"I don't think so, at least not in the near future. The kids and work keep me too busy to even think about that. And I don't believe Graham is the type to rush into anything. He seems somewhat content with things as they are."

"You know, I'm glad that we've been able to remain friends after all that happened between us," Micah said. "I know it's been good for the kids, and I think it's been good for us, too."

"I'm glad, too," she said, looking into his deep brown eyes. "We just had one of those marriages that ran out of steam. I'm happy that we were able to see that before it turned nasty like it does in so many other marriages."

They were so locked in conversation that they didn't notice Ben smacking the ball to the right-center field fence until they heard they fans cheering.

"Way to go, son," Micah said as he and Alice stood and clapped their hands. "Way to hit the ball."

Ben looked up to the bleachers from second base and could see them standing up and waving. He grinned and nervously tipped the bill of his cap.

"I can't believe I missed so many of these opportunities," Micah said as they sat down. "I must have been a fool to think that covering another sporting event was more important than being here with Ben."

"Micah, don't start feeling guilty," Alice said, patting him on the side of the leg. "Those games you had to go to were part of your job. That put food on the table, paid the mortgage and bought clothes. We can't be everywhere for our children. We have to pick and choose. I don't even make it to everything."

"I know but I think I got carried away with it," he said solemnly. "I made too many wrong choices."

"I don't think you've ever sounded this down about things," Alice said. "Is something else troubling you?"

"I don't know," Micah said, shrugging his shoulders. "Frank asked me the same thing last night."

"So I'm not the only person picking up on it?"

"Like I told Frank, I think I need a vacation or something."

At that time, Annie came up and sat down between them. Her shorts and socks were dirty from playing in the sand.

"Can you come home with us after the game, Daddy?" Annie asked.

"Oh, sweetie, I can't," he said, glancing over at Alice. "I've already made plans for the afternoon, and I'm sure that mommy has something planned for you."

"Oh, Daddy, Mommy won't mind. Do you, Mommy?"

"How would you like to go to Daddy's house next weekend?" Alice said while brushing sand off the seat of Annie's jeans.

"That'd be super," she said with a big grin.

"We'll go to a movie and then go out for some pizza," Micah said. "Would you like that?"

"Sure," Annie said. "I can't wait."

Ben's team won, 14-8, and he had two doubles and drove in four runs. He hurried over to Micah after a brief team meeting in the right field foul area.

"Did you like that game, Dad?" he asked enthusiastically.

"I thought you were great," Micah said, tapping the top of Ben's cap. "I think you play on a good team this season."

"We're doing pretty good," Ben said. "We've won five games and lost two so far. We're in second place."

"We're going to Daddy's next Saturday," Annie blurted. "He's going to take us to a movie and for pizza."

"Cool," Ben said wide-eyed.

They walked over to the parking lot. Micah and Ben talked about the Reds while Annie was telling Alice about some new beanie babies that her friends had bought in the past week.

"I'm glad you could be here this morning," Alice said as she opened the side door to let the children into her green van. "They really enjoy seeing you."

"I enjoy being with them. I'll give you a call early next week to finalize plans for next weekend."

"And please let me know if I can help you about the other stuff," she said. "Don't get depressed over things. Okay?"

"I'll talk to you later," Micah said as he turned and started to walk toward his vehicle. "Bye."

Micah waited until Alice backed out of her parking space. The children waved as they passed by his vehicle. He smiled with closed lips and waved back at them. He sat quietly in the vehicle for a few minutes, reflecting on the time he had spent with his family. He suddenly felt empty inside. He turned on the ignition in the vehicle and left the park.

Three

The phone rang as Micah unlocked the front door to his townhouse. He ran over to pick up the receiver before the answering machine clicked on.

"Hello," he said, a bit out of breath as he plopped down on the couch.

"Did you just finish a marathon?" a cheerful voice on the other end asked. "I hope you're not having a heart attack."

"Nah, I just got home from Ben's ball game," Micah said. "I was opening the door when the phone rang and hurried over to answer it. What's up, Josh?"

Josh Larkin edited Micah's book about Cincinnati's Big Red Machine of the 1970s. They developed a close friendship, occasionally going out for drinks or dinner to discuss the project and discovered they had more in common than sports.

"I was wondering if you had any plans for tonight," Josh said. "I was thinking about going down to that new pub that just opened on Fourth Street. It's close to the newspaper."

"Big Shots?"

"That's it. I've heard they've got pretty good food and the atmosphere isn't bad either. Care to join me?"

"Well, let me look on my busy social calendar and see if it's clear for tonight," Micah said with a light laugh. "It looks like I'm free for the evening."

"Do you want to meet there around seven or so?"

"Sounds fine with me. See you then."

Micah spent the afternoon writing a column for the Sunday paper. He wrote about the Reds needing to acquire some power hitters in the offseason in their rebuilding process to become contenders again. Whether they were winning or losing, people wanted to read about the Reds. He transmitted the story from his laptop to the *Register* sports department and called to make sure they received it.

"Give me a call if you have any questions," Micah told copy editor Joe Morris. "I'll be around the house for another hour or so."

"Thanks, Micah," said Joe, a crusty veteran who had been at the newspaper for thirty-five years. "I don't think we'll have any. How's everything else going?"

"I can't complain. Any messages for me?"

"I haven't seen or heard a thing. Most of the bosses are taking vacation this time of year, relaxing, drinking beer, and soaking in the sun on some beach. Boy, don't they have the life?"

"Sure do," Micah said with a laugh. "Well, I've got to be going. I'm meeting a friend for dinner tonight. I hope you get out of there at a decent hour."

"It won't be until two or so since there are a couple games on the West Coast that we have to wait for. And knowing my luck, they'll go into extra innings. See ya."

After getting off the phone, Micah showered and trimmed his beard. He gazed into the mirror over the wash basin and noticed a few gray hairs beginning to show on his chin and ran his finger over them as if they would disappear. He brushed his teeth and got dressed, putting on a white polo shirt and khaki slacks.

When Micah arrived at Big Shots, Josh was already there. He was standing at the bar, drinking a mug of dark beer, and immersed in a conversation with an attractive blonde. Micah was almost hesitant about interrupting them. She gazed at Micah through light blue eyes as he walked up behind Josh.

"Hey, buddy," Josh said after turning around and facing Micah. "Did you just get here?"

"Just arrived," Micah said, smiling and looking back at the woman.

"I'd like you to meet Cora Miller," Josh said. "She's a reporter at the *Register*. Do you know each other?"

"I don't believe so," Micah said as she shook her hand. "Where do you work at the paper?"

"I'm a general assignment reporter on the city beat," she said with a pleasant smile. "I've only been at the *Register* for about three months."

"Where are you from?"

"I worked in Charlotte, North Carolina, for the past eight years, primarily covering higher education. I hope to get back into education reporting here."

Micah glanced down at her left hand and noticed she wasn't wearing a wedding band. While she appeared soft on the exterior with her creamy complexion, he knew she had to be tough as nails on the inside to be on the city beat. She had to cover crime, political corruption and all sorts of oddball stories, something that Cincinnati was not in short supply.

"What does your husband do?" asked Micah, wanting to make sure she wasn't married. "Any kids?"

"Never married, and no children," she said. "You?"

"Single. I've been divorced for a couple of years," he said. "I've got a twelve and ten-year-old. Great kids."

"If I may so rudely interrupt," Josh said before briefly clearing his throat, "but we've got a table reserved over there. Would you care to join us for dinner, Cora?"

"I'd liked to but I'm waiting for a friend. I thought she would have been here by now."

"She'd be welcomed to join us," Micah said.

"Are you sure that won't be a problem?" Cora asked.

"Of course not," Josh said while adjusting his wire-rimmed glasses on his nose. "No problem at all. There's room enough for six."

"Okay, then," she said. "That would be nice. She works at the newspaper, too. Her name is Vanetta Wells. She's got red hair if you see her come in."

"I don't believe I know her either," Micah said. "Does she work on the city desk, too?"

"She works in promotions," Cora said. "We both live at the same apartment complex, and that's where I got to know her. She's a real sweet person."

A few minutes later, after they were seated at the table, Cora noticed Vanetta standing off to the side of the front entrance and waved at her. Vanetta smiled and walked over to them. Micah was sitting next to Cora so Josh moved over and Vanetta sat down next to him.

"Hi," Josh said. "I'm Josh and this is Micah. I believe you already know Cora."

"It's nice to meet you," Vanetta said as she eased herself on the chair.

"Micah works at the newspaper," Cora said.

"I've seen Micah around," Vanetta said with a smile. "Sports columnist."

"And Josh is a book editor," Cora added quickly.

"What publishing house do you work at?" Vanetta asked.

"Overbrook," he said. "We do a lot of sports histories and biographies. I've been there for almost twelve years. How long have you been at the newspaper?"

"Too long," Vanetta said with a hearty laugh. "It will be fifteen years next month. I never thought I'd be there that long but I guess it's a good place to work. I don't have too many regrets."

Micah ordered a round of beers for everyone and a few minutes later a waitress came around and took their food orders. The evening went by quickly as they discussed everything from sports to local politics.

"I've had a very enjoyable time," Cora said. "Thank you for inviting us to sit with you."

"No problem," Josh said. "The pleasure was ours."

"I hope to see you at the newspaper one of these days," Micah said, turning to Cora. "I'm not in the office that often. Do you usually work nights?"

"Most of the time," she said. "And usually on weekends. This was a rare Saturday night off for me."

"I hope you drop by and see me whenever you're around," Vanetta said to Micah, her emerald green eyes flashing. "I'm there during the day. Monday through Friday."

"I'll try to do that," Micah said, nodding slightly.

Josh and Micah walked the women to their cars in the parking lot adjacent to the pub. It was well-lighted and there was still some traffic whizzing by on the street. Micah stood next to Josh's refurbished 1974 yellow VW Bug as the women drove off.

"That was some evening," Josh said. "I never expected that. And Vanetta is something else. Doesn't she have the sexiest look with that red hair?"

"I never really noticed," Micah said with a laugh.

"Cora's nice, too," Josh said.

"I think so. She seems like a nice person. They both seem very nice."

"We need to do this again. I sure wish I'd gotten Vanetta's phone number."

"Well, you can always reach her at the newspaper," Micah said.

"I think I'll do that one of these days," Josh said. "Do you think she'd go out with me?"

"I don't have a clue," Micah said. "You can only find out by asking her."

"I may just do that," Josh said softly, and then as if talking to himself, said, "I may just do that."

"I need to be going," Micah said. "Thanks for giving me a call today. We'll do it again."

They shook hands and went on their way. On the way back to his apartment, Micah couldn't get his mind off Cora. She seemed so pleasant and down to earth. So many other women he knew in the media were full of themselves, always out to impress others. But Cora seemed relaxed and unconcerned about what others thought about her. And he couldn't forget her blue eyes and tender smile.

Micah stopped by the sports department the next evening to check on any messages. The sports department was located in the corner of the third floor while the city desk was at the opposite end. Front pages from the newspaper of famous events were framed and lined the walls on both ends of the floor. After getting off the elevator, he glanced over to the city desk and didn't see Cora. He knew she was probably on assignment.

There were hardly any reasons for Micah to show up in the sports department except to speak to some old friends once in awhile. His check was deposited directly into his bank account and any messages from his sports editor, Spencer Duggins, were usually sent e-mail or voice mail. But he thought it was still nice on occasion to drop by the office. Especially with a new person on the city desk.

"Hello stranger," Frank said, peeking out from behind one of the terminals. "I missed you at the ball park today."

"So how did our beloved team do today?" Micah asked. "Or shouldn't I ask."

"You should know better," Frank said, grinning. "A heartbreaker. It was 2-1 in 10 innings."

"I'll read about it in the paper tomorrow," Micah said. "I've got to run."

"See you later."

Micah walked back toward the city desk, looking around the newsroom again for Cora, but didn't spot her. He stepped into the elevator and the door closed. A moment later, Cora came out of the employee lounge and walked toward the sports department. She glanced around for a moment.

"Can I help you?" Frank asked.

"No," Cora said with smile. "I just finished my break and thought I'd see if I anybody I knew was down here."

"Any one in particular?"

"No. I'm relatively new here and just being nosy," she said, blushing lightly. "I need to get back to my desk and get back to work. Bye."

"See ya."

Four

Micah spent the next four days at the Cincinnati Bengals' summer training camp in Georgetown, Kentucky, interviewing team officials, coaches and players about the upcoming season. When he returned home Friday night, there was a pile of letters in the mailbox and the answering machine light was blinking. After thumbing through the letters, mostly bills and junk mail, he flicked on the answering machine and sat down on the couch.

Alice was the first message.

"Micah, don't forget about picking the kids up on Saturday. Ben has a ball game at 11 a.m., so you can swing by the house around two to pick them up. Of course, you're welcome to come to the game. Bye."

Then Josh.

"Hey, buddy. I hope you've had a good week down in Georgetown. I was wondering if you wanted to go back out on Saturday night. Maybe we can get lucky like last weekend. Give me a call. See ya."

And then a voice he didn't recognize.

"Good evening. I hope you remember me. We met at Big Shots last weekend. This is Vanetta. I hope you don't mind me calling. I got your phone number in the company directory. I'm not doing anything this weekend and was wondering if you'd like to go out. You can call me at 555-3237. Bye."

Micah shook his head. He couldn't remember ever being asked out by a woman. He thought times had really changed when a woman would make that request on an answering machine and leave her number. He knew he had been out of circulation too long and perhaps no longer knew the rules.

Micah went to the refrigerator and took out a can of light beer and went back and sat back down and put his feet on the coffee table. He picked up the TV remote pad and clicked on ESPN. After turning down the volume, he reached over to the end table and took the cordless telephone and called Josh.

"How was training camp?" Josh asked. "I bet it was hot and muggy down there."

"It wasn't too bad. We had some light showers every day that keep temperatures down somewhat. It was nice to get away for a few days. The Bengals have got some nice folks to deal with so it's not bad at all."

"I wish I could do something like that. I'm not going to get out until January at a book publishers' convention in Chicago. I'm looking forward to that. It can be a drag sitting in the office every day reading manuscripts and talking to agents. I need a week of nothing but fun."

"And a publishers' convention is fun?"

"Oh, we have our meetings to attend during the day, but the nights are open. And some of the big publishing houses throw some damn good parties. It's a great time for bookworms."

"I won't be able to go out tomorrow night," Micah said. "I'm picking up the kids in the afternoon and keeping them until

Sunday night. I promised Alice last week that I'd keep them while she went out with Graham."

"That's a good enough excuse. I was really looking forward to going back to Big Shots. I'd like to see Vanetta again."

Micah paused for a moment. He decided not to mention Vanetta's message on the answering machine, knowing that it might hurt Josh's feelings.

"Why don't you go on by yourself? She might show up and then you'd have her all to yourself."

"I don't know," Josh said. "I don't like going to bars by myself."

"Well, I don't either but I'm not out there trying to pick up women," Micah said.

"Hey, I'm not either," Josh said with a laugh. "We just stumbled across those two last weekend."

"If I remember correctly, you were at the bar talking to Cora when I arrived last weekend. And now you're telling me you weren't on the prowl."

"It wasn't what it looked like. I was waiting for you to get there. It was just idle chit-chat."

"You seemed to be handling it quite well," Micah said, jokingly.

"If anything, I was just lucky."

"Well, if you do decide to go, let me know how everything turns out."

"Only if I score," Josh said with a laugh. "I'll probably end up staying here and reading a manuscript."

After they hung up, Micah finished his beer while flipping through the newspaper. He looked at the rival *Cincinnati Herald* and read the sports column by Dirk Rogers. Micah and Dirk arrived in Cincinnati about the same time, and while civil with each other, they weren't friends. Dirk was nine years younger than Micah, but a receding hairline along with a beak nose made him appear older. He also had a know-it-all attitude about most things and would hardly let anyone ever express an opinion without cutting them off in mid-speech.

Dirk's column carried a San Diego dateline. He had followed the Reds on their West Coast swing. Micah wondered why he would be making that trip since the team was already out of contention. He figured Dirk must have had something else he was working on and would have to find out what it was. Micah knew it wouldn't be that difficult since sportswriters couldn't keep their mouths shut for very long.

He got up and emptied his suitcase, taking the dirty clothes and dropping them in the washer. It was still early enough to take care of the laundry and tidy the house for the children. While putting away dishes in the cabinet, the phone rang.

"Hi," a sultry voice purred after he picked up the receiver. "I see you're back."

"Uh, Vanetta?"

"You guessed right," she said with a soft laugh. "I assume you got my message."

"I did," Micah said, feeling a little uneasy about talking to her. "I was down in Kentucky the past four days with the Bengals. I just got home an hour or so ago."

"Did you have a good time?"

"I enjoyed it. How has your week been?"

"Boring as usual. My job in promotions isn't nearly as exciting as a sportswriter's."

"It's not all fun and games," Micah said. "There're lots of deadlines to deal with along with a lot of other things."

"I'm sure there are. But I bet it beats going to spelling bees, awards dinners, and other newspaper promotions."

"I probably can't argue with you about that," he said with a chuckle.

"Were you able to give any thought about Saturday night?"

"I was going to call you," Micah said, knowing he was telling her a white lie. "My kids are going to be spending the weekend with me. I'll be picking them up in the afternoon."

"Oh, I didn't realize you had any children."

"I've got a boy who is twelve and a ten-year-old daughter."

"I love children."

"You have any?"

"No," she said. "I got too wrapped up in my career when I was married and never got around to it. My husband and I didn't think we needed kids at the time. And after we divorced five years ago, there's been no reason for me to have a child. I certainly don't want to be a single mom at this stage of my life. I'm thirty-nine now so it's doubtful that I'll be bringing any babies into the world. It's funny though. My ex-hubby remarried and has two children. "

"Perhaps it's not too late for you to become a mother," he said. "You just need to find the right man."

"I know," she said slowly.

"Well, are you going out this weekend?" Micah said, wanting to change the subject.

"I don't know. I may just curl up on the couch with a good book."

"You remember Josh, don't you? He was with me at the pub last week."

"Barely," Vanetta said.

Micah rolled his eyes and paused for a moment.

"He's a great guy. He told me that he might be at Big Shots tomorrow night. You might go there and run into him."

"I'll think about it," she said nonchalantly.

"I need to be getting off here," Micah said. "I've got a few more things to do to get the apartment ready for the kids."

"You still have my phone number?"

"Yes."

"Well, if you ever find yourself wanting to do something some evening, just give me a call," she said wistfully.

"I'll do that," he said. "Bye."

"Toodles."

Micah laid the phone down on the sofa cushion. He scratched his head for a moment and grinned.

"I can't believe that woman," he said to himself while shaking his head.

Micah picked the phone back up and dialed Alice's number. It rang four times before she picked it up.

"Am I catching you at a bad time?" Micah asked.

"No," she said. "I was just putting Annie to bed. How was your trip?"

"I had a good time. It was nice getting away for a few days."

"Are you going to be able to keep the kids this weekend?"

"No problem. That's why I'm calling. I'm looking forward to it."

"Me, too," Alice said with a laugh. "I need a break."

"I'm looking at it the same way," Micah said. "I need a break with the kids."

"So do you think you'll be at Ben's game?"

"I'll try to be there."

"Okay, Micah," she said. "I'll see you tomorrow. Good night."

"Bye."

Five

After taking a long shower and getting dressed on Saturday morning, Micah drove to Shoney's for breakfast. He usually fixed his own meals when he was at home because he believed that they were healthier than what he could eat in restaurants. He also was a vegetarian and most of the menus in restaurants were limited as to what he could eat.

While sitting in a two-person booth, he glanced over his newspaper and saw Cora standing in line to be seated. He lowered the newspaper, waited for her to make eye contact with him, and grinned. She responded with a soft smile. He got up from the booth and walked over to her.

"Good morning," he said. "Would you care to join me? I've got an extra seat."

"Oh, thanks," she said. "I'm in sort of a hurry this morning. Are you sure you don't mind?"

"Of course not. I'm in somewhat of a hurry today, too."

After returning to his table, she placed an order of pancakes and coffee. The waitress warmed his coffee.

"So how have you been?" Micah asked after folding the newspaper and placing it on the side of the table.

"I've been busy. There seems to have been a lot of shootings in the past week. I guess because it's hot and tempers begin to flare. But I've been all over the city covering them. I've got to go to a news conference at eleven this morning. The mayor and police chief are going to announce some kind of beefed up enforcement to help curtail the shootings."

"What a way to spend a weekend," Micah said with a laugh.

"So what are you doing out so early?" she said.

"I've got my kids for the weekend. My son has a ball game at eleven so I'm going to go see him play, and then I'm going to take him and my daughter home with me. We'll probably take in a movie and get pizza."

"That sounds like a lot of fun. Do you get to see your kids often?"

"Not as much as I would like, but I'd like to think I'm getting more of that so-called quality time with them. I do try to see as many of their activities as I can. There was a time when I let work interfere with about everything."

"That's a common denominator I've heard since I've been a reporter."

"I think it's an excuse more than anything. I think a person can find the time to do whatever they want to do if they just make the effort. So many of us use work as an excuse to dodge other responsibilities. I know there are times when it can't be helped, but for the most part, we are victims of our own devices."

"I think you're right," she said before taking a sip from her coffee. "I think that's one reason I've never made any commitment to a personal life. I don't think it would be fair to others."

"Hey, this conversation is getting a little heavy for a Saturday morning," Micah said with a chuckle. "Is there anything on the light side we could talk about? Office gossip?"

"I don't know much office gossip," she said with a laugh. "I haven't been here long enough to pick up on much of that. Plus, I'm out of the office so much."

"That's the way it is for me. I usually work from the ball park or hotel room when I'm on the road. I seldom venture down to the newspaper anymore except to see some old friends."

"I've made a few friends," she said. "There seem to be a lot of nice people there."

"I like it. I couldn't imagine myself working anywhere else. I don't know how long I can keep up with all the travel and crazy hours, but the people there are great. Speaking of people, how did you get to know Vanetta?"

"Oh, she lives in the same apartment complex that I do. We would often see each other coming and going in the parking lot and then one day we saw each other in the company cafeteria. That's when we really spoke to each other. She's been a good friend. She's shown me parts of the city. And how did you get to know Josh?"

"We worked on a book together a long time ago," Micah said. "We hit it off real well. I consider him my best friend. Whenever I'm in town, we usually go out to different restaurants and such. We've even gone to a few ball games and concerts. He's been a great buddy. Furthermore, I think he likes Vanetta."

"He does?" Cora said with a giggle. "Well, that doesn't surprise me. A lot of guys seem to like Vanetta."

The waitress returned with Cora's order. They sat quietly for a few minutes while she took a few bites from her food. Micah picked the paper up and glanced quickly over the agate page to check on scores and the day's schedule.

"So what are your plans this evening?" he asked.

"I'll probably stay at home. I may rent a video or something."

"No hot date?"

"Not for me," she said. "I'll probably be working until early evening. There's not much of social life for this girl."

Micah looked at his watch and saw that it was 10:15.

"I've got forty-five minutes to get to the ball park and the same for you for the news conference," he said. "I think we'd better hit the road."

"Thanks for sharing the booth with me."

"It was my pleasure. It's nice to have someone to talk to in the morning."

After they paid their checks at the counter, they had to go in separate directions to their cars. They stopped at the midway point in the parking lot.

"I hope you have a nice weekend with your children," she said.

"Thanks," he said. "You have a good weekend, too."

Micah didn't move for a couple of seconds as he watched her walk toward her car. He took in her shapely figure before she suddenly turned her head and glanced back at him. Micah felt his face flush and grinned.

"Bye," he said sheepishly and waved.

Cora smiled and then walked on to her vehicle. Micah shook his head slightly and went on his way.

When he arrived at the ball park, he had to drive around for a few minutes before finding a parking space on the street. Ben's game had already started as he walked up to the playing field. He glanced over at the swings and saw Annie playing with some of her friends. She was so caught up in her activity that she didn't see him. When he reached the bleachers, he noticed Graham sitting next to Alice on the fifth row.

Graham, who was usually seen in a coat and tie, still stood out in the crowd in his bright red-and-white warm-up outfit. As with most TV personalities, he was a local celebrity and most of the fans were aware of his presence at the game. After Micah worked his way through several people to get to them, Graham stood up and shook his hand.

"Good morning," Graham said with a big smile.

"Hi folks," Micah said. "Have I missed much?"

"No," Graham said. "We're just in the bottom of the first. No score."

"That's good. It took me awhile to get parked. How are you, Alice?"

"I'm doing well," she said warmly. "Are you ready for a busy weekend?"

"I'm really looking forward to it. I hope they are."

"That's all they've talked about for the past two or three days. I think Annie looks at it as a vacation."

"So you're going to a concert at the zoo tonight?" Micah said to Graham.

"I got some real good seats from the station. We're one of the sponsors. Have you ever been to one of them?"

"Never," Micah said. "I've heard they're very good. I could never fit it into my schedule. I couldn't fit a lot of things into my schedule."

Alice didn't comment but Micah had an idea what thoughts crossed her mind. There had been so many different activities he had missed in their marriage because of his priority on work. He knew he couldn't count the times that he had to offer an excuse for not showing up at different places. After awhile, Alice didn't count on him. If he made an appearance, it was a bonus for the family.

The game was over before they realized it. Ben's team won, 12-6. They walked over to the playground to get Annie and wait for Ben's team meeting to end.

"I've already got their clothes packed, what little there is," Alice said. "I think they'll probably need to get cleaned up after we get home."

"That's fine," Micah said. "I'm in no hurry. I'll just follow you there if that's all right with you."

"Okay," she said, and then looked at Graham. "How about 5:30? I thought we'd stop and get a bite to eat before going to the concert."

"I'll be ready," Alice said with a smile.

"I'll see you then," Graham said. "Tell Ben I thought he played a good game. It was good seeing you, Micah. I'll see you somewhere down the road."

"Be careful," Micah said. "Enjoy the concert."

Graham walked on to his car while Micah and Alice stayed at the playground.

"Why don't you and Annie go on over to the house?" Micah asked. "I'll wait for Ben and he can go with me. There's no telling how long he will be."

"That's a good idea," Alice said. "Do you want me to stop and pick up anything to eat?"

"No, don't bother," he said. "I'll pick up something at McDonald's for the kids on the way to my apartment."

Ben walked up shortly after Alice and Annie left. His uniform was soiled at the knees. He had a smudge of dirt on his chin that Micah cleaned off with his thumb.

"Where's Mom?" Ben asked.

"She and Annie left a few minutes ago. You're riding with me."

"How did you like the game?" Ben said as they walked to Micah's car. "Don't you think we're looking pretty good?"

"I've been impressed," Micah said with a grin. "I think you guys are really coming together as a team at the right time."

"I'm glad you came to the game," Ben said.

"I'll be here every time I can," Micah said. "You can count on it."

Annie was already out of the shower and getting dressed when Micah and Ben got to the house. Although Micah hadn't lived there in quite some time, it hadn't changed that much. A few family photos were still on the wall and some of his books were in the bookshelf. The furniture they had purchased several years ago was still in the same place. It was a comfortable feeling for Micah.

"You played a good game," Alice said to Ben.

"What did Mr. Parker think?" Ben said. "Did he stay for all of it?"

"He watched all of the game. He thought you played well, too."

Ben went back to the bathroom and took a shower while Annie came out and sat next to Micah on the couch. He put his arm around her and gave her a gentle squeeze.

"What are we going to do tonight, Daddy?" she asked, looking at him through big blue eyes.

"I thought we'd go to a movie and get a pizza. Is that all right?"

"That's good," she said with a grin. "What movie?"

"Hmm, I don't know right now. I guess you and Ben will have to decide on that after we get to my apartment."

"Ben and I don't like the same movies," she said with a grimace.

"Well, I guess we'll just have to compromise."

"What does that mean?"

"That means you'll both have to give in a little on what you want to see."

"But what if we still can't decide?"

"That's when I'll make the decision," he said with a gentle hug.

Ben came out of his bedroom carrying a travel bag. Micah and Annie got up from the couch as Alice returned from the kitchen where she had finished washing the breakfast dishes.

"I guess we're ready to go," Micah said.

"Well, you all have a good time," Alice said as she bent down and kissed both of the children on the cheek. "I'll see you on Sunday night."

"You enjoy yourself as well," Micah said. "We'll see you."

Six

"Well, kids, why don't we go ahead and order a pizza, then we'll pick out at movie to go see a little later," Micah said as they sat on the couch watching cartoons on the Disney Channel. "What kind would you like?"

"Pepperoni!" Annie said.

"Sausage!" Ben said a half-second later.

"Pepperoni!"

"Sausage!"

"Okay, Okay," Micah said with a laugh. "Let's not argue about it. I'll order half pepperoni and half sausage."

"I didn't think you liked meat," Ben said.

"I'll order a salad," Micah said. "It's not a big deal."

Micah phoned in the order and was told it would take forty minutes to be delivered. He glanced up at the kitchen clock. Five-thirty. He knew Alice and Graham would probably be headed to a restaurant about now. He hoped they enjoyed themselves. If he had to choose a man to go out with his Alice, he knew Graham would have been a good choice because he was always a gentleman.

Micah walked back to his bedroom while the children watched television and picked up a copy of *The Sporting News*. He read several columns before the front door bell rang. He gave the deliveryman $20 and told him to keep the $4.50 in change.

He put the pizza on the coffee table and walked back to the kitchen for paper plates and soft drinks. Ben opened the container and began eating a piece from his half. Annie waited patiently for Micah to return to put some slices on her paper plate.

"The pizza sure looks good," Micah said as he took the lid off a plastic container and spread Italian dressing over his garden salad. "Have you kids decided on a movie yet?"

"I want to see that new movie with Robin Williams," Ben said. "The previews are really funny."

"Is that okay with you, Annie?" Micah said.

"I guess so," she said, crinkling her nose.

Micah picked up the newspaper in the magazine rack next to the couch and took out the entertainment section. He studied the listings in the movie guide for times of the movies.

"It looks like we can go at 7:05 or 9:10 over at the Showcase," he said. "How about the early show?"

The children nodded approval while they chewed on pizza. Micah returned to eating his salad and picked up the remote.

"Do you mind if I switch over to the news?" he asked.

"Go ahead, Dad," Ben said. "Maybe we'll catch a few ball scores."

A minute after flicking on a local station, there was an on-the-scene report from Interstate 75, near the Brent Spencer bridge that crossed over to Kentucky. Micah turned up the volume.

"A tanker truck slammed into a vehicle, causing a chain reaction involving about twenty cars," said the reporter. "Police say at least three people were killed and several others injured. Police aren't sure of the cause of the accident, but eyewitness accounts say the truck driver apparently lost control of the vehicle coming down Death Hill in Covington. We'll have more details at eleven."

"I sure hope your mom and Graham were able to miss that accident," Micah said. "That will back up traffic for hours. They would probably miss the concert at the zoo."

"That concert sounds boring," Ben said between bites.

"Now you shouldn't say that," Micah said. "I think it would be very enjoyable."

"Do you think they'll be able to see any animals?" Annie asked with wide eyes.

"Probably," Micah said. "But they wouldn't have that much time to do it."

"Would you take me sometime, Daddy?" Annie asked.

"I'd love to," Micah said with a gentle smile.

"Can I go, too?" Ben asked.

"I thought you said it would be boring," Micah said with a laugh.

"It could be but I'd still like to go," Ben said. "I'd go look at the lions and elephants while you and Annie listen to the music."

"If you say so," Micah said, grinning.

The station went directly to the weather report and then sports. No other mention was made of the accident.

"Well, kids, let's get this mess picked up and get out of here," Micah said. "We'd better hurry up if we're going to make the seven o'clock show."

They arrived at the cinema about fifteen minutes before the movie was to begin and got their tickets. Micah bought Annie some popcorn and a soft drink and got some red licorice sticks for Ben.

"I don't see how you kids can eat after that pizza," Micah said.

"Daddy, you can't watch a movie without popcorn and a soda," Annie said with a grin.

"You're probably right about that, sweetheart," he said as he patted her gently on the top of the head. "Let's go find some good seats."

They sat midway in the middle section, with Micah sitting between the children.

They liked the movie, laughing in all the right scenes. Micah enjoyed it too, having been a Robin Williams fan since the old *Mork and Mindy* television show.

"That movie was a good choice," Micah said to Ben as they walked out of the theater under the glow of the lights in the parking lot. "It was very funny."

"I thought it would be," said Ben, feeling good about picking out the movie. "I think it got two thumbs up by those TV guys."

"I thought it was okay," said Annie. Ben rolled his eyes and shook his head while Micah smiled at both of them.

"Ready to go home?" Micah asked. "It's nine so all the malls will be closing soon."

"I'm ready," Annie said. "I get the TV when we get home."

"That's not fair!" Ben said.

"I called it first," Annie said smugly.

"Listen, kids," Micah said. "Let's quit the arguing. Annie can have the TV until ten and Ben can decide what to watch until 11. And then it's bedtime. Understood?"

"Okay," Annie said. "Let's hurry up and get home."

"Take your time, Dad," Ben said while making a funny face at Annie. "We're in no hurry."

"Would you kids quit it?" Micah said, shaking his head. "I've never seen you guys argue like this."

Ben hurried and got in the front passenger seat when they reached the car while Annie sat in the back. Micah turned on the radio and caught the end of the 8:55 news.

"Police have confirmed that six people were killed and thirteen injured in the traffic pileup on I-75 early this evening. Authorities say the brakes apparently went out on a tanker-trailer and then rammed into several vehicles. The names of the victims have not been released. The driver of the truck was not injured."

When Micah opened the front door to his apartment, he noticed the light was blinking on the answering machine. As he went over to listen to the messages, Annie picked up the remote and turned on the TV, increasing the volume.

"Turn that down, Annie," Micah said, raising his voice. "I'm trying to listen to some messages."

Annie looked at him sheepishly and turned down the volume.

"Micah, this is Reg Taylor on the copy desk. Could you give me a call? It's about 7:40 right now. It's important so please get back with me."

A second message came on:

"Mr. Stewart, this is Officer Riley of the Cincinnati police department. Please call me as soon as you get home. My number is 555-4017. Thank you."

Micah felt an emptiness in his chest. His hands began to tremble. He knew something was wrong. He picked up the telephone.

"What's the matter, Dad?" Ben said with a serious look.

"I don't know, son. I've got a call from the police."

He dialed the number, waiting impatient for it to be answered.

"Officer Riley speaking. May I help you?"

"Officer Riley, I'm Micah Stewart. You called my home this evening. Is there something wrong?"

"Mr. Stewart, are you married to Alice Stewart?"

"She's my ex-wife. Has something happened to her?" Micah asked with tenseness in his voice.

"Well, Mr. Stewart, she was involved in an accident tonight on I-75. You may have heard about it on the news. She was seriously injured. She's in ICU at University Hospital."

"Oh, my God!" Micah's legs felt wobbly as he moved to sit down on the couch. "I'm going right over there."

"Mr. Stewart, one other thing please."

"What is it?"

"The companion in her car is dead."

"Graham Parker?"

"Yes, sir. He died at the scene."

"Oh, my God! Oh, my God!"

Micah put down the receiver and the children darted over to him. They had caught part of the conversation and their eyes were brimming with tears.

"Children, mommy's in the hospital," Micah said as he bent down and wrapped his arms around them. "She was in a car accident and she was seriously injured."

"Mommy's going to be all right?" Annie said in a pleading voice as tears streamed down her cheeks.

"Yes, Mom is going to be fine," Micah said, trying to reassure the children.

"How about Mr. Parker?" Ben said in a quivering tone. "Is he all right?"

Micah hesitated for a second and said, "Mr. Parker died."

"I want to go see Mommy," Annie said as tears streamed down her cheeks.

"We're going to see her right now," Micah said. "She's at University Hospital. Come on and let's go."

Seven

Ben and Annie could hardly keep up with Micah as he briskly walked into the hospital. He glanced back to make sure he wasn't getting too many steps ahead of Annie, who was practically at a run to keep pace with him.

"Where's ICU?" Micah asked the receptionist at the information desk.

"It's straight down the hallway and to the right," an elderly white-haired woman said. Micah was already headed that way before she could finish. "Sir, children aren't allowed in ICU."

Micah went directly to the nurses' station. Hospital personnel were scurrying about all over the unit. Most of the injured in the traffic pileup had been taken to University Hospital.

"Ma'am," Micah said impatiently to a nurse while leaning over the counter. "I'm Micah Stewart. My ex-wife is here. Her name is Alice Stewart. Can you give me some information?"

"Please wait a minute Mr. Stewart while I get her chart," she said while forcing a tight smile.

The children stood next to Micah for what seemed like an eternity as the nurse went to an adjoining room.

"Is Mommy going to be all right, Daddy?" Annie asked. "Can we see her?"

"I hope we get to see her, sweetie," he said while gently patting her on the cheek. "Mom's getting good care right now."

A minute later, the nurse returned with a man in a light blue surgical uniform.

"I'm Dr. Willis. Your wife is in serious condition but she has stabilized. She suffered a broken bone in her right leg. She's also broken her left arm and severely strained her back and neck. We don't believe there are any internal injuries although she has quite a few abrasions from the accident."

"When can we see her?" Micah asked.

The doctor turned away from Micah and looked at the nurse. He paused for a few seconds before saying anything.

"You can visit with her for five minutes," the doctor said as he turned back to Micah. "No longer. She's awfully weak and needs rest. Please don't try to make her talk. I think it's important that she knows her family is here though."

"Thank you, doctor," Micah said.

As the doctor walked away, the nurse took Micah by the arm and led him to Alice's room. Ben and Annie were one step behind.

"I'm Aly Johnson," said the short and chubby nurse. "I've been looking after your wife. I don't want you to be alarmed by her appearance. She looks a lot better than she did several hours ago. She's coming along fine considering what she's been through."

They hesitated in the doorway before walking to her bed. Several intravenous tubes were coming out of Alice's arms. Her arm and leg were already in casts and both were elevated. Her face and upper chest were badly bruised, her eyes black and puffy.

Micah quietly walked up to the bed, gently touching her hand. She turned her head slowly toward him.

"Micah?" she moaned softly.

"Everything is going to be all right," he said, bending over and kissing her on the cheek. Ben and Annie stood next to him, clutching his hands.

"Don't say anything," Micah said. "The kids are here with me. You need to rest. The doctor said you're coming along just fine. "

Alice tried to force a smile but couldn't with her swollen lips. She turned her hand over and squeezed his hand lightly. Micah glanced at the kids and motioned with his eyes for them to touch her arm.

"I love you, Mommy," Annie said softly.

"I love you, Mom," Ben said, fighting back tears.

"Mr. Stewart," the nurse said, "We need to go now."

Micah nodded to her as the children stepped back.

"Alice, we'll be back in the morning," he said. "You get your rest now." He kissed her again gently on the cheek before stepping quietly out of the dimly-lit room.

"How long will she be in intensive care?" Micah asked the nurse.

"We'll probably move her to a private room later tonight since she's coming along so well. What she needs now is sleep and rest."

"Has anyone else been notified?" Micah asked. "Her parents live in Cleveland."

"I don't think so, Mr. Stewart," the nurse said. "You may want to make some calls."

Micah went to a pay phone in the lobby and called Alice's parents while the children stood next to him. Her parents said they would leave immediately and be in Cincinnati in about six hours. Micah wanted to tell them to wait until morning but knew they would want to be at their daughter's side as soon as possible. They told him they would call their son in Florida and another daughter in Indiana.

It was nearly midnight when Micah returned to his apartment. The children were emotionally exhausted after seeing their mother in a near death-like state. Josh called a few minutes after Micah put Annie to bed in the guest room.

"How is Alice?" he asked. "Is she all right?"

"She's got a few broken bones and cuts but the doctor says she going to make it," Micah said. "She's at University Hospital. We just got back from there."

"Is there anything I can do?"

"If you wouldn't mind, could you come over and stay with the kids tonight while I go back to the hospital?"

"I'll be over in less than an hour," Josh said. "Don't you worry about anything."

"I'll wait until you get here. I just got Annie in bed. I need to make a few more phone calls."

After putting down the receiver, Micah saw Ben on the couch staring blankly at the television. He sat down and put his arm around him.

"Mom is going to be okay," Micah said. "I know she looks bad but she's going to get better."

Ben looked up at him mournfully and then buried his head in his shoulder and started to cry. Micah held him more securely and rocked gently. He kissed the top of his head.

"Why don't you go on to bed now, son? It's been a long day."

Ben didn't say a word. He got up and walked with his head down to Micah's bedroom. A minute later, after taking off his clothes, Ben clicked off the overhead light and got into bed.

Micah picked up the telephone and called the newspaper's sports department and told them that he wouldn't be at work the next day because of the accident. He didn't have to explain what happened.

Josh was at the front door a few minutes later and came on in without knocking or ringing the doorbell.

"The kids are in bed," Micah said. "I really appreciate you doing this. Alice needs someone with her tonight. Her parents will be here in a few hours."

"Buddy, let me know if I can do anything," Josh said. "I heard about Graham Parks. It's just tragic. He was such a great guy. The best sportscaster this town has had in years."

"They were going to the concert at the zoo," Micah said. "I guess they must have driven over the bridge for dinner. I saw him at Ben's ball game this morning. I can't believe all this has happened."

Tears began welling up in Micah's eyes. Josh came up to him and put his arm around his shoulders.

"I know it's difficult," Josh said with a comforting hug. "I wish I could say something because I can't imagine the pain you and the kids are going through right now. We should be thankful that Alice is going to get through this."

"I should get back to the hospital now," Micah said. "I'll give you a call early in the morning to let you and the kids know how she's doing."

"Tell her we love her," Josh said.

On the drive to the hospital, Micah thought about his years with Alice. Although they were no longer married, he still cared very much about her. She was a wonderful mother. She had always put him and the children first and made sacrifices for the family. She never complained because it was always out of love for others. Tears began to fill his eyes again.

Aly Johnson, the charge nurse, was still at the nurses' station when he returned to the intensive care unit. She pursed her lips in a soft smile. There was much less activity in the unit than when he was there earlier with the children.

"She's sound asleep, Mr. Stewart," she said. "We decided to keep her here overnight as a precaution. She'll probably go to the med-surg floor in the morning. But there's nothing to be concerned about right now. We just thought it would be better to keep her here under observation for the next eight hours or so."

"That's good to hear," he said with a sigh of relief. "I've got someone staying with my kids. I'm going to spend the night here."

"There's a waiting room just down the hall and to the left," the nurse said. "You can stay there. It's fairly crowded right now because some of the other families from the accident are here, too. But we'll keep you monitored on any changes in her condition."

"Thanks for everything," Micah said with an exhaustive look in his eyes. "Would it be okay if I looked in on her one more time?"

"Only if you just look from the door. She really doesn't need to be disturbed."

"Thanks."

Micah walked to Alice's room. He stood there for a minute gazing at her battered body, then closed his eyes, thankful that she was still alive.

Eight

Micah was asleep in an upright position on a couch in the waiting room, his head over the back and turned away from the light coming through the hallway. The room was full of people sleeping on the other couches and chairs; some even leaned up against the wall and on the floor. A few were awake, staring aimlessly at the walls while others were whispering back and forth about the condition of the victim they were visiting.

An older man came up and tapped softly on Micah's shoulder several times. Micah almost felt he was in a dream as his half-open eyes tried to focus on the surroundings. A few more taps and he realized it wasn't a dream. He gazed up at the figure standing next to him. It was George Murphy, Alice's father. Her mother, Nora, was standing at the doorway. Micah gazed down at his watch and saw that it was 5:15.

Micah shook his head and rubbed his eyes for a second, then slowly stood up. His body was stiff after sleeping a few hours on the couch.

"Good morning, George," he said lowly after clearing his voice. "I'm glad to see you and Nora made it all right."

"We got here as soon as we could," George said quietly.

They walked to the door, where Micah put his arms around Nora and hugged her. Although he had been divorced from Alice for two years, he had maintained a good relationship with her parents. They were in their late fifties, and both were still very active. George, tall and slender, was balding but he had strong chiseled look on his face that made him look ten years younger. Nora was silver-haired but had striking features that she had passed on to Alice.

"Alice has a broken leg and arm, lots of bruises and cuts, but she's going to be fine," Micah said. "You probably know that Graham didn't live."

"Yes," George said somberly. "It's just unreal. I still can't believe what happened."

"It's horrible. Simply horrible," Nora said, wiping away tears from her eyes.

George put his arm around Nora's shoulders and squeezed lightly.

"She's going to be all right, honey," he said.

Micah took them down the hallway to Alice's room. They stood at the door and watched her lay motionless in the bed. Several monitors were plugged into her, setting off beeps and blinking red lights. A nurse was checking her vital signs and administering a pain killer through one of the intravenous tubes. She looked up at Micah and motioned for them to come over to the bed.

"You can come in for a couple minutes," the nurse said softly. "Mrs. Stewart is coming along nicely. We should be moving her out of here a little later this morning."

"Thank you," Micah said.

Nora stepped over to the bed and gently touched Alice's bruised hand. George stood behind her, placing his hands on her shoulders while Micah went to the foot of the bed.

"Thank God she's alive," Nora said softly. "My poor baby. I can't believe what's happened."

George squeezed her shoulders firmly.

"She's going to be all right, Mom," he said. "She's going to be all right."

The nurse returned to the door and pointed to her watch that they needed to leave the room. Micah touched George's arm and motioned with his head that they had to leave the room.

They walked down the hallway to the vending-machine room. Micah took out a pocketful of change and bought coffee for all of them. They sat down at a small table that hadn't been cleaned off. George picked up the empty cups and wrappers and put them in the trash can while Nora took a paper napkin and brushed crumbs off the top of the table.

"How are the children?" George asked. "How are they handling this?"

"They're at my apartment," Micah said. "A friend of mine stayed with them last night. They're upset but I think they're going to get through it after a nurse told them she was going to recover. I'll go get them in a little while and bring them back. Do you want to go back with me and get freshened up or anything?"

"No thanks, Micah," said Nora, with tired eyes. "We need to be here when Alice wakes up. We also called Bud and Carrie. Bud should be arriving here shortly."

Bud and Carrie were Alice's brother and sister. Although they had gone in different directions, they still remained close. Every year the family always got together at a beach house on the outer banks in North Carolina that George would rent for a week.

They saw each other every year at Christmas, taking turns on which home would host the get-together.

It was 6:45 on the wall clock. There was more activity in the hallways as a shift change was approaching for the hospital personnel. Several people that Micah recognized from the waiting room were coming into the vending area to get coffee. Others were heading to the cafeteria.

"I guess I need to be going," Micah said. "The children will be getting up shortly and my friend needs to go to work. I'll probably shower and get breakfast for the kids before I come back."

"Just take your time," George said. "I know you must be exhausted. We'll let you know if anything changes."

They got up from the table and Micah shook hands with George. Nora came over and hugged Micah and kissed him on the cheek. Their eyes began to fill with tears again.

"She's going to be fine," Micah said. "Don't you worry about anything. Alice has always been a strong woman."

"I know," Nora said, pursing her lips.

Micah walked slowly to the parking lot. The night had seemed a blur. He glanced back at the hospital, trying to let it sink in that Alice was inside and seriously injured. And he thought about Graham and how fragile life is when a friend unexpectedly dies. Micah got inside his vehicle and took a deep breath. Then he wiped away a tear.

When Micah unlocked the door to his apartment, Josh stirred slightly on the couch. He had the couch throw over him and his head rested on a cushion. The children were asleep in the bedrooms.

Josh opened his eyes and sat up quickly. He yawned and stretched his arms. "How is Alice?" Josh said while replacing the throw on the back of the couch.

"She had a good night. They'll be moving her to a private room this morning. Her parents are with her now."

"That's good. The kids haven't made a sound."

"I appreciate you coming over last night. I don't know what I would have done."

"Hey, what are friends for? I'll be here as long as you need me."

"Thanks," Micah said with a weary smile. "I'm going to take the kids back to the hospital a little later. You can go ahead and leave if you want to. I thought I'd get cleaned up and eat some breakfast. Of course, you're welcome to some breakfast."

"I need to be going. I have an appointment with an agent at eleven so I need to take care of a few things. I plan to go over to the hospital this afternoon. Do you need for me to stay with the kids again tonight?"

"I don't believe so. I think Alice's mom will probably look after them. I'm sure they'll be staying over at Alice's place. But if there's a change, I'll let you know."

"Don't hesitate," Josh said. "Call me anytime."

Micah opened the newspaper he had picked up on the front porch. The banner headline read, *Tragedy on Death Hill*. A small photo of Graham Parker was shown alongside a large photo that graphically illustrated the tangled mass of cars in the pileup.

"I still can't believe this all happened," Micah said, shaking his head while handing the newspaper to Josh. "I can't believe Alice is in the hospital and that Graham is dead."

"I know it's difficult. It's hard for me, too. It will take a little while for it all to sink in."

"I don't know if it will ever sink in," Micah said. "I feel so empty."

"I had a good friend who was killed in a car accident when I was in high school," Josh said. "It shocked the entire community. I didn't think I'd get over it but after awhile you find that you'll be left with good memories of the person and forget the tragic death."

"I sure hope so, especially for Alice. It's going to devastating for her."

"I think she's stronger than you think," Josh said.

"I hope so."

Nine

Alice was in a private room on the third floor when Micah returned to the hospital with the children later in the morning. George and Nora were sitting next to the window. As Micah walked toward the bed, Alice slowly opened her eyes. Her right leg and left arm were in traction. A crooked smile came across her bruised and bandaged face.

"Hi," Micah said in warm and low voice. "How are you?" He put his hand on her hand and gently squeezed.

"I'm sore," she said. "Are the kids okay?"

"They're out in the waiting room. I wanted to come in first and make sure everything was all right. They came with me last night and saw you."

Nora and George walked to the door and said they were going to go see their grandchildren and would bring them back in a few minutes.

"You know about Graham?" Micah asked.

"Yes," Alice said sadly.

"I know all of this is difficult but thank God you survived."

Tears filled Alice's eyes as she gripped Micah's hand. He took a tissue off the bed stand and softly touched her eyes and cheeks.

"Mommy!" Annie's cry came from the doorway. She ran up to the bed while Micah put out his arm to make sure she didn't disturb Alice's position.

"Be careful, hon," Micah said. "We don't want to Mom to hurt anymore."

"Okay, Daddy," she said. "I'm sorry Mommy."

"Hi, Mom," Ben said as he slowly approached her.

The children stood next to her. She raised her hand and touched each child on the cheek. George and Nora stood at the doorway, both of them fighting back tears.

"When are you coming home?" Ben asked.

"The doctor said I shouldn't be here for more than a couple days," Alice said.

"That's a hospital for you," Micah said, shaking his head. "With the way insurance is, they want you out when you can mend at home."

"I really don't mind," Alice said. "I'd rather be in my own bed."

"I can't say I blame you," Micah said. "It will be good for you to get back to familiar surroundings."

There was a knock on the door railing and a man peeked in.

"Mrs. Stewart's room?"

"Yes," George said.

"I've got some flowers for her."

He brought in four flower arrangements and laid them on the counter against the wall. Alice knew who sent her the one filled with white daisies. That was her favorite flower and it came from Micah. She also received flowers from the *Register* sports staff, the real-estate company she worked, and Josh.

"They're all so beautiful," Nora said as she looked at the cards.

"They are lovely," Alice said. "Thank you, Micah. Please tell everyone at the paper how much I appreciate the flowers."

"I will," he said with a warm smile.

A nurse came in and said she would be bathing Alice in about five minutes.

"I guess we need to go," Micah said to the others. "Alice could use some rest now."

"We'll take the kids and go to Alice's house," George said. "Is that all right with you?"

"That's fine," Micah said. "I need to stop by the newspaper and do a few things."

Micah returned to Alice's side and held her hand for a few seconds.

"Is there anything you need for me to do?" he said.

"I think I'm fine," she said. "I'll see everyone later."

Annie and Ben went over next to Micah, who picked up Annie and let her kiss Alice on the cheek. Ben then kissed her on the cheek as Alice touched his arm. Nora and George kissed her while the nurse returned with a pan of warm water, large sponge, and towels.

"We'll see you later," Micah said after the others had walked to the hallway. "Get some rest."

Micah drove directly to the newspaper office from the hospital. Along the way he was thinking about what a long weekend it was because of the tragedy. He almost felt as if he had lost touch with what was going on in sports because his thoughts had been entirely on his family.

"How's Alice?" asked Spencer Duggins, the *Register* sports editor.

"She'll probably be going home in a couple days," Micah said. "Thanks for sending the flowers. She really appreciates them."

"Why don't you take some time off?" Duggins asked. "I know you must be exhausted."

"I was going to ask you if I could return on Thursday. Graham Parker will be buried tomorrow and I plan to go to his funeral. And Alice may be going home on Wednesday and I want to help her."

"Why don't you just take the entire week off?" Duggins said. "We'll be able to manage without you here. I think we'll be able to sell a few newspapers without your column."

Micah laughed. Duggins had always used sarcastic remarks to get his point across to those on his staff. He had been at the newspaper for more than twenty-five years, climbing the ranks after covering high school sports. Although he was in his late forties, he looked older because of the crazy hours he worked and lack of exercise. He was on the heavy side and his gray hair was thinning on top. He had quit smoking years ago but was still a heavy coffee drinker.

"Okay, Spence," Micah said. "You've made your point."

"Just let me know if you need any more time. Alice and your kids need you more right now than the newspaper."

"Thank you," Micah said. "I appreciate it."

As Micah was heading toward the elevator, he heard someone call his name from the newsroom. Cora waved for him to wait and quickly walked up to him.

"I'm so sorry about your ex-wife," she said. "I had to cover the accident and I didn't know who she was until someone on the copy desk told me. How is she?"

"She's much better," Micah said. "She broke a couple bones but she may be able to go home in a couple of days. Thank you for asking."

"If there's anything I can do, please don't hesitate to ask me," she said.

"Thanks for the offer but everything seems to be under control. Alice's parents are here now to look after the kids. All we need now is time for her to get over this."

The elevator door opened. Micah smiled and stepped inside.

Once home, he played back messages on his answering machine. Most of them were friends asking about Alice's condition and offering to help. The last message was from the funeral home. Micah would be one of the pallbearers. They wanted him to call back and confirm that he would serve. He called back and told them he would.

Ten

Graham's funeral was attended by more than five hundred people. Besides family and friends in the media, several officials and athletes from the Reds and Bengals were in attendance to pay their respects to the sportscaster.

After the service and burial, Micah drove to the hospital to see Alice. Color was beginning to return to her face. The swelling had gone down around her mouth and eyes. She was wearing a gown that her parents had brought back from her home. Nora had brushed her short, dark hair to give it some bounce.

"How was the funeral?" asked Alice, who was propped up although her leg was still in traction.

"It was very moving and touching," Micah said with a soft smile. "There were a lot of people there. He was very well liked and thought of."

"I wish I could have gone. It's like we never said good-bye."

Micah patted her lightly on the hand.

"I know it's not easy for you," he said. "I brought back something for you."

He took a funeral announcement from his inside coat pocket and handed it to her. It had Graham's name, those who survived him, and the list of pallbearers and honorary pallbearers. Tears welled up in Alice's eyes.

"Thank you, Micah," she said. "I don't know how I could have gone through all of this without you. You've been a true friend."

"We'll always be friends," he said. "Nothing will ever change that. We've gone through too much together."

Alice smiled sweetly and squeezed his hand.

"I know that," she said softly. "It's a shame we couldn't have worked things out better in the past."

"It was mostly my fault," he said. "But that's all in the past. What we've got to do now is get you out of the hospital. Have you heard anything from the doctor?"

"Dr. Willis said I should be able to go home on Thursday," she said. "He said everything looks good. He doesn't believe I'll need much rehabilitation because the bones set properly. And he doesn't think my arm will take hardly any time to heal."

"How long will your parents be here?"

"They said they'd stay as long as I need them. Dad may go back this weekend and pick up a few things. I'm sure Mom will stay as long as I need her."

"You know you can call on me anytime. Spencer told me to take the rest of the week off. I'm taking him up on it."

"I want you to get some rest. I know these past few days have been very hard on you, too."

"I plan to do that."

"Why don't you go out and do something? Call Josh and go out for dinner. Just get away from it all for a few days and clear your head."

"That sounds like a good idea. Will you promise me that you'll call me if something comes up where you need me?"

"I promise," she said with a tender smile.

"I guess I should be going and let you get some more rest," Micah said.

"Thanks for coming by," she said.

"I'll see you later," Micah said, then kissed her on the forehead and left.

Micah got home early in the evening. He turned on the television and caught the end of the local newscast. Scenes from Graham's funeral were replayed as the credits scrolled on the screen. He saw himself along with the other pallbearers carrying the casket to the long black hearse. Then it ended with Graham's smiling face before switching to the national news feed.

Micah turned off the TV and walked to the kitchen. He opened the refrigerator but there was nothing there that appealed to him. He wasn't in the mood to prepare dinner and he didn't want to call out for pizza or Chinese. He took out a can of soda and opened it.

The phone rang and he went over and picked up the receiver before the answering machine could click on.

"Micah speaking."

"Hi, Micah. This is Vanetta. How are you tonight?" she said cheerfully.

"I'm fine, thank you."

"Did you get my message?"

"I just got home and I haven't played back my answering machine. I'm sorry. Anything important?"

"I was wondering if you wanted to go out and get a bite to eat. I'm still at the office. I'm going to leave in about ten minutes. I thought perhaps I could meet you at Big Shots or somewhere."

Micah paused for a moment.

"You still there?" she said with a laugh.

"Sorry about that," he said. "I was just thinking. Well, sure, I guess I could meet you there. Seven o'clock?"

"That would be great. See you then."

After he put down the receiver, Micah wondered what in the world came over him to accept her invitation for dinner. He didn't feel like going but he was getting hungry. Then he remembered Josh's remarks about her. He wanted to call her back and decline the offer but knew he couldn't do that.

Vanetta was sitting in a booth when Micah arrived at the pub. A large, autographed photograph of Sparky Anderson was on the wall above the table. Photos of players, magazine covers and sports memorabilia covered the wall from end to end. Micah saw her before she noticed him and headed toward the table.

"I'm a little late," he said. "I apologize."

"That's okay," she said, flashing a wide smile full of deep red lipstick. "I just got here a few minutes ago."

A waitress came over and they each ordered a mug of dark beer and an appetizer of fried mozzarella cheese sticks.

"Thanks for inviting me," Micah said. "I was wondering what I would eat tonight. You made it easy."

"Do you eat out a lot?" she asked.

"I guess I do because I'm on the road a lot. I really prefer eating at home though."

"I'll have to invite you over some evening. I'm a pretty good cook if I do say so myself," she said with a wide grin.

Micah gave a half smile and took a swallow of beer. He cleared his throat.

"How has everything been at work?" he said. "Do you stay busy this time of year?"

"We stay busy all the time. It doesn't matter what time of year. There's always some kind of promotion."

"Just like different sports seasons, I guess."

"That's right. My calendar is full of different things we promote during the year, whether it's sports, gardening, outdoors, holidays. Just about everything."

"Have you seen Cora lately"?

"No, I haven't. She works a lot of nights. We really don't see each other that often."

"I saw her at the paper on Monday. That's the first time we've ever crossed paths to my knowledge. Of course, before we met last week I didn't know who she was."

"Are you ever near promotions?"

"I have no idea where the promotions department is located," he said with a laugh.

"We're on the second floor. You need to come down and visit sometime."

The waitress returned with their appetizer and took their orders. Micah ordered a veggie burger and side salad while Vanetta got a steak and baked potato.

"Don't you eat meat?" she asked.

"I've been a vegetarian for several years. I don't have any desire for meat."

"I don't know how I could ever do that. I love steak too much."

"About the only think I miss is the protein."

Micah gazed around the pub, looking for any familiar faces.

"Expecting someone?" Vanetta asked.

"No," he said before taking another sip of beer. "It's sure taking a long time for our food."

"It hasn't been that long. Are you in a hurry?"

"I guess I'm just hungry," he said with a nervous laugh.

"Do you like movies?"

Micah hesitated before answering. He had a large collection of videos in his apartment but he didn't want to get into a lengthy conversation. And he didn't want it to lead to a date.

"I go hot and cold," he said.

"How are you now?"

"Cold."

"Okay," she said, flicking her hair back lightly.

The waitress returned with their food. They didn't say much while eating, which suited Micah fine. After attending the funeral, he wished he was alone.

"I apologize," he said.

"What for?"

"My mind is a million miles away. After going to the funeral this afternoon, I'm really not thinking straight."

"Was it the funeral for that sportscaster?"

"Yes. He was a friend of mine."

"Oh, I'm sorry. You should have told me. I've just been rattling on about all sorts of trivial things. No wonder you seemed so distracted."

"My ex-wife was injured in the accident," Micah said. "She's at University Hospital."

"I hope she's doing all right," Vanetta said with a look of concern.

"She'll be going home in a couple of days."

They finished their meal and waited for the check.

"I'd like to have you over to my place sometime," Vanetta said.

"Perhaps one of these days," he said.

"I'll even fix vegetarian," she said with a light laugh.

"I'll keep that in mind."

After paying the bill, Micah drove directly to his apartment. He hoped she wouldn't invite him over. He felt bad enough about meeting her, knowing how Josh felt about her. He didn't have any feelings for her.

He hit the message button on the answering machine and sat down on the couch and put his feet up on the coffee table. He flicked off his shoes and spread out his arms on the back cushions.

Vanetta's message was first. She had called about three o'clock. There was another message from a communications company wanting to change his long-distance telephone service. And then there was Cora.

"Hi, this is Cora. I'm just calling to see how your ex-wife is doing. Please let me know if I can do anything. You can reach me at the office. Bye."

Eleven

It was hot and humid as Micah drove to work on Monday. He ran the air-conditioner on high all the way. When he got out of the car three blocks from the newspaper building, the blast of heat nearly took his breath away. He hurried down the street to find some relief inside the building, sweating by the time he opened the front door.

In his office, he checked his mail before going see if Spencer had anything on his mind. He was ready to get back into the routine of writing his column. The Reds were still on the West Coast while the Bengals were in Kentucky at preseason camp.

Spencer had the day's sports section on his desk, marking through any errors on the pages and making suggestions with a red pencil. It was the first thing he did when he arrived at the office. He wanted to make sure that the staff knew that he was aware of everything that did and didn't make it into the section each morning.

"Busy?" Micah asked at his doorway.

"Come on in. I'm just going through the paper. How's Alice?"

"She's doing very well. She's at home now. It will take some time before she is up and about without crutches but she looks good and is feeling better every day."

"Well, that's great. I just can't imagine what she's gone through. It must be really difficult."

"She's handled it very well. Her parents came down from Cleveland to stay with her. Her brother and sister also came in for a few days."

"So what have you been up to?"

"I took your advice and just tried to spend time with Alice and the children. I also got some rest. I appreciate your concern in all of this."

"I learned a few years ago that the family should come first. A person who has his priorities in the right order is a better newspaperman. They have more of sensitivity to other's feelings when they allow themselves to experience things on their own."

"That's a good philosophy. I wish I had learned it a few years ago."

"Micah, I learned it from experience. I've had some trying times in my career. I didn't want others to make the same mistakes. So many people in this business get so wrapped up in deadlines, stories and whatever that they lose sight of other things in their life."

"Why do you think that is?"

"I've thought about it some and I've come to the conclusion that so many of us enter the profession when we're young and fresh out of college. We don't know anything else and then we slowly get immersed in it all. By the time we get married and have families, we've made the newspaper the most important part of our lives, whether we realize it or not. By the time we do, it's often too late."

"I agree. I certainly made my mistakes."

"Haven't we all."

"Any ideas on what I should write about this week?"

"Hmm," Spencer said as he put his hand to his chin. "I think we should leave the Reds alone for a while. They're suffering enough. You could drive down to the Bengals' camp. The University of Cincinnati camp begins on Wednesday, so that's something you could consider. If you go to the Bengals, you also could drive on down to Lexington and go to a Kentucky practice. I believe they're having media day on Friday. Check with the desk and double check that."

"That's a good start. I think I will go down and see the Bengals and swing over to Kentucky. If it's all right with you, I'll write my first column for Wednesday. I thought I'd do a farewell piece about Graham. Do you believe that'd be okay?"

"He's been gone for more than a week but I don't see a problem with that. I know it's probably something that you feel you must write."

"I do," Micah said. "Because of all the circumstances surrounding his death, I wasn't able to write a column after it happened."

"I understand."

"I need to take care of a few things around here. I'll let you get back to marking up those pages," Micah said with a light laugh.

"It's good to have you back." Spencer smiled. "Let me know if I can do anything."

"Thanks."

Micah walked over to a computer terminal. There was hardly anyone in the newsroom except for editors. Most of the copyeditors and reporters would be coming in later in the afternoon, combining all their talents to put out a newspaper that would roll off the presses at three a.m. and be delivered to most homes and newsstands by seven.

He perused the wire-service stories to see what was happening around the National League and at various NFL training camps. There were some stories from around Ohio, Kentucky, and Indiana that sounded promising. He printed off those he thought were possible fodder for columns.

On his way out, he glanced over to the city desk. Cora was sitting at a terminal, poring over her notebook while writing a story.

"Hi," she said with a bright smile as he approached her.

"Hello. I just wanted to let you know that I got your message last week. Alice is doing fine. She's at home now."

"That's great. So you're back at work now?"

"Yep." Micah said, tucking his hands in his front pockets. "First day back. What brings you in this time of day?"

"News conference," Cora said. "State officials announced plans to relieve the congestion at the accident site where Graham died."

As Micah opened his mouth, a voice came from the entrance to the newsroom.

"Micah!"

Vanetta spotted him from the elevator.

"I see you're back at work," she said. "Hello, Cora."

"I got back today," Micah said.

"I really enjoyed the other night," Vanetta said. "We need to go out for dinner again real soon."

Micah smiled, uncertain if her remark was directed to him or Cora. He didn't reply but glanced at Cora to see her reaction. She had turned her head toward the computer screen.

"So when are you going to come over for dinner?" Vanetta asked.

"I don't know," Micah said, blushing lightly. "I'm going to be pretty busy the next few weeks trying to catch up on a few things."

"I've been going through my vegetarian cookbooks and trying to find something just right for you. Do you like vegetable lasagna?"

"Yes."

"So why don't you come over this week. You're invited too, Cora."

"I've got to go down in Kentucky on Wednesday and I'll probably be there for a few days."

"So why don't you come over tomorrow night? Do you have any plans?"

"Hmm, I don't think so," Micah said, realizing that he wasn't going to get out of it easy. Vanetta was just too persistent.

"How about you?" Vanetta said, looking at Cora.

"I guess I could be there," she said. "I don't have anything to cover unless there's some breaking news."

"Would you mind if I bring my friend?" Micah said.

"Who?" Vanetta said with a quizzical look on her face.

"Josh."

"Who's Josh?"

"You met Josh with me at Big Shots."

"Oh, I remember. Sure, bring him along. Is he a vegetarian?"

"He doesn't eat red meat."

"How about 7:30?"

"Sounds okay with me," Micah said. Cora nodded in agreement.

"Toodles," Vanetta said as she walked back to the elevator. "I'll see you then."

"You'd better show up tomorrow night," Micah said softly to Cora after Vanetta got on the elevator. "I don't think I could manage an evening with her without some support."

"I do think she has an eye on you," Cora said, grinning.

"I don't know what to say. She seems like a nice woman but she's certainly not my type."

"I'll try to make sure that nothing big happens tomorrow so I can be there," Cora said.

"I'd better let you get back to work on your story. It was nice seeing you."

Micah left the building and drove back to his apartment and worked on his column about Graham. He reminisced about how Graham was compassionate in his reporting and avoided sensationalizing events he covered. He wrote about Graham's wry sense of humor and how he would be missed by those who knew him.

When he was finished, he picked up the telephone and called Josh at his office.

"I figured you'd still be there," Micah said when Josh answered, knowing that the office was usually best place to reach him. He knew it wasn't unusual for Josh to spend the night there on the couch after getting so wrapped up in reading manuscripts he lost track of time.

"Hey, what's going on?" Josh said. "Great to hear from you!"

"I'm back at work now."

"I talked to Alice this afternoon. She really sounded good."

"She is getting a little more upbeat. She's coming along real well."

"Anything else going on?"

"I was wondering if you had plans for tomorrow evening?"

"Are you kidding?" Josh said with a laugh.

"Remember that redhead that we met at Big Shots a couple weeks ago?"

"Sexy Vanetta?"

"You remembered," Micah said with chuckle.

"How could I forget? She's been in my dreams ever since."

"Well, she's invited us over for dinner along with Cora."

"Great!"

"How about if I pick you up around seven?"

"That's good."

"Home or office?"

"Office."

"See you then."

Twelve

"How did you ever arrange this?" Josh said after he got into Micah's car in front of his office.

Micah turned down the volume on The Moody Blues' *I'm Just a Singer (In a Rock 'n' Roll Band),* playing on an oldies station.

"I saw her yesterday at the newspaper," Micah said. "I was over in the newsroom talking to Cora when she came dropped by. I didn't think you'd mind going."

"You thought right," Josh said with a laugh. "I think she's hot."

Micah didn't say anything for two blocks. He knew he had to tell Josh about meeting Vanetta at Big Shots. He didn't want him to find out about it at her apartment.

"I need to get something out in the open with you," Micah said.

`"What's that? You like her, too?"

"I think she's a very attractive woman but that's it."

"So what do you want to tell me?"

"I had dinner with Vanetta at Big Shots last week. I had just come home from the hospital and hadn't had anything to eat. Then she called and I met her there. We ate and then I went home."

"That's interesting," Josh said, arching his eyebrows slightly. "That's it?"

"Yes, Josh, that's it."

"Thanks for telling me," Josh said with a puzzled look.

"Is everything okay?"

"Sure. It just kind of surprised me a little."

"Josh, I have no interest in her. Okay?" Micah said. "I didn't give it any thought when I met her at the pub. There was nothing to it."

"Hey, I believe you."

George Thorogood's *Bad to the Bone* came on the radio. Josh reached over and cranked up the volume. They both started singing, "*Ba ba ba ba bad...*" and laughed.

Vanetta opened the door when they arrived, wearing a bright, yellow tank top and tight green shorts. Micah noticed she wasn't wearing a bra. Cora was sitting on the couch, wearing a light blue blouse and jeans.

Vanetta hugged Micah and gave him a quick kiss on the cheek. He wasn't expecting it and blushed. She smiled at Josh.

"I'm glad you're here," she said. "The lasagna is still in the oven. Would you care for something to drink? I have some red wine, beer, coke, and iced tea."

"I'll take a beer," Josh said.

"Iced tea for me," Micah said.

As Vanetta went back to the kitchen, Micah and Josh went into the living room. Micah sat next to Cora on the couch while Josh leaned back in the easy chair.

"How was your day?" Micah asked Cora. "Chasing down any big stories?"

"Pretty routine for me," she said. "How about you?"

"I finished a column about Graham Parker. I'm going down to Kentucky tomorrow to work on a few stories."

"How about you, Josh?" Cora said.

"I can't say I did anything exciting today," he said. "My days are pretty much the same."

"But I bet it's interesting," she said. "Reading all those manuscripts and meeting authors."

"I enjoy it," he said. "Of course, you get to read some bad manuscripts. But, by and large, it's not a bad job if you love to read."

Vanetta walked into the living and handed a can of beer to Josh, and then turned and looked seductively at Micah before handing him a tall glass of iced tea. Cora saw the look she gave him.

"Anything else?" Vanetta asked, keeping her eyes on Micah.

"I'm fine," Josh said with a smile that went unnoticed. Micah nodded.

Vanetta sat down on the middle cushion between Micah and Cora and crossed her legs.

"So, Micah, did I hear that you're going to Kentucky?"

"I'm going to spend couple days in Georgetown and Lexington. I'll be back this weekend."

"I love Lexington," she said, almost to the point of ignoring Josh and Cora. "Have you ever been to Keeneland for the races?"

"I usually go there in the spring and fall," Micah said. "It is a lovely race track. Have you been there Cora?"

"No, I haven't but I've heard a lot about it."

"I've been there a few times," Josh chipped in.

A shrill buzz went off in the kitchen.

"The lasagna must be ready," Vanetta said. "Let me go turn off the oven. I think everything will be ready in about five minutes."

"Can I give you a hand?" Cora asked.

"I could use a little help putting the salad out on the table."

Cora got up and walked back with Vanetta to the kitchen. Josh got out of the chair and went over to Micah.

"I think she's got the hots for you," Josh said.

"Who?"

"Vanetta. That's who. Don't tell me you haven't noticed the way she's been acting around you."

Micah ran his hand over his forehead for a few seconds. He was well aware of Vanetta's behavior toward him and was embarrassed by it all.

"I don't know what to say," Micah said. "I hardly know her."

"I guess I can mark her off my list because she's certainly marked me off of hers."

"Oh, don't give up so easily."

"Dinner's ready," Vanetta said cheerfully from the dining room. She had a small oval table and had Micah sit across from her as she poured wine into the glasses. Cora brought over the tossed salads and placed them next to the plates that held generous portions of vegetable lasagna.

"Everything sure looks and smells good," Josh said.

"It sure does," Micah said.

"Why, thanks Micah," Vanetta said. "I hope you like it. I looked around for the best recipe for lasagna that I could find. I ended up getting it from Elizabeth Gormley, the food editor at the paper. Do you know her?"

"I think I've seen the name," Micah said. "I never go to that department. How about you, Cora?"

"I've seen her but I don't know her. I think she puts out an interesting food page."

Josh quietly began eating after being ignored by Vanetta on his other comments.

"Do you ever edit cookbooks?" Cora asked Josh.

Josh finished chewing some salad, swallowed, cleared his throat and then took a quick sip of wine.

"Never," he said. "We occasionally receive query letters about them but that's as far as it goes with us. But I know there's a pretty good market for them."

"What's your favorite sport, Micah?" Vanetta asked before taking a sip of wine.

"Probably college football."

"Why is that?"

"I like the strategy of eleven players lining up against eleven and both sides having plays to counteract one another."

"I think football is so complicated to understand," Vanetta said. "It just doesn't make any sense to me."

"View it like a chess game. The offense moves and then the defense moves. It keeps up that way until the offense scores or when the defense gains control of the ball."

"I never thought of it that way," Vanetta said, propping her head on her hand and smiling broadly. Josh glanced over at Cora and slightly rolled his eyes. They both smiled.

"Uh, what's your favorite sport?" Micah asked Cora.

"I think I like football, too," she said. "But I think I may like it for different reasons. I like the pageantry at the games with the bands, cheerleaders, and everything that surrounds it like the tail-gating."

"Tail-gating?" Vanetta asked, looking over at Cora. "What in the world is that?"

"That's when fans bring food to the game and eat out in the parking lot," Cora said. "Some people cook out. People set up picnic tables and really have a good time before going to the game."

"That seems like so much trouble," Vanetta said. "I think I'd prefer eating inside the stadium."

"You should try tail-gating," Josh said. "It's actually a lot of fun."

"Have you tried it, Micah?" Vanetta said. Josh grinned at Cora.

"Actually, I haven't," Micah said. "When I go to the stadium it's to watch the game from the pressbox so I really don't have the opportunity to do it."

"How about dessert?" Vanetta said glancing at each of her guests. "I have some apple pie and ice cream."

"I'll take both," Josh said.

"A small piece of pie for me," Cora said.

"I'll have a small slice of pie," Micah said.

Vanetta got up from the table and reached over and took each of their plates. Cora stood up and took the salad bowls and followed her into the kitchen.

"Am I invisible?" Josh whispered, shrugging his shoulders.

"I'm sorry," Micah said. "I don't know what to say."

"That's okay. I think it's kind of humorous now."

Vanetta and Cora returned with the desserts. Vanetta held Micah's pie and set it in front of him. She casually brushed her leg against him.

"Very good," Josh said after taking a bite of apple pie.

"It's delicious," Cora said with a smile.

Vanetta stared at Micah, awaiting his assessment of the dessert.

"It's very good," he said with a silly smile.

"Oh, that makes me happy," Vanetta said. "I was so worried that the crust wouldn't turn out flaky enough."

"It's just fine," Micah said.

Vanetta beamed widely at Micah.

After dessert, they went back into the living room. Vanetta sat next to Micah on the couch. They talked for about twenty minutes about what was going on the newspaper's promotion office.

"I need to be going," Micah said, looking down at his watch and wanting to get out of the conversation. One thing he never cared to discuss was the newspaper, especially when he was away from it.

"So early?" Vanetta said. "It's only ten."

"I need to get up early if I want to get to the Bengals' practice on time. I'm also going to drop by and visit my ex-wife on the way."

"Well, if you must," Vanetta said. "I do hope you can make it over again."

"We'll see," Micah said.

"Thanks for inviting me," Josh said.

"You're welcome," Vanetta said.

"Me, too," Cora said. "Do you need any help with the dishes?"

"No thanks," Vanetta. "I'll just put them in the dishwasher. It won't take me a few minutes to get everything cleaned up."

Vanetta accompanied Micah and Josh to the front door. Micah turned to shake her hand but she hugged him and kissed him on the cheek again. Josh opened the door and stepped outside.

"Thanks again," Micah said before turning and following Josh to the car.

"Good night," Vanetta said. "Toodles."

Micah got into the car and turned on the ignition. A commercial was playing on the radio and he turned it off.

"Interesting evening," Micah said as he drove out of the parking lot.

"For you," Josh said with a laugh.

"I never expected any of this. I'll never go over to her place again. I hope Cora got through it all right."

"I think Cora had a good time. She was picking up on what was going on and got tickled by it all."

"What do you think about her?" Micah said.

"Cora? I think she's a nice lady. Do you like her?"

"I like her."

Thirteen

Micah took his laptop computer out of the backseat of his car and walked across the hot pavement to the media center at the Bengals' training camp. As he entered the work area, he noticed Dirk Rogers talking to Fred Moore, the team's press relations officer. Fred threw up his hand and waved while Dirk simply looked through him. Micah found space on the table to set up his computer, took it out of the case and plugged the cord into a receptacle.

Fred came over and shook his hand, and gave him a couple press releases.

"Glad to see you, Micah," he said. "How's everything been?"

"I'm just getting back into the swing of things after Graham's death. But I'm doing all right."

"I hadn't realized your ex-wife was in the accident until a few days ago. How is she doing?"

"She's much better, thank you. She's at home now. It will probably take several months before she gets back to work. She broke an arm and leg so she's going to have some problems getting around."

"I sure hope she has a quick recovery."

"Thanks," Micah said. "So how has camp been going?"

"Most of the players are here. We're still waiting to sign our No. 1 draft choice. It seems like we go through this every year. These agents seem to think we should sign over the franchise to these kids."

"I guess that's part of the game. Try to grab all you can."

"The players are out of the practice field right now. They'll be coming off around noon. You can grab them as they head to the locker room."

"How about Jake Simmons?"

"Coach Simmons has a press briefing around 12:20 or so. It's in the room over there," Fred said, pointing to a room to his right.

"It looks like I have about twenty-five minutes before practice is over. I think I'll go out there and catch the end of it."

"Let me know if you need anything."

"Thanks, Fred," Micah said as he headed out the door to the practice field. There were about five hundred fans outside a fence watching the practice. Inside, next to the sidelines, members of the media were huddled in small clusters, chatting away about all sorts of newspaper gossip while waiting for practice to end. Coaches were blowing whistles as they worked with their different groups. Quarterbacks and receivers were together. Offensive linemen and running backs worked on timing. Defensive linemen and linebackers were slamming their bodies against tackling dummies. The secondary players were batting down passes.

"So what have you been up to?" Dirk said as he walked up to Micah. "I haven't seen you around in a few weeks."

"My ex-wife was injured in that accident that killed Graham," Micah said while keeping his eyes on the players.

"Were they together?"

"Yes. They were going to a symphony concert at the zoo."

"I hadn't realized they were dating."

"It's not something people advertise."

"Sorry," Dirk said. "I didn't mean to offend you."

"You didn't offend me. It's just a private matter that people don't normally discuss with everybody. What have you been up to?"

"I went with the Reds on their West Coast swing. It looks like there may be some shakeups at the end of the season."

"It wouldn't surprise me. I'm sure there'll be quite a few changes."

"Did you see my piece about Jack Colson probably on his way out as manager, possibly before the end of the season?"

"I'm sorry but I didn't," Micah said. "I was probably busy with other things."

"You should read it," Dirk said. "Quite revealing."

"I'm sure it is," Micah said while keeping his eyes focused on the practice field. "I'll make a point of looking it up when I'm back at the office."

Miles Jackson, the Bengals' beat writer for the *Register*, spotted Micah and came over. He had been covering the Bengals for eight seasons and was one of the first blacks hired by the sports department. He had covered high schools for three years before getting the Bengals' beat. He seemed out of place around the big and burly football players, being about 5-foot-6 with a slight build that carried no more than one hundred and thirty-five pounds. But he was a persistent reporter who wasn't afraid to ask tough questions. He had gained the trust of most of the players because of his straightforward and honest reporting.

"Hey, Micah," he said with a smile. "Good to see you. Hi Dirk."

Dirk nodded and walked away.

"How's camp been?" Micah asked.

"Same old stuff," Miles said. "It never changes. It's always hot, humid and miserable out here. The players really don't feel like standing around talking to us after practice and we really don't like hanging around out here either. It's kind of a peaceful coexistence."

"So what are you writing about today?"

"I thought I'd do something on Maurice Jones, that new cornerback they got from the Lions," Miles said. "He's supposed to be the guy who really takes the secondary to a new level."

"That sounds interesting. I was thinking about doing a column on what the coaches want to accomplish while they're here for three weeks."

"Go for it. I've got a few notes and quotes that I've picked up the past few days that you can have."

"Thanks. I need all the help I can get," Micah said with a laugh.

"Did Dirk have anything to tell you?"

"Not really," Micah said. "I think he was a little peeved that I hadn't read one of his columns."

"So what's new? That guy is really a pain in the you-know-what. I don't know why they put up with him at the *Herald*. He thinks he's God's gift to sports writing."

"Well, he is a good writer."

"I know he is but he doesn't have to tell people how good he is."

"Probably a little insecure."

"Could be. I just think he should let his writing speak for itself."

At that moment, a horn sounded that signaled the end of practice. The players took off their helmets and started a slow jog to the locker room. They wanted to get out of the midday sun and under the cold showers. Along the way, a few of them stopped to sign autographs for the fans. A few of the reporters and camera crews walked alongside some players for interviews as they made their way off the field.

Micah was able to run down the offensive and defensive coordinators for a few questions about preseason goals before they headed off to meet with Coach Simmons and talk with him before the press briefing. Micah went on to the press room and waited for Simmons.

Simmons, a big man who had been an offensive tackle for the Eagles back in the 1960s, spoke in a measured tone. He didn't say anything the reporters didn't expect. The team was coming along fine. There hadn't been any injuries. All the players will be given a fair shake. He hoped to start making a few cuts by the weekend. It was the same thing coaches were saying at the other NFL camps. It lasted about fifteen minutes, then the coaches went to lunch for thirty minutes before breaking the squad up for team meetings. The reporters also grabbed a bite to eat, and then started pecking away stories on their laptops.

Micah got a few quotes off the press briefing, and along with the information from Miles, was able to write an 18-inch column about the team's expectations in camp.

"I think I've written this column before," Micah told Miles.

"Hey, it's about the same story every year. About the only thing that changes are the names, and that doesn't always happen."

Micah put his laptop back in his case. He and Miles walked out to the parking lot.

"Care to join me for dinner?" Micah asked.

"I wish I could but I brought my wife with me and she's waiting at the motel. I think she's already made plans. Thanks for asking."

"Well, I'm going on to Lexington. I'll be staying at the Marriott until Sunday. I'll be back over here tomorrow, and then I'll be going to UK for its media day."

"I'll see you in the morning. Don't get into any trouble tonight," Miles said with a laugh.

"I wouldn't worry too much about that. I'll probably be in bed by ten."

Micah got into his car and headed south on I-75 to Lexington. He arrived about twenty minutes later at the hotel and checked in. He carried his bags to the elevator and rode it up to the third floor. He walked slowly to his room, unlocked the door, and put the bags down, then sat on the bed and fell backward. He stared at the ceiling.

Micah realized he was lonely.

Fourteen

Micah returned to Cincinnati on Sunday afternoon. It was another sultry day. The sun was beating down hard. The Ohio River moved at a sluggish pace as the sweltering heat nearly took a person's breath away. Before going home, he swung around to Alice's home to see how she was doing.

George came to the door a few seconds after Micah rang the doorbell. He was wearing a T-shirt and knee-length plaid shorts.

"Come on in, Micah," he said. "Pardon my appearance but I just had to cool down. How have you been?"

"I just got back from Lexington," he said. "I thought I'd drop by for a few minutes and check in on Alice."

"I saw your column from Lexington in today's paper. It's hard to believe that it's almost football season. Is Kentucky going to have a good team?"

"I think they may be decent. They probably won't be talking about basketball down there midway through the season. But it's hard to tell. I've thought other Kentucky teams would be decent but they folded in conference play. So how is Alice?"

"She's doing much better. She's a little uncomfortable right now with this heat and having to wear those casts. But she's coming along nicely. She's taking a nap right now. Do you want to slip back into her room and see her?"

"No, that's okay. More than anything, I just wanted to check on her condition. How are the kids?"

"They're fine, too. Nora took them down to the neighborhood pool. They've been gone for about an hour."

"That sounds like the smart thing to do today. I think I may to go my apartment pool after I get home. Will you tell Alice I came by?"

"Of course, Micah. Why don't you call a little bit later?"

"I'll do that. I'd better get going. You take care."

Micah stopped by a drive-through Chinese restaurant and picked up a vegetable plate and egg roll. After he got home, he picked up a handful of mail and magazines from his mailbox and newspapers that had been left at his front door. He sat them on the table as he got a plate and silverware to eat his food. He noticed the red light blinking on his answering machine but decided to wait until he finished his lunch before playing back the messages. He already knew Alice was better and that's all he cared about at the present time.

While eating his food, he sorted through the mail, placing bills in one stack, junk mail in another, and magazines in a small stack. He flipped through *The Sporting News* quickly. He picked up *Men's Health* magazine, studied the cover of a muscular man holding some dumbbells, and wished he had a body like that. He knew he was getting too soft around the belly from so much inactivity. He used to play basketball a few years ago, but once he turned forty, he gave it up for fear that he would hurt himself. He knew of too many older guys who had severely sprained ankles, broken bones and torn up knees trying to play a young man's sport. He had also read about a few guys dropping dead from heart attacks.

After finishing his meal, he went back into his bedroom and took off his clothes. He looked in the full-length mirror on one of the closet doors, and flexed his muscles.

"I need to get this body back in shape before it's too late," he said out loud to himself. He went to the chest of drawers and pulled out a pair of swimming trunks and put them on, then opened the closet door and found his beach thongs. He glanced out his bedroom window to the courtyard area and noticed that there were a few people using the pool.

He grabbed a towel and headed out the front door. After getting to the pool, he found a lounge chair and placed the towel across it and took off the thongs. He went directly to the pool and jumped in. It seemed as cold as ice but his body quickly adjusted to the change in temperature. He began swimming from one end to the other, feeling the tension beginning to ease in his shoulder and leg muscles. After swimming six laps, he got out of the pool and returned to the lounge chair. He toweled off and eased slowly into the chair.

"Need some suntan lotion?" a soft voice asked. "You might get terrible sunburn if you don't."

Micah peered over to his right where a stunning blonde in a red bikini was lying on her stomach a chaise lounge four feet from him. He guessed her to be in her late twenties. Her body had a shimmering golden glow from the lotion that covered her from head to toe. She was wearing dark sunglasses.

"Hm, thanks," he said, trying to keep eye contact with her under the glare of the sun. "This is my first time out here this summer and I forgot to bring any with me."

Micah was sure she could tell that he hadn't spent any time at the pool. He had a farmer's tan, with only his arms, neck and face showing any signs of being out in the sun. His chest and legs had a pale olive tint.

"I didn't think I had seen you here before," she said while handing him the bottle of lotion. "My name is Tammy."

"I'm Micah."

"Have you lived here long?"

"I've been here for a couple of years," he said while spreading the lotion over his body. "How about you?"

"I moved in last winter. I really like it here."

"I do too. It's relatively quiet and most of the people are nice."

"So what do you do for a living?"

"I'm a sports writer."

"Oh. Where?"

"*The Register.*"

"I must confess that I don't read sports that often."

"That's okay. I don't always read the sports section either," he said with a laugh. "What do you do?"

"I'm a nurse at university hospital. I work in intensive care."

"That's interesting. My ex-wife was there last week. She was involved in that traffic pileup that killed six people."

"What's her name?"

"Alice Stewart."

"I vaguely remember that name. It was so hectic around there. Didn't she have some broken bones?"

"Yes. Arm and leg. She's home now."

"That's good. So does she live here?"

"She lives over in Mount Healthy."

"I have a few friends who live there. That's a nice family neighborhood."

Micah handed the lotion to her and leaned back in his chair. He had forgotten his sunglasses so he had to keep his head down. He could feel her eyes on him and it made him feel uneasy.

"Do you swim?" he asked.

"Not much," she said. "I usually get into the water to cool off."

"It sure feels refreshing today. This must be the hottest day of the summer."

"I heard it was about ninety-five."

"Well, I think I'm going to take one more dip in the water and then get out of this sun."

Micah walked over to the side of the pool and jumped in head first. He swam eight laps, lingering in the water for a few more minutes. Several people were pitching a beach ball back and forth on the other side of the pool.

When he returned to the chair, Tammy had already left. He picked up the towel and a small note was under it. It read: "I live in apartment 206. Call me sometime. Tammy." Micah looked around and she was nowhere to be seen. He dried off, put on his thongs, and went back to his apartment.

As he walked in, he saw the answering machine light blinking and remembered he had forgotten to replay the messages after lunch. He put Tammy's note on the end table and pushed the replay button. He figured he would have a message from Vanetta.

And he was right. The first one to play was from her on Wednesday night.

"Hi, Micah. I want to thank you for coming over last night. I hope we can do it again real soon, just you and me. Toodles."

The next message was from a roofing company, followed by a telephone survey, and Micah pushed the fast-forward button.

"This is Josh. I'm calling on Friday night. I'm not sure when you're supposed to get back, but if you return this weekend, give me a call. I've got a couple tickets to Riverbend to see Jimmy Buffett on Sunday night."

The next message was from Vanetta again.

"This is Van, calling on Saturday afternoon. I was hoping you'd be back by now. Call me when you get back. Toodles."

Micah shook his head.

"Hello, Micah. This is Cora. I hope you don't mind me calling. I was wondering if you'd like to meet for dinner on Sunday. Please give me a call if you'd like to. Bye."

Micah smiled and went back to the bathroom and turned on the shower. He wanted to get the remaining lotion and chlorine off his body. He lathered up his hair with shampoo and washed all over. He was thinking what he should do for Sunday evening. Concert with Josh? Dinner with Cora? He could even call up his new friend Tammy.

He turned off the faucet, stepped out of the shower and dried off. He put on some lightweight jeans, T-shirt and sandals, combed his dark brown hair and went back to the living room. He turned on the television and caught the beginning of *The Big Chill*. He sat back in his recliner, and before too long, was sound asleep. He woke up at nine o'clock. The concert had already started and it was too late to call anyone for dinner.

Micah picked up the phone and called Alice.

"Stewart's residence," Ben said after picking up the receiver.

"Hi, Ben. This is Dad. How are you doing, buddy?"

"Hi, Dad! We won another ball game yesterday. I wish you could have been there. I had a triple and two singles. Grandpa watched me."

"What a great game. I would have been there if I could," Micah said, realizing he had uttered those words many times. "Is your Mom awake?"

"Sure, Dad. Hold on a minute."

Ben took the cordless phone back to her bedroom. Alice was sitting up in the bed watching a movie.

"Your father tells me you're doing better," Micah said.

"I feel like I am," she said. "It's such a burden with the casts. I'll be glad when I get them off."

"It's going to be awhile."

"I know. I may as well get used to them."

"Do you need me to do anything?"

"I really can't think of anything. If you get a chance, you might drop by and take the kids out for dinner. They get to be a handful for Mom and Dad at times."

"That's no problem. How about Tuesday night?"

"That would be nice. I'll let the kids know."

"Well, you take care of yourself. Don't hesitate to call me for anything."

After he hung up the phone, Micah was thankful that he was able to be doing something for his family. But he knew that the situation really hadn't changed. If they had still been married, he probably would have been doing the same thing. His work would have prevented him from being with them every day. The phone rang and he picked it up.

"Where have you been?"

Micah quickly recognized the voice. It was Vanetta.

"I was out of town. I just got back today."

"Did you get my messages?"

"I did but I feel asleep in the recliner and realized it was too late to return any calls."

"Micah, you can call me anytime."

"Thanks, Vanetta. I just don't like calling people late at night."

"But I just called a few minutes ago and your line was busy."

"I called my ex-wife to see how she was doing," said Micah with a little irritation showing in his reply.

"Oh."

"I need to be getting off here," he said. "I've got a few things to do."

"Well please call me when you get a chance."

"I'll do that, Vanetta. You have a nice evening."

"Toodles."

Fifteen

"Hi, Dad!" Annie said, wrapping her arms around Micah's waist as he stepped into the living room. "Where are you going to take us to eat tonight?"

"It's up to you and Ben," he said, then kissed her on the top of the head. "It doesn't make me any difference."

Alice's parents had gone out for a break. They were going out for dinner and then do some shopping at one of the malls. Alice rolled into the living room in a wheelchair.

"My, don't we look like a queen on her throne," Micah said with a laugh.

"I don't feel like a queen but this sure beats being in bed all the time," she said, smiling. "Dad picked this up for me this morning. It's nice to get around."

"I'm sure it is. I wouldn't want to be confined in bed all the time."

Ben came through the front door carrying his ball glove. He was dirty all over.

"Take those shoes off at the door," Alice said. "I don't want you tramping that dirt through the house."

"Sorry I'm late Dad," Ben said while removing his shoes. "I had ball practice tonight and it ran a little late. Can I take a shower?"

"You'd better," Micah said. "I don't want you in my car like that."

Ben took off his shoes and went back to his bedroom. A minute later, the shower came on in the adjoining bathroom.

"So what have you been doing?" Alice asked as Micah went over and sat on the couch. "Dad said you were here Sunday."

"I was down in Georgetown and Lexington," he said. "Doing about the same things I do this time of year."

"How's everything at the office?"

"About the same. Spencer and a few of the guys asked about you."

"Josh called me over the weekend."

"He called me, too. He had some tickets for the Jimmy Buffett concert at Riverbend but I fell asleep on the recliner and didn't call him back."

Ben came out a few minutes later, his hair still wet, but looking fresh and clean.

"I'm ready," he said. "Where are we going?"

"It's up to you and Annie."

"How about Applebee's?"

"Is that all right with you, Annie?"

"That'll be okay."

"Will you be all right while we're gone?" Micah said to Annie. "Can I run out and get you something to eat before we leave?"

"I'll be fine," she said. "Dad and Mom won't be gone that long. I'll just sit here and watch TV. I've got the phone next to me."

"You won't try anything foolish?" Micah asked.

"I promise," she said with a smile. "I don't think I'm in the condition to do too many foolish things. Now you all just run along."

While waiting for their food at the restaurant, Ben talked about his baseball season while Annie told Micah about her beanie doll collection. Micah always enjoyed these kinds of moments with them.

"Dad?" Annie asked.

"What is it sweetie?"

"Why don't you and Mommy get married again?"

Micah paused for a second. From what had been childish talk about beanie babies turned very serious.

"That's a difficult question to answer," he said. "Why do you ask?"

"I just would like for you to be home again."

"Me, too," Ben said.

"Well, children, your Mom and I got divorced because we didn't share a lot of the same things you need in a marriage. I probably wasn't the best husband because of my work. Mom felt that I needed to be around more. She was probably right."

"Don't you love her?" Annie said.

"I still love Mom, but it's a different kind of love. It's just not the kind of love that married people have for each other."

"I don't understand," Annie said.

"It's hard to explain. You'll know what I mean when you get older."

The conversation ended as the waitress brought their food. Micah dug into his salad while the children ordered hamburgers and fries. They ordered hot-fudge sundaes for dessert.

George and Nora's car was in the driveway when Micah returned to Alice's house. He dropped the kids off in front, kissing Alice on the cheek and patting Ben on the knee. Ben had let it be known in the past year that he didn't want to be kissed in public by his Mom and Dad. He felt he was getting too old for that kind of affection. Micah knew it was a phase that he would grow out of in a few years.

George opened the front door as the children ran up the steps. He waved at Micah, and Micah waved back as he backed out of the driveway. Micah thought about what the children asked him about remarrying Alice on the way back to his apartment. He couldn't tell them that there wasn't any passion left between him and their mother. That had slowly drained from their relationship in the final years of their marriage. He still cared for Alice and wanted the best for her, but he knew that he could never live with her again. Micah wasn't sure if he was capable of maintaining any kind of relationship with anyone.

Micah pulled into O'Malley's bar a few blocks from his apartment. He stopped there occasionally after games to drink a beer to wind down before going home. It had been nearly a month since he had been there but it didn't matter because the place always seemed the same and usually had a few of the regulars around the bar or throwing darts.

"Where have you been stranger?" asked Tommy Wilson, who had been the bartender for as long as Micah could remember. "Ball games?"

"That's about it," said Micah, not wanting to bring up the traffic accident.

"Draft?"

"You got it."

"Josh was in here a little earlier. He was telling me about that Buffett concert he went to. He said it was excellent. I've always liked Buffett. Cool dude."

"I haven't seen Josh in a few days. I need to give him a call. Was he by himself?"

"Yeah. He was trying to make some time with a little blonde honey at the bar but wasn't getting anywhere with her," said Tommy, a big man with a full beard and salt-and-pepper hair than came down over his ears. He looked like a person you wouldn't want to meet in a dark alley but Micah found that he was gentle for the most part unless there was some disturbance in the bar. When that happened, he wouldn't hesitate to step in and break up the fight.

"How's business?"

"With this heat, people have been coming in to cool off," Tommy said in a raspy voice. "Usually business drops off in the summer because people are outside doing things. But it's been different the past few weeks."

"I know what you mean. I don't even like to be out in it for five minutes."

"You going to Riverfront this week?"

"I think I'll go out tomorrow night. The Dodgers are in town. It's still a decent rivalry despite being in different divisions."

"I may go out there this weekend. I haven't seen a game since May."

Micah finished his beer and got up from the stool.

"Sure you don't want another one?" Tommy said. "It's on the house."

"Thanks but I need to be getting home," Micah said as he took two dollars out of his wallet and laid it on the counter. "I'll see you later."

"Have a good one," Tommy said. "And don't be such a stranger."

"I'll try not to," Micah said as he headed out the door.

The answering machine was blinking when Micah got home. He imagined it was Vanetta. She was getting to be a regular. He touched the message button for the playback.

"Hi, Micah. This is Vanetta. Just calling to see if you're going to be busy this week. If you'd like to come over or go out and do something, you know where to reach me. Toodles."

"Don't hold your breath," Micah said while shaking his head. "You just don't give up."

The tape clicked and another message played.

"This is Josh. What have you been up to? You missed a great concert. Catch you later. Bye."

Micah was hoping that there would be one more message, but the machine went silent. For some reason, he wanted to hear from Cora but he knew she wasn't the type that would come on strong. Like Vanetta.

Sixteen

Micah covered the game between the Dodgers and Reds the next evening. It turned out to be a long, drawn-out affair lasting nearly four hours. He didn't leave the ball park until nearly one a.m. His column was about the longtime series rivalry between the two clubs and how it made the game interesting despite the teams being out of the pennant race.

He stopped by O'Malley's on the way home. Tommy was behind the bar and the place was nearly empty. A few of the regulars were sitting at the end of the bar talking about the game. A George Strait song was playing on the jukebox too loud for that time of the morning.

"How was the game?" Tommy asked as he set a mug of beer on a napkin in front of Micah.

"Long," Micah said with a laugh. "The gods of baseball have been talking for years about shortening the game but it just seems to drag on and on. I wouldn't be surprised if one of these days they don't bring in some kind of gimmicks to entertain fans between pitches."

Tommy laughed heartily.

"So what else are you going to be doing this week?" Tommy asked, leaning on the bar with his elbows. "Other than the Reds, it seems like things are kind of dead around town."

"I may go over the UC's football practice," Micah said after taking a swallow from the mug. "I was even thinking about driving up to Columbus and see the Buckeyes. But I'll probably end up going back out to Riverfront. There's still something magical about sitting in a ball park and watching a game unwind."

Tommy took Micah's mug and filled it back up.

"What do you ever do when you're not around here?" Micah said.

"Nothing much. I've got a motorcycle and I like to ride out in the country when I have time. I also go to concerts over at Riverbend whenever I get the chance."

"I've always wanted a cycle. I never got around to buying one. It looks like the epitome of freedom."

"I guess a lot of people look at them that way, and they are to some extent. But they can be dangerous as hell on the highway. I couldn't count the times I've nearly been run over by someone. You've really got to keep your eyes open out there. But I love riding."

"I may end of buying a cycle one of these days but I think I'll wait until I'm right smack in the middle of my mid-life crisis," Micah said with a chuckle.

They talked a few more minutes about what kind of motorcycle would be good for him to purchase before Micah finished his beer and went home. He didn't play back any of the messages on the answering machine. He went straight to bed and didn't wake up until ten.

He fixed a small pot of coffee and two pieces of toast the next morning, then opened the front door and picked up the newspaper. He glanced up at the sky and saw some big, puffy clouds. It was already warm and humid.

Pouring a cup of coffee, he sat down at the kitchen table and opened the newspaper. The lead story was about plans to ease the congestion coming off the Brent Spence Bridge. It carried Cora Miller's byline. He read the story but couldn't help but think about Cora. It had been awhile since he had seen her.

After finishing with the newspaper, he put the cup and plate in the sink and showered. While under the hard spray of the water, he decided he would give Cora a call and see if she would like to go out for dinner.

But after he got dressed, Micah decided to drive to the newspaper and ask her in person. He had been out only a few times since his divorce and felt somewhat uncomfortable about calling someone up on the phone. He preferred engaging them in a conversation in person and let it lead up to a date. But after he got to the newspaper, he found out it was her day off. He picked up the company directory and wrote down her home phone number on the back of his reporter's notepad.

"What are you doing in here so early?" Spencer asked. "Didn't you go to the game last night?"

"I just had to check up on a few things," Micah said.

"How's Alice?"

"She's coming along real well."

"Tell her I asked about her."

"I will. She's got a wheelchair now and wheeling about the house."

"What are you doing for lunch?"

"I don't have any plans. I need to make a few calls but it will only take a few minutes."

Spencer gazed at the clock on the wall and saw that it was 11:45.

"Can you wait around until noon?" he asked. "I have a couple of things to do myself. We can walk down to Big Shots."

"Sure. Just let me know when you're ready."

Spencer turned and walked back to his office. Micah picked up the phone and dialed Cora's number.

"Hello," she said after the fourth ring.

"Hi. This is Micah. Am I calling at a bad time?"

"No, no. I was just sweeping off the balcony."

"I saw your story this morning about the bridge. Nice job."

"Thanks," she said sweetly. "My city editor told me they've come up with plans for years but nothing ever changes."

"That's probably right. At least they're still talking about it. I hope some good comes from what happened to Graham and all the others."

"I do, too," she said.

Micah could sense the conversation beginning to stall.

"I've was out at Riverfront last night," he said.

"I saw that," she said. "I read your column this morning."

"Well, uh, I was wondering if you had any plans for this evening?"

"Give me a second to look through the listings in TV Guide," she said with a laugh.

"Would you care to go out for dinner?"

"Sure," she said, cheerfully.

"How about if I pick you up around eight?"

"That would be fine. What kind of place do you have in mind?"

"I was thinking of some casual restaurant. Is that okay with you?"

"Sure. I see you at eight."

After putting down the receiver, Micah looked through the *Herald* and read Dirk's column about the need for some changes in the Reds. Micah thought it was well-written although he didn't care for Dirk's preachy tone. Spencer finally came out of his office at 12:15.

"Ready?" he asked Micah as he put on his sports coat. "Sorry it took longer than I expected. The publisher called."

"Anything important?" Micah asked as they walked to the elevator. He knew that Williams Andrews, the newspaper's publisher, was a big sports fan. It wasn't that uncommon for him to suggest stories to Spencer about the Reds and Bengals.

"Apparently he read Dirk's column and thinks we should hit the Reds a little harder," Spencer said as they rode the elevator down to the first floor. "I guess we'll have to do something for the weekend."

"I wrote a column several weeks ago about that. Didn't he see that?"

"You know how he is," Spencer said as they stepped out of the building and on to the hot pavement. "His memory bank when it comes to sports lasts about forty-eight hours."

They found a table in Big Shots and both ordered iced tea while waiting for
meals.

"How's everything these days?" Spencer asked after taking a big swallow of tea.

"About the same," Micah said. "Why do you ask?"

"Sometimes you don't seem as enthused."

"The accident took a little out of me but I feel like I'm getting back my vim and vigor."

"To be honest, Micah, you've seemed a little disinterested for several months."

"Really?"

"Your copy has read very well but you seem to be down about something. I was wondering if there's something I could do."

"I'm fine, Spence. Honest. I guess I got a little depressed after the divorce but I think I've bounced back from that."

"Well, if there's ever anything I can do, just let me know. We've been friends for a long time."

"I appreciate that," Micah said with a smile.

Their food arrived and they talked about the upcoming football season and some other areas related to the newspaper's coverage. When they finished, Spencer went back to the newspaper while Micah returned to his apartment.

He thought about what Spencer had said about his attitude. Micah didn't sense any big changes in himself. He still covered the same teams and wrote on a variety of topics. But he realized that he was getting into a rut. There were hardly any stories that really got him excited anymore. And he thought about the restlessness in his personal life. He knew it was similar to his work at the newspaper. He was simply going through the motions most of the time. He didn't have focus.

After he got to his apartment, he went through his compact disc collection and put a Garth Brooks CD on the stereo. He lay down on the couch and closed his eyes for a few minutes. He was looking forward to the evening with Cora. It would be something different. A smile crossed his face.

Seventeen

Micah arrived at Cora's apartment five minutes early. She came to the door wearing khaki slacks and a lime-colored blouse. She had a relaxed look on her face, unlike the times he had seen her in the office when she was working on stories.

"Come on in," she said with a bright smile. "Make yourself comfortable. Can I get you something to drink?"

"No thanks," said Micah as he walked over and sat down on the couch. He picked up a *Cosmopolitan* magazine and flipped through the pages while she went back to the bathroom to make a final check of her makeup. A Celine Dion CD was playing softly on the stereo.

"How was your day?" she asked, sticking her head out the door.

"I haven't done much. I had lunch with my boss. How about you?"

"I took care of my laundry and tried to clean up around here a little bit."

"You've got a nice place," Micah said, looking around the living room at the tasteful furnishings.

"Thank you," Cora said as she returned to the living room. "I'm ready."

She turned off the stereo and all the lights except for a lamp before locking the front door. They got into Micah's car and drove slowly out of the parking lot. As they entered the highway, a red sports car was coming in. It was Vanetta. If she noticed them, she didn't let on. But they saw her.

"She's getting home late," Micah said. "Are you two good friends?"

"I wouldn't call us good friends," Cora said. "We're friendly to one another but we seldom see each other. I think she likes you more than she likes me."

Micah laughed.

"Why do you say that?"

"You know why," she said, grinning. "She can't keep her eyes off you."

"She's called me several times at home."

"Really?"

"She's invited me to go out with her."

"Hmm."

"I really don't plan to. She's not my type."

"Okay."

Cora smiled a Micah. He could feel her eyes on him. It made him feel a little uneasy.

"I don't know why I'm volunteering all this information to you," he said.

"That's okay, just keep talking," she said with giggle. "I don't have my tape recorder on."

They both laughed.

"If we can change the subject, I thought we'd go to that new Tex-Mex restaurant on the west side of town," Micah said. "It's called El Poncho's. Is that all right with you?"

"Sure, I like Mexican," she said. "I know a couple of reporters who've been there and they liked it."

After arriving at the restaurant, they had to wait ten minutes before getting seated. They each ordered a margarita, which they finished in the waiting area before they got their table. They ordered another one while the waiter left them some salsa and chips.

"How do you like Cincinnati?" Micah asked.

"I think it's a wonderful town. There's so much to do here and the people are friendly."

"I know what you mean. I've been here for a few years now and I don't think I'll ever leave, unless it's to Florida or Arizona after I retire."

"How is your ex-wife doing?"

"She's coming along just fine. She gets about in a wheelchair now. I think she's going to be okay."

"That's good to hear. I know that had to be an awful strain on you, her and your kids."

"It was. It's something you have to deal with. Life isn't always easy. We all have to deal with tragedies of some sort."

"I guess you're right," she said. "I remember how difficult it was on my family when my father died from prostate cancer. He was only fifty-six at the time. It really left a big void in our lives."

"Can I ask you a personal question?"

"Go ahead. Don't reporters always do that when they're talking to each other?" she said with a soft laugh.

"You're right about that," he said. "Have you ever been married?"

"Never," she said. "I've had a couple of close encounters that never reached the altar. In our jobs and the hours we work, it's kind of difficult to have a meaningful relationship."

"I can attest to that. The longer I worked for the newspaper, the more distant I became from my wife. I didn't even realize it until it was too late."

"Do you still care about her?"

"We're still good friends. I can honestly say that there were hardly any bad words between us during our marriage and while we were going through the divorce. We simply grew apart as a couple. Kind of sad, I guess."

"Do you think you'd ever remarry her?"

"That's funny you say that because the kids asked me the same thing the other day."

"And what did you tell them?"

"I told them I wouldn't. I didn't go into detail but I tried to tell them that we're just going to be friends from now on."

"Why is that?"

"This is beginning to sound like an interview," Micah said, arching his eyebrows playfully. "Are you sure you don't have that tape recorder running?"

"I'm sorry," she said. "We can talk about something else."

"That's all right. I don't mind talking about it. I guess Alice and I simply fell out of love with each other. We still care for each other but the romantic part of it died. It's hard to explain. I never thought it would happen but I guess it's something that occurs in a lot of marriages and relationships."

"That's sad."

"So, do you have a boyfriend?"

"Hmm, you interviewing me now?" she asked with a giggle.

"Just wondering."

"I've been out a few times with several guys but I don't have anything serious going on. I'm too busy at work to have much of a social life."

"And that's sad."

"I plan to start making time for myself," she said. "You know how it is when you first start a job. You have to get to know the territory and everything about the workplace. I'm getting more comfortable as time goes on."

The waiter returned with sampler platter for each of them. Micah ordered another round of margaritas.

"You may have to carry me back to my apartment," Cora said with a laugh. "I usually don't have more than two drinks."

"I'm sorry. I can order you a soda if you'd like."

"I'll be okay as long as I pace myself."

"So where are you from? Tell me a little about yourself unless you want to be grilled," he said with a chuckle.

"Let's see, I'm from Virginia. I went to the University of Virginia and got my bachelor's degree in English. I've worked at papers in Virginia, Georgia and Florida. Anything else?"

"What do you like to do?" he said. "Hobbies and such."

"I like to travel when I have the money," she said. "I went on a three-week vacation to Europe three years ago and I definitely want to go back. I like to read. I like going to concerts. Anything else?"

"How old are you?"

"Now that's really personal," she said with a light laugh. "A woman never gives out her age!"

"Sorry," he said with a mischievous grin.

"Thirty-four."

"You sure don't look it."

"You know how to say the right things," Cora said, smiling. "I feel forty-four most of the time."

"So how old are you?"

"Forty-two"

"And what do you like?"

"I think I'm probably a dull boy," he said. "All work and little play."

"Oh, come on, I know you enjoy doing certain things."

"I like to read," he said. "I like music."

"What kind of music?"

"I like oldies and some country."

"I like oldies but not too keen on country except for some of the girl singers like Trisha Yearwood, Mary Chapin Carpenter, Patty Loveless, and Pam Tillis."

They finished their margaritas and ordered coffee. Micah glanced down at his watch and saw that it was nearly 10:30.

"We've been here more than two hours," he said.

"Where has the time gone?"

"Lively conversation and good company. Time flies when you're having fun."

"And I have enjoyed this evening," Cora said.

"Perhaps we can go out again soon."

"I guess we'll have to check our schedules."

"Don't remind me," Micah said, shaking his head slowly.

Eighteen

Cora had just changed into her nightgown when she heard loud knocks on her front door. It startled her at first because she wasn't accustomed to seeing anyone past eleven. She put on a yellow bathrobe and walked softly to the front door and looked into the peep hole. Standing under the outdoor light was a grim-faced Vanetta.Cora slowly opened the door about six inches and looked at Vanetta. She kept the door chained.

"May I come in?" Vanetta asked tersely.

Cora unhooked the chain and backed away as Vanetta stepped inside her living room.

"Did I see you leaving the parking lot with Micah tonight?" she asked in a demanding voice.

"Yes, you did," Cora said calmly. "Is there anything wrong?"

"Perhaps for you there isn't, but I'm a little bewildered. I didn't know you were interested in him."

"I think Micah's a nice man. He asked me out for dinner and I accepted."

"I can't believe it," Vanetta said, shaking her head angrily. "I've had him to my apartment for dinner and I've called him several times. And this is what he does to me. It's like a slap in the face."

"A slap in the face?"

"Yes," Vanetta said, getting a little flustered. "I've shown him all this attention and he asks you out."

"It's nothing serious. We're just friends."

Vanetta turned and walked toward the door. Her face was flushed by what had transpired. She glanced back at Cora, tears in her eyes, then opened the door and stormed out without another word. Cora stood in amazement, hardly able to believe what she had just heard.

Cora went to the refrigerator and took out a two-liter bottle and poured herself a small glass of soda. She sat down at the kitchen table. She pondered on whether to call Micah and tell him about what had happened. She felt uneasy about the situation because she had never really considered herself a rival with Vanetta. She hadn't been chasing after Micah. At least she didn't think so. Her calls to his home were out of concern for his ex-wife and family. She had never invited him over. And in the newsroom, she had never made it a point of checking in the sports department to see if he was ever around. She finished her drink, washed the glass out in the sink, and went on to bed.

The next morning, she got up, showered, got dressed and went on to work earlier than usual. On the way to the parking lot, she saw Vanetta walking to her car. Vanetta looked in her direction and turned her head quickly.

"Well, be like that," Cora said to herself as she opened the door to her car.

After arriving at work, Cora got a cup of coffee in the employee lounge and went to her desk. She picked up a newspaper to read in for the day. It was something every reporter did to know what was going on in the city. A few minutes later, the phone rang.

"City desk, this Cora Miller. May I help you?"

"Good morning, Cora," Micah said.

A big smile beamed across her face. She wasn't expecting a call from him.

"Oh, hi," she said.

"I just wanted to thank you again for going out with me last night," he said.

"You're welcome but you don't need to say that. I had a very enjoyable time."

"I'm going to be out the next few nights but I was wondering if you'd like go back out next weekend?"

"I can't," she said dejectedly. "This is my weekend to work nights. I'm sorry."

"That's okay, I guess. That's part of the business."

"I had a visitor last night after you dropped me off."

"A visitor? Who?"

"Vanetta."

"Vanetta? What did she want?"

"Hmm, she's a bit peeved at us. She saw us leaving the parking lot. Did you know that she likes you? I mean she likes you a lot."

"Well, I must admit that she has been coming on to me a little strong. She's called me several times at home."

"That's what she told me. I believe she thinks that I've done something to undermine her."

"That's nonsense. You've haven't done anything."

"Well, she said that what we've done is a like a slap in the face. I guess it's a pride thing."

"Good grief!" Micah said with a chuckle. "You know, I like Vanetta but that's as far as it goes. She really doesn't interest me in the least bit. The person who had goo-goo eyes over her was Josh, and she's totally ignored him. Perhaps she's getting a little bit of her own medicine."

"Could be," Cora said. She then noticed George Underwood, the city editor, nodding at her. "I need to go now. The boss is calling."

"Okay. Do you mind if I give you a call later in the week and see what your schedule looks like?"

"Of course not," she said with a soft laugh. "You can call me anytime."

"I'll talk to you later. Bye."

"Bye."

~ * ~

Micah drove up to Columbus and spent part of the day attending preseason football practice at Ohio State. He always enjoyed the trip because he would occasionally see some of his sports writing friends. After filing their stories, they would meet for dinner and talk about the Buckeyes and then exchange information about the comings and goings of other sportswriters in the region.

Micah returned to Cincinnati late in the evening and made a stop at O'Malley's. Tommy was behind the bar, and had a mug of beer in front of Micah almost before he sat down at bar stool.

"Whatcha been up to today?" Tommy said. "Any big story?"

"Only football practice at Ohio State."

"Are the Buckeyes going to be tough this year?"

"I think so. They should contend for the Big Ten again, as they usually do."

"Screw the Big Ten. Can they beat Michigan?" Tommy said with a big laugh.

"I wouldn't bet on that," Micah said with a grin before taking a swallow of the ice-cold beer. "Has Josh been around?"

"I haven't seen him for several days."

"He must be busy editing a book. He sometimes disappears for several days when he's in the final stages of editing."

Tammy, wearing her nurse's smock, came through the door. She had let down her long blonde hair and appeared soft and delicate in the dimly-lit bar.

"Hi, Tam," Tommy said. "The usual?"

"Thanks," she said as she sat down four seats from Micah. Tommy brought over a wine spritzer and sat it in front of her on a napkin.

"Long day?" Tommy asked.

"Very long," she said. "I thought I'd stop by to relax for a few minutes before I go home and crash." She glanced down the bar and noticed Micah, who was looking at her while she was talking.

"Have you been back to the swimming pool?" Micah asked with a smile.

"Hi," she said. "No, I haven't had time. How about you?"

"Same here. I've been too busy."

"I assume you two know each other," Tommy said.

"We live in the same apartment complex," Micah said. "We met at the pool a week or so ago."

"Do you come in her often?" she asked Micah.

"Several times a week when I'm in town. This is my place to unwind. How about you?"

"I stop by about once a week."

Micah finished his beer and got up to leave.

"It's time for me to go," he said. "It was nice seeing you again."

"Good to see you. Perhaps I'll see you at the pool this weekend."

Micah smiled warmly at her and waved at Tommy before walking out the front door. Tommy took Micah's mug and wiped off the surface of the counter where he had been sitting.

"He seems like a really nice guy," Tammy said.

"He is. A real gentleman."

Tammy smiled to herself and finished her drink.

"I'll see you later, Tommy," she said.

"Do you need a walk to your car?"

"Thanks but I'm parked right out front."

"Good night," he said as she left.

Nineteen

During the next several weeks Micah covered the Brickyard 400 at Indianapolis and went with the Bengals on exhibition games at Denver and Jacksonville. The only contact he had with Cincinnati was with the sports department after he filed his columns and several phone calls to Alice to see how she was coming along from her injuries. The weather was beginning to cool, especially in the evenings, and the humidity during the day wasn't nearly as bad as it had been before he went out of town.

When he returned home Sunday evening, the answering machine was loaded with messages. Josh had called several times. There was a couple from Ben, telling him about the upcoming soccer season. He wasn't expecting anything from Vanetta, and he didn't have anything. But neither were there any messages from Cora.

It was still early in the evening. The sun was slowly setting. Micah picked up the telephone and called Josh.

"Hello, stranger," Josh said. "What have you been up to?"

"Sorry I haven't called but I've been on the road the past couple of weeks."

"I saw where you've been to a few different cities. How are things going?"

"About the same. I was wondering if you wanted to go over to Big Shots and get a bite to eat."

"Sounds good to me. I was just sitting here watching TV and going through a couple of manuscripts. Nothing really pressing."

"I'll see you over there. About 8:30."

"See you then."

Micah had forty-five minutes to get over to the pub, which was just a fifteen-minute drive. He went ahead and called his children. Alice answered.

"Ben is spending the night with Larry," said Alice, referring to one of Ben's neighborhood friends. "Annie and Mom went over to Baskin-Robbins. They should be back in a half an hour."

"I'm going out to eat with Josh about that time. I guess I can call them tomorrow. How are things with you?"

"I'm doing much better. I had a checkup last Friday and the doctor said the bones are healing well. I may be able to get the cast off my arm in a few weeks."

"That would be nice. I'm sure it would help you get around a lot better."

"It sure would. I'm tired of lugging all this extra weight around," she said. "Plus I've put on some extra weight because I haven't been able to exercise. I hate to see what I'll look like when all this is over."

"Oh, you'll look fine. And you've never had any problem taking off pounds."

"You're being kind," she said with a soft laugh.

"So is anything going on?"

"That's about it. I just wish I could get back to work. I'm tired of being cooped up in here. I'm going a little stir crazy."

"How about if we go out to dinner sometime this week?"

"That would be nice but it's such a hassle right now. Perhaps after I get the cast off my arm. Thanks for asking."

"Well, just let me know when you're ready to go out. My schedule is somewhat better now."

"I'll do that."

"I'd better get off of here. Tell the kids I called."

"I will. Thanks for calling."

After hanging up the receiver, Micah took a shower and put on some clean clothes. He wore jeans, light yellow polo shirt and new brown western boots he bought while in Denver. While walking to the parking lot, he saw Tammy taking some books out of her car.

"Need any help?" Micah said.

"Oh, hi Micah!" she said while flashing a big smile. "No thanks, I'm fine. Where have you been? I haven't seen you in awhile."

"I've been on the road with the Bengals and covered a race in Indianapolis. I've been pretty busy. How about you?"

"I haven't been anywhere but I've been busy. I haven't even had time to eat since I got home from work six hours ago."

"I'm meeting a friend for dinner," Micah said. "Why don't you come along?"

"Oh, I couldn't do that. What would she think if you walked in with me?"

"Well, first of all, it's a he," Micah said with a chuckle. "I don't think he'd mind."

"Can you give me a few minutes to change into something else?"

"No problem. I told him I'd meet him at Big Shots at 8:30. We've still got thirty minutes."

"Okay," she said while closing the door to her car. "I'll be back in just a few minutes."

Tammy returned in ten minutes and they got into his car and drove to Big Shots.

"Have you ever been to Big Shots?" Micah asked.

"No, I haven't," Tammy said. "I've heard about it from several of my friends at the hospital."

"They serve pretty good food and the atmosphere is nice for a pub."

Micah knew Josh would be surprised to see him walking into the pub with a gorgeous blonde. He figured that Josh wouldn't mind meeting her. Josh had been down on his luck with Vanetta so perhaps he would be able to strike up something with Tammy.

They got to Big Shots right on 8:30. Josh already was sitting in a booth. He waved his arm to get Micah's attention. Micah noticed a puzzled look on his face when he and Tammy reached the table. His mouth was half open when he saw her next to the table. She was wearing tight jeans and denim shirt over a bright pink tank top.

"Josh," Micah said with a grin, "I'd like you to meet Tammy. She's a neighbor of mine. I hope you don't mind that I invited her to join us for dinner."

"Uh," Josh said as he stood up and put out his hand. "Uh, nice to meet you. No, I don't mind."

"I apologize Tammy but I don't know your last name," Micah said.

"It's Meeks," she said.

Tammy crinkled her nose and smiled with a knowing look about how she was affecting Josh.

"It's nice to meet you, too," she said while shaking his hand.

"Uh, my last name is Larkin," Josh said quickly.

"How about a pitcher of beer?" Micah said to Josh. They both glanced at him and nodded.

Micah sensed some chemistry between Josh and Tammy. They both couldn't seem to take their eyes off each other and both wore silly grins.

"Been busy?" Micah asked Josh.

"Oh, yeah, real busy," Josh said without elaborating.

"Tammy is a nurse at University Hospital," Micah said.

"Really?" Josh said. "I bet that's interesting work."

"I enjoy it," she said. "Are you a sportswriter, too?"

"Nah," Josh said. "I'm a book editor. I'm sure that's not as interesting as your job."

"I don't know about that," Tammy said. "If you like to read, then it would be very enjoying."

"I guess so," Josh said. "I do like to read."

The waitress brought over a pitcher of beer. Micah poured the beer into tall, slender mugs. A little later, their food arrived. Josh and Tammy dominated most of the conversation but Micah didn't mind because he was still a little road weary. Micah smiled when Tammy gave Josh her telephone number.

"It was really a pleasure meeting you," Josh said to Tammy after they walked to the parking lot after finishing their meals. "I hope we can do it again."

"Same here," she said with a grin.

"I'll give you a call tomorrow," Josh said.

"I'll be working from seven in the morning until about seven in the evening so I probably won't be home until eight or so," Tammy said.

"Perhaps I'd better call some other time," Josh said.

"No," Tammy said quickly. "Call me after eight. I was just letting you know that I wouldn't be home during the day."

"I'll do that," Josh said. He nervously shook her hand. "Bye."

"Good bye," Micah said to Josh.

"Oh, yeah, bye Micah," Josh said. "I'll talk to you later."

Micah and Tammy returned to the apartment complex after dinner. Josh returned to the bar and had another beer with a literary agent he had worked with on several books.

"Thanks for inviting me," Tammy said after they got to their apartment complex. "I really like your friend."

"I figured you would," Micah said with a smile. "To be honest, he's my best friend. And I think he likes you, too."

They parted and went to their apartments. Micah was glad that Josh may be finding someone. He also was happy that it was Tammy because she seemed to be a good person. Micah had never played matchmaker because he never liked to interfere in other people's personal lives.

Sitting on the couch, he turned on the TV. ESPN's SportsCenter was just coming on so he watched it for thirty minutes while going through the Sunday newspaper. On the local page, he noticed Cora's byline. He wondered if she was at home or working on some story. He put his hand on the telephone receiver for a few seconds, then took it off. It was getting late. He knew he had to be getting to bed. Perhaps he would call her this week.

Twenty

"Where in the world did you meet that lady?" Josh asked Micah the following night at O'Malley's.

"She's just a neighbor," Micah said with a laugh. "We met at the pool a few weeks ago. So you think Tammy's nice?"

"Man, she's a knockout. I was thinking about asking her out. Do you think she'd go out with me?"

"Hmm, I don't know her that well, but the way she was looking at you last night I think she might. And she did give you her phone number so that should tell you something."

"I'm going to call her this week. I need to think of a decent place to take her."

"You shouldn't have any trouble with that. Just remember that she works odd hours at the hospital. You'd better be flexible."

"I'd be flexible for her anytime of the week," Josh said with a grin. "So how are things with you?"

"I've been busy, as usual. It never lets up."

"You don't sound so enthused," Josh said. "Are you getting tired of it all?"

"I think I'm at the burnout stage. Perhaps I'm past it."

"Why don't you look into doing something else?"

"What am I going to do at my age?"

"Your age? Damn, you're still young. You're far from being over the hill."

"Well, I feel like an old forty-two," Micah said with a half-hearted laugh. "And besides, what can I do? Journalism isn't exactly the best field to make a career change."

"You're nuts, friend," Josh said. "Writing is still at a premium. You can do a lot of different things."

"I guess I should just get up off my duff and do something about it," Micah said while shrugging his shoulders. He nodded over to Tommy for two more mugs of beer.

"You've been in the doldrums for quite a while," Josh said. "I thought you would snap out of it by now. I think Alice's accident kind of brought things to a head for you. Am I right?"

Micah didn't reply as Tommy brought over the beer. He walked back the cash register and lit up a cigarette. Mary Chapin Carpenter's *I Feel Lucky* was playing on the jukebox.

"That could be part of it," Micah finally said. "If I may be perfectly honest, and I've never told anyone this, but my life seems so empty."

"Empty? What do you mean?" Josh said with furrowed eyebrows.

"Well, work isn't that satisfying anymore," Micah said, wrapping his hands around the mug and looking straight ahead. "It seems like I'm in a rut. And my social life is practically non-existent. It just seems like I work and that's all there is."

"Don't we all feel that way at times? Aren't you dating?"

"I haven't had a date in several weeks."

"I thought you were going out with Cora. Haven't you heard from her?"

"No. I've been out of town and I'm sure she's been busy at the paper."

"Why don't you call her up?" Josh asked before taking a swallow from the mug. "I think she's nice woman."

"I think so, too. I probably should give her a call."

"Have you ever thought about getting back together with Alice?"

"We're just friends. I did invite her to dinner after she gets the cast off of her arm. But there's nothing there between us. We lost any fire between us long before we got divorced. We're better friends than lovers."

"Well, she's a helluva friend for you," Josh said.

"No doubt about that," Micah said. "It's a shame that she lost Graham. He was good for her."

"I think you're good for her, too, but that's really none of my business."

"It's hard to explain my relationship with Alice. I think you'd have to be involved with a person for a long time to understand what can happen in a relationship."

"I suppose so," Josh said.

"Have you gotten over Vanetta?" Micah said with a laugh.

"Geez, what a weird woman she is. I felt like the invisible man around her. But she has a great body. You should ask her out."

"No, thanks," Micah said raising his hands. "No way! She's trouble."

They finished their beers and Josh paid the tab. It was raining when they stepped outside. Lightning flashed in the distance. They dashed to their cars and drove home.

Micah's answering machine light was blinking when he walked in the door. He was wet and went back to the bathroom to take off his clothes and dry off. He put on his bathrobe and went back to the living room and hit the message button.

"Micah, this is Vanetta. I'd like to know what I've done? I saw you with Cora the other night. I don't understand. Would you call me or see me at my office and explain why you are doing this to me?"

Micah shook his head. It was the first time he'd ever met a woman who wouldn't let go after a date. He didn't feel he had let her on. He couldn't understand why she was acting this way toward him. He decided it would be better to call than visit her at the newspaper because he wasn't sure how she would react to him.

The tape clicked and the next message came on. Micah knew from the first word it was Cora. It brought a warm smile to his face.

"Hi, Micah. I guess we've both been busy the past few weeks. I see where you've been on the road. I've also had a several assignments that have kept me busy. Give me a call when you get a chance. Bye."

It was nearly midnight, too late to be calling anyone. Micah went on to bed, deciding he would go into the newspaper office in the morning and check mail. And perhaps Cora would be working.

The storm passed through the area during the night. The sun shone brightly in a clear, blue sky when Micah left his apartment at ten. Despite his recent doldrums, he felt good as he drove to the newspaper office. After getting off the elevator, he went directly to the sports department and checked his mailbox. Spencer was in a news meeting with other department editors, mapping out the news for the next edition of the paper.

Micah quickly looked over the mail. They were all press releases, people trying to push story ideas on him. They all ended up in the trashcan. He walked over to the city desk and saw Cora poring over some statistics in a spreadsheet. She didn't see him approaching.

"You look busy," he said lightly.

"Oh, hi Micah," she said while turning her head toward him. "Good morning. I didn't expect to see you today."

"I needed to check on my mail and messages," he said. "That's about all. I got your message."

"It seems like ages since I've seen you."

"What's your schedule look like this week?"

"I'm free in the evenings and this weekend."

"Would you like to do something?

"Sure. I'm up for about anything."

"Would you like to go the races over at Turfway on Saturday?"

"That would be fun."

Micah sensed that someone was staring at him. He turned around and looked at the entrance to the newsroom. Vanetta was standing there, glaring at both of them. She stood motionless for a few seconds, and then stomped off.

"I think we've lost a friend," Cora said, raising her eyebrows.

"I don't know if we need friends like her," Micah said. "She left a message on my answering machine yesterday, asking me to call her or see her at the newspaper. I think I may have to call her."

"What did she want?"

"She wants me to explain to her about why I'm treating her the way I have. I really don't know what in the world she's talking about. I never had any kind of relationship with her."

"But she didn't see it that way," Cora said. "She fell for you hard. What are you going to tell her?"

"Don't you think the truth would be the best thing?"

"Probably. I hope she can handle it."

"Enough about her. I'll pick you up around six on Saturday. We'll eat at the track dining room. The races start at 7:30."

Cora smiled sweetly.

"I'll see you then."

There was a bounce in Micah's step as he left the newspaper office. Less than twelve hours earlier he had been lamenting to Josh about his sorry state of affairs. Now he had something to look forward to on the weekend.

Micah spent part of the afternoon attending football practice at Moeller High School, the traditional football power in the area. He interviewed the head coach and several players, and then worked up a column at his apartment about how confidence can play so much in a school's success. After transmitting the story to the sports department, he picked up the phone and called Vanetta. She answered the phone in a cheerful tone but quickly sounded unmoved after realizing it was Micah on the other end.

"What do you want?" she asked curtly.

"You asked me to call you so that's what I'm doing," Micah said in a calm voice. "You wanted some explanation."

"I really don't think that's necessary now."

"Well, if that's the way you feel, then so long."

"Why are you treating me like this?" she asked quickly.

"I really don't understand what you're talking about, Vanetta."

"You've just totally ignored me since I had you over to my home. I don't know why you've done this to me. I don't deserve to be treated this way."

"Vanetta, I don't understand why you're acting this way. There has never been anything between us. I accepted the invitation to your house out of friendship. There was nothing to read into it."

"Well, thanks a lot," she said with a tinge of anger. "You dump me and go to Cora."

"What in the world are you talking about? Dumping you? There was never anything between us. As for Cora, that's really none of your business."

"You can go to hell!" Vanetta said and slammed down the receiver.

"Be that way," Micah said as he put the receiver down. He went back to the kitchen and took a can of beer out of the refrigerator. He walked back to the living room and turned on the television.

Twenty-one

Micah arrived at Cora's apartment five minutes early. He couldn't get over how youthful she appeared when she was away from work. She had a radiance about her, pearly white teeth and pure complexion.

"Do you feel like you've got some winners tonight?" Micah asked as he stepped inside. "Have you studied the entries in today's paper?"

"What are entries?" she asked with a laugh. "I've never been to a race track in my life. About the closest I've been to horse racing is watching the Kentucky Derby on TV when I can."

"I think you're going to enjoy it then," he said. "I don't get out to the track as often as I would like. I just love to watch the horses run."

"Do you bet much?"

"This may surprise you but I very seldom bet. When I'm working, I don't bet because I find it a distraction. And this may sound odd, but when I'm covering something at the track, I feel I'm there to work instead of betting."

"That sounds reasonable to me, I guess," she said. "Ready to go?"

Turfway Park was a twenty-five minute drive from her apartment. On the way there, he tried to explain to her the basics of handicapping although he knew most of it was going right over her head. At the track restaurant, they were seated close enough to watch the races. They ordered drinks and watched the grounds crew go over the track's surface in their tractors and prepare it for the first race.

"I called Vanetta last night," Micah said.

"Really?" Cora said as her eyes opened wide. "What did she have to say?"

"She couldn't understand why I supposedly dumped her," he said, shaking his head. "I tried to explain to her that there was never anything between her and me. She told me to go to hell and hung up on me."

"Oh, my goodness. I never thought she'd be that way."

"I learned a long time ago that you can't really judge people," Micah said. "They all react differently to situations. They may be reasonable in some circumstances and totally irrational in others."

"I suppose you're right," she said. "I told you she had it bad for you."

"Oh, cut it out," Micah said, grinning. "She didn't know me well enough to feel that way."

"I hope she doesn't bother you anymore."

"And I hope she doesn't bother you. You're more likely to see her than I am."

"She'll get over it."

Micah ordered a vegetarian plate of broccoli, carrots, corn and a baked potato and a large glass of ice water when the waitress came around as Cora was still mulling over her decision.

"I think I'll have the same," she said. "I need my veggies."

"Are you sure?" Micah asked. "Please don't feel you have to eat vegetarian because of me."

"I do it quite often," she said. "It's no problem for me."

After the waitress left, Micah scooted over next to Cora and opened *The Daily Racing Form*. He began going over all the entries in the first race, taking out a pen and marking off the horses he didn't think had a chance of winning. He went over the past performances, showing her how the horses did in recent races, the distances and times. He smelled the faint scent of her perfume as she moved a little closer to him, momentarily causing him to lose his train of thought.

"Uh, are we ready to bet?" he asked. "What horse do you like?"

"Oh, I don't know. Why don't you make the first pick and we'll see how it does."

Micah pointed out to the tote board and showed her the odds on the horses and how many minutes until post-time. He explained to her how the horses would pay off if they won.

"How about if I bet $6 across the board on Royal Regret?" he asked.

"What does that mean, across the board?"

"If the horse finishes first, second or third, we will get the payoffs on him. It's a fairly safe bet since he's the second favorite at three-to-one."

She walked with Micah to the betting window and listened to him make the bet. They walked back to the front window and watched the horses being loaded in the gate for the six-furlong race. The bell sounded and the horses were off. Royal Regret stayed close to the leaders, running fourth in the eight-horse field in the backstretch. As they turned for home, Royal Regret made his move. Cora started jumping up and down and yelling.

"Come on! Come on!" she screamed as the horse was closing in on the leader in the homestretch. Royal Regret came on strong and won by a head. Cora turned and gave a big hug to Micah. He started laughing.

"Was that exciting?" he asked while his arms were wrapped around her.

"Oh, that was wonderful," she said. "I've never seen anything like it."

After the race became official, Micah went to the window and got his payoff and went back to the table. Their food had already arrived.

"Well, this pays for dinner," he said with a laugh as he put a wad of money on the table from his winnings.

"That was so much fun," she said. "Is it always that easy?"

"Easy?" Micah said with a smile. "You've got to be kidding. It was pure luck!"

They stayed through the seventh race and decided to leave early and beat the traffic out of the parking lot. Micah won more than $200, the best he had ever done.

"Do you want to go to Big Shots or someplace?" Micah asked as he pulled out of the parking lot. "It's still fairly early."

"Would you rather come to my place?" she asked. "I've got some beer in the refrigerator and some wine."

"Sure," Micah said as he glanced over at her. "It would be a lot more peaceful."

After they got to her apartment, Cora went back to the kitchen and got him a beer and poured a glass of red wine for herself. She handed him the beer and walked over to the stereo. She put on a James Taylor CD and kept the volume low.

"I like JT," Micah said. "I saw him in concert a few years ago at Riverbend."

"I love James Taylor's music," she said as she sat down next to him on the sofa. "I've got most of his CDs. I've probably seen him about five times. I think he's great."

"So you like concerts?"

"I love going to concerts but in this job it's kind of hard ever finding the time to go to them."

"The Moody Blues are going to be playing in Louisville next month. Would you like to go?"

"I'd love to see them," she said. "Let me know the date and I'll see if I can arrange to be off that day."

"I'll let you know in the next day or so."

Micah took a swallow from the can and laid it on the coffee table. Without a thought, he put his left arm behind her on the couch. She kicked off her shoes, leaned back a little and put her feet up on the coffee table.

"So do you have a busy week ahead of you?" she asked, resting her head resting against the couch.

"Not really," he said. "I get into a routine that hardly changes from year to year."

"Is that good or bad?"

"It does get a little monotonous but at least I know what I have coming from week to week. Occasionally I have to write a column on breaking news, such as a manager being fired or a player traded. I really don't mind though. That keeps the job interesting. What does your week look like?"

"A few meetings and whatever happens around town," Cora said. She took a sip of wine and put the glass down on the coffee table.

She put her head back on the couch and smiled at Micah. The dimly-lit living room cast a soft glow over her face and her brown eyes sparkled as she gazed into his eyes. Without hesitation, Micah turned slightly toward her and put his lips on hers. They closed their eyes and partially opened their mouths. His heart was racing and he could feel her heartbeat. Their mouths parted for a second, and then Micah turned even more and put his right arm around her waist and gently pulled her toward him. They kissed again, this time longer and with more passion.

Micah straightened up on the couch and Cora rested her head on his shoulder as his arm rested on her shoulder.

"That was nice," he whispered. "I've wanted to do this all evening."

"I'm glad you did," she said softly. "I've been waiting for you to do it."

They sat without talking for several minutes while being serenaded by James Taylor on the stereo. They closed their eyes and savored the special moment in their relationship. Micah put his hand under Cora's chin, lifting her head up and kissed her again. He couldn't remember kisses being so tender and sweet. He savored the moment.

"I guess I should be going," Micah said as he glanced at his watch. It was 11:45 p.m. "We both have to work tomorrow."

"I wish you didn't have to leave so soon but I guess you're right," she said with a sigh, and kissed him on the cheek. "I've really enjoyed this evening."

"Me, too," he said with a warm smile. "Can I call you tomorrow?"

"Micah, you can call me anytime," she said with a soft laugh.

"Perhaps we can go out to dinner again this week?"

"I'd love to."

Cora walked with Micah to the door. They kissed again in the doorway before he left. He smiled all the way as he drove to his apartment.

Twenty-two

Micah was awakened the next morning by a phone call from Spencer Duggins. It was unusual for him to be calling in the morning. About the only time that ever happened was when there was some breaking story.

"It looks like there's going to be some changes with the Reds," Duggins said in his deep raspy voice. "A few sources have told Frank Smith that Jack Colson is out as manager, effective sometime today. I need you to make some calls and write something about what is going down."

"Sure, Spence," Micah said, clearing his throat. "I'll hop right on it. Where is Frank?"

"He's at home making some calls. He got tipped off last night from someone in the organization."

"Anything from the competition?"

"Nothing so far but I'm sure they'll get wind of it pretty soon."

"Well, let me make a few calls and I'll get back with you."

"Thanks, Micah. Bye."

Micah took out a small black address book that he always carried with him that contained names and phone numbers of people he came into contact with on various stories. There were names of players, coaches, front-office personnel, and community leaders along with those "unnamed" sources that always seemed to end up in stories.

It took only a few calls before Micah was able to find out that Colson was out as manager. Micah wasn't surprised because the team had failed to perform up to expectations this season. He liked the manager but somehow felt that he had lost control of the team. There wasn't the cohesiveness, chemistry and camaraderie that was usually part of contenders. He was told that Colson was expected in the clubhouse at ten to pack his personal belongings.

Micah called Frank and Spencer and told them what he had learned and that he would be heading down to the stadium to interview Colson. Frank would be there, too, while Spencer said he would bring in a general assignment writer to write a sidebar about Colson's career.

Colson was behind his desk when Micah knocked on the door frame. The only other people in the clubhouse were the trainers. Colson nodded for him to come on in and sit down.

"I'm sorry to hear what's happened," Micah said while opening his notebook.

"Not as much as me," Colson said with a forced laugh. He had been around baseball for nearly thirty-five years, first as a player who bounced around the majors for eighteen seasons, then as a coach and finally as a manager. He was well-liked by the players, probably too much, and had been popular with the fans until the team started losing. He was in his late fifties, but the leathery look of his skin and gray, thinning hair made him appear ten years older.

"Surprised?"

"Oh, yes and no. When you look at our record, it's what you'd expect. But I guess that any manager believes that they need one more season to turn it around. I still feel like this team has the potential to compete for the division title. Perhaps someone else can do it."

Frank stepped into the tiny office that seemed more like a transient's quarters. The walls were bare except for a clipboard holder for the starting lineup. A closet contained a few uniforms. Colson sat behind a gray metal desk that was bare on top.

"Hiya, Frank."

"Hi, Jack. What are your plans now?"

"I've been thinking about that. I'll probably go back to Texas for a while. Maybe I'll try to get a real job," he said. "I think the first thing I'll do is get out my fishing pole and get away from it all."

"I can't say I blame you," Micah said, wishing he could do the same.

Micah and Frank spent about thirty minutes with Colson while he finished packing his gear.

"I've always appreciated you guys," Colson said while leaning back in his chair. "I may not have always agreed with what you wrote, but I've always respected you. I felt you were being fair with me. I can't say that about everyone."

Micah knew Colson was referring to Dirk, who had spent quite a bit of time with the Reds in recent weeks, hinting about the firing of Colson but not supporting his stories with anything other than hunches. Micah was sure Dirk would be hot under the collar after being scooped on a story he felt he had been on top of for the past month.

"Jack, you've always been fair with us, for the most part," Micah said with a grin. "And when you weren't, you always let us know in some way there was more to a story. I hope everything goes well for you."

Micah and Frank shook hands with Colson and left. On the way back to the newspaper office, Micah used his cell phone to call Spencer and give him the details. Spencer told him that the newspaper was coming out with a rare bulldog edition about Colson's firing and that they had until noon to write their stories.

Micah didn't mind deadline writing. He always felt he excelled in those situations. It would get his adrenaline flowing and the computer keyboard would almost sing as his fingers hit the keys in an up-tempo rhythm. Micah and Frank finished their stories by noon. Thirty minutes later, a pressman brought out the newspapers with the banner headline: *Reds Fire Colson.*

Cora came in from covering a government agency meeting when she saw Micah along with several other editors in the sports department. They had just watched the noon news and none of the three stations in town had the story about the firing.

"What's all the commotion?" she asked one of the copy editors, who then held up the front page to show her. She saw Micah's column down the left side of the paper.

Micah glanced over to her direction and smiled, and then walked over to her.

"It looks like you had a busy morning," she said with a grin. "Congratulations."

"Thanks," he said. "I guess we got a little lucky."

"You're too modest."

Micah blushed. He felt good about what the newspaper had accomplished. In today's electronic journalism, it was difficult for a newspaper to beat television and radio with a story. More than anything, he was happy to get the story before the *Herald.*

"Hey, Micah," Spencer said, motioning him to come back to the sports department. "ESPN radio wants you for a quick interview."

"I'll see you later," Micah said to Cora as he turned and walked back to the sports department.

Micah, Spencer and Frank spent the next two hours on radio interview shows. After it died down, Micah looked in the newsroom and saw that Cora had already left. He returned to his apartment, happy that the Reds had a day off and would be going back on the road for a six-game swing. He lay on the couch and dozed off to sleep, not waking until dusk. He was hungry and decided to go down to Big Shots.

He got a seat at a bar table and ordered his usual veggie burger, fries and a mug of beer. While looking around nowhere in particular, he was startled by someone addressing him from his rear, and turned around.

"Congratulations. You really scooped everyone on Colson's firing."

Dirk was holding a beer and stared grimly at Micah. Micah knew it must have taken everything for Dirk to say something to him about the story.

"Thanks, Dirk."

"I've been working on that damn story for weeks. I can't believe what happened," Dirk said with anger building in his voice.

"Those things happen. Next time, you may get the story. You know how those things go. I'm surprised TV or radio didn't get the story first."

"It still pisses me off," Dirk said before taking a big swallow of beer. "You work your ass off to get something and this happens. It's just not right."

Micah didn't want to gloat, at least outwardly, but he felt a great deal of inner satisfaction for the story. He knew that Dirk would have been laying it on him heavily if he had broken the story.

"Ah, it'll be old news tomorrow," Micah said. "I wouldn't lose too much sleep over it."

"Then why don't you tell my editors that? I'm sure that's an explanation they'd like to hear," Dirk said sarcastically.

"You know what I mean," Micah said. "No malice intended."

A waitress brought over Micah's food and another mug of beer. Micah took a bite out of the veggie burger, hoping Dirk would see he was eating and go away.

But it didn't happen. Dirk was getting drunker by the minute. And more obnoxious.

"Damn, this really pisses me off," he said loudly, drawing attention from several people sitting close by. "Work your ass off on a story and someone pulls the rug out from under you. I'm going to find out who did this to me."

Micah didn't say anything. He took a big bite from his burger and chomped on it slowly. He didn't want to get into an argument with Dirk in a crowded restaurant where most of the patrons knew them. He then dipped a French fry into ketchup and ate it slowly.

Micah looked up at the front entrance and saw Vanetta standing at the doorway. She had already spotted him and was making her way to his table.

"Hi, Vanetta," Micah said as she came up to him. "Care to join me?"

She hesitated for a second as if she wasn't going to take his offer, then pulled out the stool and sat down. Dirk smiled but she ignored him.

"I see where you made headlines today," Vanetta said very businesslike.

"I wouldn't say I made headlines but it was a big story," Micah said.

"It should have been my story," Dirk said, slurring his words. "I got screwed."

Vanetta stared at him and raised her eyebrows.

"Why don't you go over to the bar and sit down?" Micah said quietly to Dirk. "You need to sober up some."

"Kiss my ass!" Dirk said. "You don't need to be telling me what to do." The area around the Micah's table got quiet. The night manager came over and took Dirk by the arm and escorted him to the corner of the bar. He had the bartender bring over a cup of coffee.

"Who's that creep?" Vanetta asked.

"That's Dirk Rogers. He works for the competition. He feels like he got burned."

"I know the feeling," she said.

"Can I order you a drink?"

"I'll have a mug of light beer."

Micah got the attention of the waitress and ordered two more mugs of beer. He offered Vanetta some of his fries but she declined.

"Can't we just be friends?" he asked.

"I don't know if I can be just friends with you."

"Why do you say that? We never had anything going between us."

"Do you honestly believe that?"

"Yes. I've never had any feelings for you out of the ordinary."

"Well, thanks a lot," she said, her face reddening in the cheeks. "I guess I really misread your signals."

"Signals? What signals?"

"The way you looked at me the first time we met. The little things you did when you came over to my apartment."

"Listen, Vanetta, I apologize if I gave you the wrong impression about anything. That was never my intention. I was just being myself."

"So all along you liked Cora?" Vanetta put the mug to her mouth and took a long, slow sip.

"I'd rather not discuss Cora. That's a whole different matter and it's personal."

"Be that way," she said.

Micah didn't respond. He glanced at the corner of the bar and saw Dirk passed out, his head buried in his arms. Micah motioned for the waitress and asked her for his bill.

"I need to be going," he said to Vanetta. "I hope we can still be friends."

Vanetta's eyes were welled up with tears. She turned away from him.

"Perhaps," she said. "We'll see."

Micah paid his bill and left money to cover Dirk's bill and left. When he returned to the apartment complex, Josh and Tammy were talking in the parking lot. They had just returned from dinner at a seafood restaurant near the Ohio River.

"Hi," Micah said.

"Hello," Tammy said. "How are you doing?"

"Just got back from Big Shots. Nothing much else going on."

"Way to kick butt on the Colson story," Josh said. "That's been the talk of the town."

Micah knew better than to think people were talking about the Register coming out with the story first. Most of them wouldn't be able to tell you who had it first since it was already on radio and television. But it still felt good.

Micah left them talking in the parking lot and went up to his apartment. He didn't want to infringe on Josh's time with Tammy.

Twenty-three

"Would you please cut this out!" Cora said into the telephone mouthpiece. "Enough is enough!"

"Are you all right?" Micah asked

"Oh, Micah, I'm sorry. I thought it was another prank call. That's all I've been getting since I got home tonight. About every five minutes or so someone calls and doesn't say anything. It's been going on for more than an hour now."

"Do you have any idea who it could be? Did you write something that would have ticked somebody off?"

"I don't think so. And if I did, I don't think the people I've been writing about in the past week would be doing something so juvenile."

"How about if I we go out and get a bite to eat?"

"That would be nice. I don't know if I can stand this much longer."

"Do you have a beeper from work?

"Yes. Why?"

"Then why don't you turn off the ringer on your phone. If they need to reach you from the paper, they can beep you."

"That's a good idea," she said. "But how will you reach me?"

"Just give me your beeper number," Micah said with a laugh.

"Stupid me," Cora said with a sigh.

"I'll be over in about twenty minutes."

Micah put the receiver down and went back to the bathroom to brush his teeth and comb his hair. A minute later, his phone rang.

"Hello," he said. "Hello."

There was silence. He hung up the receiver and went back to the bedroom. He changed his shirt and headed to the front door. The phone rang again. He hesitated for a moment and then went back and picked it up.

"Hello," he said. Again there was silence at the other end. He put the receiver back down on the phone.

"Okay, we're going to have someone playing games with me too," he said to himself as he headed out the front door. Cora was sitting on the couch reading the *Columbia Journalism Review* when Micah arrived at her apartment.

"I'm so glad you're here," Cora said as she opened the front door. "Those phone calls were getting on my nerves. I've never had anyone do it to me before."

"Well, you've got company," Micah said. "I got a couple of those calls after talking to you."

"Who could it be?"

"I've got an idea."

"Tell me."

"There is only one person I know who is mad at both of us."

"Vanetta?"

"That's right. She's the only person I could think of who might do something like this."

"Surely, Vanetta wouldn't do something so silly and immature. I know she's upset that we're dating but to do these things with the telephone is stupid."

"I agree that it's stupid but she's the only person who would have any reason to do it."

"Perhaps you're right," Cora said with a look of concern. "What do we do about it?"

"Let's just wait it out and see if she stops. If she doesn't, I guess we'll have to confront her about it."

"Well, I'm famished now," Cora said, forcing a smile. "Can we go get something to eat?"

"Let's go," Micah said as he got up and walked to the door. "Any place in particular?"

"I don't care. McDonald's would be okay with me."

"How about Wendy's?"

"That's okay."

"Wendy's has a salad bar," Micah said with a laugh.

A Wendy's was about five minutes from Cora's apartment. They went inside and placed their order. Some noisy teen-agers in one corner of the dining area were playing a boom box. The night manager went over and asked them to turn it off, and after a slightly heated exchange, the teen-agers stormed out of the building.

Micah went over and fixed a salad while Cora unwrapped a chicken breast sandwich and took a bite from the French fries. An elderly couple was sitting two tables over, quietly eating their food as if they were afraid to disturb anybody after the manager had the run-in with the youngsters.

While standing at the salad bar, Micah glanced over at Cora for a few seconds. She was the first woman he had any feelings for since his divorce from Alice. There was a self-assuredness about the way she carried herself. Being a reporter on the city beat took a certain amount of confidence and inner strength because they had to deal with all kinds of people and situations. But there was still softness about her when taken away from the newspaper element.

"If you don't mind me saying, I'm surprised that you've never been married," Micah said after returning to the table and sitting down next to her.

"I've had a few close calls," she said with a laugh. "I guess I'm still married too much to the business to get settled down with any one person."

"Dated anyone here?"

"Nobody at the paper. I've gone out with a couple of lawyers I met over the courthouse. That's about it."

"I'll try not to hold that against you," Micah teased.

"Oh, they were nice guys although a bit full of themselves."

"It's hard to have any kind of relationship in this business," Micah said. "It's even more difficult with a family. I know that first-hand."

Cora took a bite from her sandwich and looked directly into Micah's eyes. She took a sip from the straw in her soda as she continued to look at him.

"Impossible?" she said.

Micah cleared his throat and took a drink from his iced tea. He felt a slight tension in his neck.

"Well, I guess nothing's impossible."

"You don't like to take chances?"

Micah felt a little uneasy. He wasn't used to someone throwing questions his way but he decided to play along with her.

"I took chances the other night and won," he said with a grin.

"I wouldn't say you scored big."

"What do you mean? I won more than $200."

"You're talking about the horse racing," she said with a coy smile.

"Of course," he said. "What did you think I was talking about?"

"Hmm."

"And after that, I figured I got to first base."

"I don't remember a ball game."

"I don't remember one either," he said, arching his eyebrows ever so slightly.

"But you didn't score."

"I usually don't swing for the fences the first time out."

"Afraid you'll strike out?"

"Not really," he said. "I prefer to get runners in scoring position. Doing that I have a better chance of hitting a grand slam."

Cora giggled.

They finished eating their meals, and Micah took Cora back to her apartment. He remained in his vehicle as she opened her door to get out.

"Do you care to come in for a little while?" she asked. "I've got some beer in the fridge."

"Thanks for the offer, but I've got to get up early in the morning and run a few errands," he said. "Let me know if you get any more of those phone calls."

"I'll do that," she said with a smile. "Thanks for coming over."

"Anytime," he said.

"Good night," Cora said, flashing a big smile before closing the door.

"Wait a second," Micah said as he opened his door and got out. He walked around to her and kissed her tenderly on the mouth.

"That was worth waiting for," she said.

Micah was tempted to stop at O'Malley's on the way home but figured if he didn't have the time to go up to Cora's place he sure didn't have any business stopping off for a beer. After he got home, the answering machine light was blinking.

After pushing the message button, the first two calls were silent. The third was from Josh. Micah guessed that the mystery caller figured that he wasn't at home and quit calling. Micah returned Josh's call.

"Evening, Josh," he said. "Sorry I wasn't home when you called but I was out with Cora. We went out and got a bite to eat. What's up?"

"I was wondering if you'd be interested in doing a quickie book about Colson?" he asked. "If you could knock something out in three weeks, say 30,000 words or so, we could get it out by the first of October."

"I don't think so," Micah said. "I think too much of Colson to write something that quick. Plus, I really don't have the time. Thanks for asking. You might try Frank Smith at the paper."

"I'll do that," Josh said. "I just wanted to give you first dibs."

"Cora and I have been getting crank phone calls," Micah said.

"Any idea who it could be?"

"Just between us, I think it could be Vanetta. She's upset with both of us."

"I wouldn't be surprised. She's weird."

"I don't know what to do."

"Do you have a caller ID on your phone?"

"No," Micah said. "I never had a need to get one. That's a good idea. I could find out right away if it was her."

"And if she continued, you could get caller block to prevent her from ringing your phone."

"You're a genius, Josh," Micah said with a laugh.

"I know," Josh said, chuckling. "Now if others could only see it."

"I'll get that caller ID tomorrow. I need to go now. Any chance you can make it over to O'Malley's sometime this week?"

"Just give me a call," Josh said, and then added with a laugh, "Toodles."

Twenty-four

Alice answered the doorbell, standing erect with crutches, when Micah came by to see how she was doing. She was wearing a paisley granny dress, and her hair was nearly touching her shoulders. All the bruises and cuts from the accident had vanished. Except for the leg in a cast, she was radiant. The sparkle was back in her blue eyes and she had a rested appearance.

"My, my," Micah said, "Don't we look wonderful."

Alice smiled. Micah gave her a hug as he stepped into the living room. Nora was sitting on the loveseat watching a soap opera. She turned downed the volume with the remote as Micah made his way to the couch.

"Hi, Nora," he said. "How are you doing?"

"Just fine, thank you," she said. "What do you think of Alice?"

"I'm really amazed she's doing so well," Micah said, glancing over at Alice with a smile as she eased herself down on the couch.

"I'm feeling much better," Alice said. "I'm getting used to these crutches now. "

"How much longer will you have the cast on?" Micah said.

"Eight to twelve more weeks," she said. "It won't be over soon enough for me."

"I can imagine," he said.

"The kids should be getting home from school pretty soon," Alice said. "They've been asking about you."

"I'm really sorry I haven't been over any sooner," he said. "I've had all sorts of things happen at the office."

Nora's attention was on the television as she turned up the volume slightly. Micah was always amused just watching her facial expressions during different scenes while watching a soap opera. She had been watching them for as long as he could remember.

"I hear you've got a girlfriend," Alice said.

Micah blushed lightly.

"Where did you hear that?"

"Josh called the other day and mentioned that you had gone out with a reporter at the newspaper. I believe he said her name is Cora."

"We've gone out several times," Micah said. "It's not anything serious by any means."

"I think you should go out," Alice said with a soft smile. "You've been consumed by that newspaper way too long. You need to start enjoying life. I've been telling you that for years."

"I know you have. It's just hard to let go. But I'm trying."

Ben and Annie burst through the front door. They had seen Micah's car parked in front of the house from a block away, and both made a dash to the house.

"Daddy!" Annie said as she jumped on his lap and kissed him on the cheek.

"Hi, sweetie," he said, giving her a gentle hug. "How's school?"

"I like my teacher. She's real nice."

"Hi, Dad," Ben said, sitting down between Micah and Alice. Micah put his arm around him and patted him on the shoulder.

"Hi, son. What have you been up to?"

"I'm on the soccer team," he said. "And I guess my teachers are okay."

"You've got several teachers?"

"Yep," he said with a grin. "I'm in junior high now. Didn't you know that?"

"Uh, I remember," Micah said. "It just slipped my mind. You kids are just growing up too fast for me."

"Can you stay for a while, Dad?" Ben said.

"I think so unless your mother has other plans for you."

"Just get that homework finished," Alice said. "That's the house rule this school year."

"Aw, Mom," Ben said with a grimace.

"Don't 'Aw, Mom,' me," she said with a laugh. "You and Annie go to your rooms and do your homework. It won't take that long. Dad will still be here."

The children went to their rooms and closed their doors. Nora was still caught up in the soap.

"Have you been able to do any work?" Micah asked.

"I've done some copyreading of ads," Alice said. "I usually spend about twenty hours a week on it. They've been able to e-mail me different things. I'm really looking forward to getting back out and showing homes again."

"Do you have enough money?"

"I'm doing fine," she said.

"I'll be glad to give you whatever you need," Micah said. "I don't want you and the kids to do without. Will you let me know if you need anything?"

"I will," she said. "That's awfully nice of you to make that offer."

"Well, we're still family, regardless of our status. I still care very much for you and the kids."

"I know you do."

A little later, after the children had finished their homework, Alice ordered out for pizza and breadsticks. Micah wasn't crazy about pizza but he never complained because he knew how much they liked it. They sat around the dining room table and ate it, and talked about what was going on in school. Micah left around seven.

On the way home he stopped at a phone mart in the mall and bought a caller ID box. The salesman showed him how it worked. Micah wasn't always that good with gadgets but this one didn't appear too complicated. He hooked it right into the telephone when he got home. He waited around the phone for the first caller, and it was Cora's number that registered on the readout.

"Hi, Cora," he said answering the phone.

"How did you know it was me?" she asked with a laugh.

"I bought a caller ID," he said. "Now we'll find out who's been pulling these prank calls."

"Good," she said. "I haven't received any today so perhaps we won't get any more."

"I hope that's the case but you never know. I want to be ready if it happens again."

"So what have you been up to today?"

"I went over to see Alice and the kids. I stayed and had pizza with them."

"That's nice. How's she doing?"

"She looks great. She's getting around great with the crutches. Her leg will probably be in a cast for another three months."

"I bet your children were glad to see you."

"I was glad to see them. I hadn't been over there in several weeks. I really felt bad about it. I need to make more time for them. They'll be up and grown before I know it."

"That's right. You'd better make the time now."

"Would you like to meet them?"

"Perhaps at a later time. I don't know if they'd be ready for me right now."

"You might be right. Children have a tendency to be a little jealous at times."

"I know I was when my parents got divorced," Cora said. "I remember crying myself to sleep when my Dad showed up one evening with his girlfriend. I couldn't bear to be around them. I feel bad about it now because she was really a nice woman. She died a few years back from breast cancer. She was as sweet as she could be."

"We'll just play it by ear then."

"I think we need to get to know each other a little better. And I think you should prepare them for me before it ever happens. Have they ever met any other woman?"

"Nope. There's never been anyone that I've been around as long as I've known you."

"That's surprising. I thought you'd have women lining up outside your apartment to be with you," she said with a light laugh.

"Dream on," he said. "I was too busy for a wife, so why should I have had time for girlfriends?"

"Well, you've made some time for me."

"That's been a conscious effort. I'm trying to change my ways."

"I'm thankful," she said. "I hope I've been worth the time."

"I'm not complaining," he said with a chuckle. "But they know about you."

"They do?"

"At least I think they do. Alice mentioned your name. Josh had told her that we've gone out a few times."

"How did she take it?"

"Oh, she doesn't mind. She's dated since we split. She's always felt I needed to get out and enjoy myself."

"Well, I just wanted to call and see how you were doing. Are you working tomorrow?"

"Yes, I need to write about what the Reds should look for in a manager. I haven't a clue about it but I'm sure I'll come up with some answers," he said with a laugh.

Smiles were on their faces as they hung up the phones. Micah sat next to the telephone for about an hour, reading the newspaper, and hoping to get another call to check out the caller ID. But the phone sat silent, and he finally turned off the lights and went to bed.

Twenty-five

Tommy was talking to several regulars when Micah entered O'Malley's and sat down at the bar. He nodded at Micah and a minute later brought over a frosty mug of beer. A George Strait song was playing on the jukebox. It was still early in the evening and many of the patrons hadn't arrived.

"Staying busy?" Micah asked.

"It's getting a little more busy around here now that the kids are back in school and people aren't out doing things at night," Tommy said while wiping off the counter with a white washcloth. He was perpetual motion behind the bar. When he wasn't cleaning off the counter, he would be washing and drying glasses or fixing pre-mixed drinks for shots. Occasionally he picked up a broom and started sweeping. He couldn't stand still for very long.

"Any of the new bars hurting business?" Micah asked.

"Probably some but not that much," Tommy said. "We have our regulars we can count on all the time. You've got to have those core customers to stay in business. Did I tell you I'm thinking about having karaoke a couple nights a week?"

"No you didn't. How come?"

"Just to try something new. I've been to a couple of establishments with it and people seem to be having fun."

"I guess so," Micah said. "I've seen it around the country at hotel bars. It can get on your nerves after awhile because there are some really bad singers out there. I think karaoke is a magnet for them."

They both laughed. Micah finished his beer and Tommy poured him another one in a new mug. Josh and Tammy came through the front entrance, and Micah joined them at a table. Josh ordered a pitcher of beer and some cheese sticks for an appetizer.

"What brings you guys over here tonight?" Micah asked.

"We both worked late and didn't feel like going to any place fancy," Josh said. "I didn't expect to see you."

"I was over at Riverfront today talking to some officials about when they're going to hire a new manager," Micah said. "Then I went to the office and wrote a column. I got here about fifteen minutes ago. How about you, Tammy? How's everything at the hospital?"

"Busy," she said. "It never really lets up, except that some days are busier than others."

"Did you ever find out who had been making the prank calls to you and Cora?" Josh asked.

"I still don't have an idea. It stopped after I bought the caller ID. And that's fine with me."

"That happened to me one time," Tammy said. "I think it was either a disgruntled relative of a patient or a nurse I was working with. It stopped after a few days."

"It can be a pain," Micah said before taking a sip from his mug. "I never understand why people do those things."

"Where's Cora?" Josh asked. "I haven't seen her in awhile."

"She's working on some big investigative project. They've kept it hush-hush around the office. I haven't even asked her what it's all about."

The cook brought out the cheesesticks and took their orders. Tammy and Josh both ordered a cheeseburger and fries while Micah got a small salad. A couple of guys were playing pool in the rear of the bar and occasionally the pop of the cue ball against another ball could be heard in the front. George Jones was playing on the jukebox.

Tammy sat close to Josh and would touch his arm when telling him something. There was a sparkle in Josh's eyes when he looked at her. Micah hadn't seen warmth in Josh's relationship with any woman to compare to what was going on with Tammy.

"Did you find someone to knock out that book for you on Colson?" Micah asked.

"I finally did," Josh said. "Frank said he was too busy so I found one of the free-lancers from around town. Do you know Bill Wright?"

"I've talked to him several times at the ball park," Micah said. "He'll do a good job for you. Plus, I'm sure he can use the money."

"I sure wish I could get you to write something for us. Any chance of that happening?"

"I wouldn't totally rule it out," Micah said. "I just don't have the time or the energy to devote myself to a project like that. I don't want to do something half-baked."

"I understand that. I wouldn't want you to do that. Just let me know when you think you've got something."

"You'll be the first to know."

They got their food and began eating. Josh poured each of them some more beer from the pitcher. They talked about upcoming concerts and other things going on in the city before they left together. It was dark when they stepped outside and walked to their cars in the side parking lot. Josh pulled out of the lot first and arrived at the apartment complex before Micah. They were already inside Tammy's apartment by the time Micah got home.

Micah was disappointed there weren't any messages on the answering machine. He was hoping to hear Cora's voice. He sat down on the couch, picked up the TV remote and surfed through the channels. There was nothing that interested him so he turned off the TV. He picked up the phone and called Cora. There was no answer.

A minute later, there was a knock on the door. He got up and gazed through the peep hole and there was Cora. He quickly opened the door.

"I just called your house," he said excitedly. "What are you doing out this time of night." He kissed her lightly on the cheek.

"It's not that late," she said as she stepped into the living room. "It's only nine o'clock or so. I just left the newspaper and thought I'd pay a surprise visit on you. I hope you don't mind."

"Hardly," he said with a smile. "Can I get you something to eat? There's not a whole lot in the refrigerator but I could probably come up with something. Or I could order a pizza."

"I'm really not that hungry," she said. "But if you want to order a pizza that would be fine as long as you would help me eat it."

"What do you want on it?"

"How about pepperoni and green peppers? Oops, forgot you were a vegetarian."

"That's okay," he said. "I'll order half with pepperoni and green peppers and the other half with just green peppers."

Micah picked up the phone to place the order while Cora sat down on the couch. She flipped through *Esquire* magazine as he was put on hold. He finally got off the phone and sat down next to her. She put the magazine on the coffee table.

"How was your day?" he asked. "Still working on that big story?"

"We're about finished with it. We've got a few more calls to make. It's supposed to run this Sunday."

"Can I ask you what it's about or should I wait?" Micah asked with a grin. "I'll promise not to tell anyone."

"It has something to do with some politicians getting kickbacks from building contractors. It's an important story."

"I think it is," Micah said. "It's safe with me."

Cora smiled and kissed him gently on the lips.

"I know it is," she said. "I don't worry about that."

Micah turned toward her and pulled her closer to him. Their mouths met in a warm passionate kiss. She rested her head on his shoulder as he softly rubbed his hand along her arm.

"I'm glad I met you," he whispered.

"I feel the same way," she said with her eyes closed. He kissed her again on the forehead and squeezed her gently. He savored the silence and the closeness of their bodies for the next few minutes. It was broken when the pizza was delivered.

Micah carried the pizza to the kitchen table and took a couple of sodas from the refrigerator. Cora sat down across from him at the small oval table. They each took a slice of the pizza.

"I've got a confession to make," Cora said between bites.

"Go ahead."

"When we first met at Big Shots that evening, I thought you liked Vanetta."

"Really?"

"You seemed somewhat aloof to me."

"If I was that way it was because of Vanetta," he said with a laugh. "She tried to control the conversation."

"And then when you came over to her apartment, I thought there might be something going on between you and her."

"You've got to be kidding," Micah said with a chuckle. "I couldn't wait to get out of her apartment. The only reason I stayed as long as I did was because of you."

Cora beamed.

"Is that so?"

"Honey, I'm not so keen at this dating game. I really haven't gone out that much since my divorce. I'm still uncomfortable about a few things."

"Such as?"

"Well, I don't know how often I should call you," he said. "I don't want to bug you all the time."

"You don't bug me," she said with a soft smile. "I love hearing from you. Don't ever think that I get tired of that. You can call me every day as often as you like."

"I even feel a little uncomfortable about what is expected from me."

"What do you mean?

"Well, this is a little embarrassing," Micah said, feeling his face getting a little red. "From the stories I've heard, it seems like a lot of people get intimate right from the start and hop right into bed. I'm not used to that."

"I think you're doing just fine," Cora said. "A woman appreciates a man taking his time, especially if she cares about him. I think it's a sign of respect and I like that."

"So you don't think I'm old-fashioned?"

"There's nothing wrong in being old-fashioned in things like that."

They finished the pizza and cleaned up the kitchen. It was nearly eleven o'clock.

"I need to be going," she said. "I've got to be at the office early tomorrow."

"Thanks for coming over."

They embraced at the door, kissing long and passionately several times, before she left. Micah almost asked her to spend the night. He wanted her. He knew there would be another time.

Twenty-six

O'Malley's was packed on its first evening with karaoke. Micah, Josh and Tammy found three stools at the bar. Tommy brought in some extra help to handle all the customers that showed up to sing.

"Hell, I wish I had done this a long time ago," Tommy said to Micah as a customer tried to sing *You've Lost That Loving Feeling* but failed miserably. It didn't matter since everyone in the bar cheered heartily after every song.

"It's sure attracted a crowd," Micah said. "I think it was a good idea. When you get a chance can you bring us a pitcher of beer?"

"No problem," Tommy said while wiping his brow. "Coming right up."

"Do you plan to sing?" Josh asked Micah.

"I don't think so," Micah said with a laugh. "If I got up there it would clear out the place. Why don't you get up there Tammy?"

Tammy was turning pages through the binder that contained all the songs and writing down a few of the titles of songs that she knew.

"I may do it," she said with a grin. "I've done it before. It's a lot of fun."

"I'll do it if you do," Josh said.

"Why don't we do a duet?" Tammy asked.

"Pick out a song and I'll give it a shot," he said.

Tammy flipped through a few more pages and found a song she thought they could sing.

"How about Sonny and Cher's *I Got Your Babe*? she asked. "That shouldn't be very difficult."

"I'm game," Josh said with a laugh.

Tammy wrote down the song and number on the disc and took it to the disc jockey. After two songs, Josh and Tammy were on the makeshift stage singing the Sonny and Cher tune. Tammy did fine taking Cher's part of the song but Josh was nervous and he was off-key through much of Sonny's verses. But when they finished, they still got a nice round of applause.

"I don't think I'll do that again," said Josh, a little red-faced from the experience. "It's more difficult than what it looks like."

"I can imagine," Micah said with a chuckle. "That's why you're not going to get me up there."

"Oh, Micah, you can do it," Tammy said. "I'm sure there are some oldies that you can do."

"Perhaps after I've had a few more beers," Micah said. "I'm not going to make a fool of myself right now."

"You've done it many times before, so what's the difference now?" said a man sitting next to Micah. He had a preppy look about him, his collar up around his neck and wearing khaki slacks without socks.

"I beg your pardon," Micah said. "Were you speaking to me?"

"I sure as hell wasn't talking to myself."

Micah sensed that the guy had been drinking too much and decided to ignore him. But the man, who appeared to be in his mid-thirties by his smooth complexion and flecks of gray hair, turned his bar stool toward Micah and stared at him. His eyes were droopy and he slurred his words.

"Listen, friend," Micah said. "I'm sitting here with a couple of friends minding my own business. I don't know you from Adam."

"So fucking what! And don't call me friend."

Micah turned his stool toward Josh, who had been oblivious to what was going next to him. The man tapped Micah on the shoulder.

"Are you ignoring me?" he asked.

Micah didn't respond. The man knocked him on the shoulder.

"Who in the hell do you think you are?" he asked, his voice growing louder. "I'm speaking to you!"

Josh turned and saw that Micah was having problems. Micah rolled his eyes to let him know that he needed some help with the drunk.

"Help," he said in a whisper. "This guy is trying to pick a fight."

"I'll let Tommy know," Josh said.

"Hurry," Micah said with a slight grin.

The man took a big swallow of beer and gave a push against Micah's stool, turning him toward him.

"Are you a coward or something?" he asked. "You afraid to talk to me?"

"I don't know what you're talking about," Micah said, trying to remain calm. "I don't even know you."

"So what!" the man said.

Tommy saw Josh motioning to him and came over. The man didn't notice Tommy standing across from him and continued to torment Micah.

"I'd like to kick your ass," he said. "You want to do something about it?"

Micah didn't say anything and glanced at Tommy.

"That's enough," Tommy said. "Another word and you're out of here. Do you understand?"

"Fuck you!" the man said loudly.

"I beg your pardon," Tommy said, his eyes getting wide. "You get out of here right now."

"And who's going to make me?"

"You're looking at him."

The man gave a lingering look at Tommy and sobered up to the point that he knew he was arguing with the wrong person.

"Hey, man, no problem," he said while getting up from the stool. "I wasn't trying to cause anything."

"Just keep moving right out the door," Tommy said sternly.

The man eased away from the bar and walked away without looking back from anybody. He was tipsy as he made his way to the front door, but staggered out without any word.

"That's the downside to having karaoke," Tommy said to Micah. "You start bringing in people like that."

"I didn't know what to do about him because I've never been around a drunk like that," Micah said. "The guy was totally obnoxious."

"You did the right thing. There's no sense in trying to argue with someone like that."

Josh and Tammy got back on the stage and sang *Islands in the Stream*. It barely resembled the original tune by Kenny Rogers and Dolly Parton but they had fun trying to get through the song.

Micah finally got the nerve to put up a song, and sang Buffalo Springfield's *For What It's Worth*. He hit a couple of flat notes but managed to get through the song without too much trouble.

"I don't think I'll be getting a recording contract for that," he said to Josh and Tammy.

"That wasn't so bad," Tammy said. "You're too hard on yourself."

"Yeah, you sounded great," Josh said.

"I think you've been drinking too much," Micah said, grinning. "You know what they say about karaoke."

"What's that?" Josh said.

"Karaoke is people who have been drinking too much and singing badly," he said with a laugh.

"I think you've made a good point," Josh said before taking another sip from his mug.

"That guy who was messing with me really looked familiar," Micah said. "I've seen him somewhere."

"I know what you mean," Tammy said. "I've seen him on TV or in the newspaper."

"All I know is that he's an asshole," Josh said with a laugh. "I'm glad he's gone."

"I hope that's the last we hear from him," Micah said. "I can't stand to be around obnoxious drunks."

"I'll drink to that," Josh said with a big laugh, then taking a big swallow from his mug.

Twenty-seven

Micah finished cleaning the kitchen and straightening his bedroom when the phone rang. He hurried to the living room to answer it.

"Hello?" he said after letting it ring twice.

"Good morning, Micah," Nora said. "I hope I'm not catching you at a bad time."

"No, ma'am," Micah said. "I've just been trying to make my apartment livable again."

"I was wondering if I could see you a little later today?"

"Just tell me when and where," Micah said. "Is something the matter with Alice?"

"No, no" Nora said quickly. "It's nothing like that. I just would like to sit and talk with you for a little while."

"How about if I meet you at Denny's around eleven? Is that a good time?"

"Is it the one near Alice's house?"

"That's the one," Micah said. "Do you think you can find it all right?"

"That shouldn't be any problem. I'll see you at eleven. Bye."

Micah put down the receiver and sat down on the couch. He couldn't imagine what Nora would want to talk about. He hadn't sensed any friction between him and Alice's parents while visiting her after the accident. He had two hours before he had to be at the restaurant so he finished cleaning the apartment. He took a quick shower and got dressed and headed to the restaurant.

Micah waited inside the front entrance for Nora. She arrived ten minutes late but that didn't surprise Micah because she was notoriously for arriving late to appointments. Micah opened the door when she got to the entrance and kissed her on the cheek.

"Thanks for taking the time to talk to me," Nora said. "I hope it isn't a bother."

"You know better than that," Micah said.

A waitress took them to a booth. The restaurant was between the breakfast and lunch crowd and wasn't busy.

"Are you hungry?" Micah asked.

"No," Nora said. "I just want some coffee. Go ahead and eat if you want to. I don't mind."

"I think I'll have some toast with my coffee," Micah said. A minute later, the waitress took their order.

"So what's up?" Micah asked.

"Are you happy, Micah?" Nora asked.

"I think so. Why do you ask?"

"After spending the past few weeks with Alice and the children, I thought how nice it would be if you and Alice got back together."

Micah squirmed a little and cleared his throat.

"Er, I don't know what to say," he said. "I feel that Alice and I have a very good relationship right now. Has she said something to you?"

The waitress returned with their orders, creating several seconds of silence as they put cream in their coffee and Micah spread grape jelly on his two slices of toast.

"Alice hasn't said anything," Nora said after taking a sip of coffee. "She doesn't even know I'm here."

"I can understand your concern," Micah said. "But we do have a good relationship. We're very close friends. I think the world of her."

"Then why don't you and Alice try to get back together?" Nora said with a pleading look on her eyes. "It just doesn't make any sense to me. I know couples who don't get along and they've been married for years."

"Because we're better at being friends than being married to each other," he said. "Alice is a fabulous mother but I'm not so great as a dad. You know that."

"The kids love you," Nora said. "I know they would love to have you back at the house."

"Perhaps so, but I wouldn't be around for them like a father should."

"You're too hard on yourself," Nora said. "George had to make sacrifices when our kids were growing up. That's part of being a family."

"I agree, but there's more to what happened between Alice and me. I don't know how you will take this but we just fell out of love with each other."

A tear trickled down Nora's cheek and she wiped it away with a napkin.

"Sometimes we lose sight of what love is all about," she said. "You and Alice could still be in love and not realize it."

"It's a different kind of love," Micah said. "It's not the love that should be shared between a husband and wife."

"But you and Alice were married for seventeen years. Why throw it all away? You've had more than two years to sort things out."

"I think we have sorted things out, Nora. That's why we have such a good relationship right now. And you know how much Alice disliked me going on the road and leaving her to raise the children."

"I know she did but I think that she would change her mind now."

"She's also developed a very good real-estate business and has done quite nicely without me," Micah said with pursed lips.

"Well, I wish you would reconsider," Nora said. "I'm sorry for sticking my nose in your business. I just want the best for Alice, you and the kids."

"I know you do, Nora," Micah said with a tender smile and reaching over and touching her hand. "You're a very caring person and you've been a wonderful mother-in-law. I think the world of you and George."

"We love you as a son, Micah," she said. "We will always hold you dear to our hearts."

"I appreciate that. You know I will always do what I can for Alice and the children. They are very important to me."

"I know that," she said.

Micah finished his toast. The waitress warmed their coffees. They talked a few more minutes about Alice's condition before leaving the restaurant.

"You know you can call on me for anything," Micah said in the parking lot.

"You're a very kind man," Nora said. "I hope you'll forgive a foolish woman for prying in your business."

"You're not prying," Micah said. "You're just being a concerned mother. I understand completely where you're coming from."

Micah hugged Nora gently and kissed her on the cheek before they got into their cars and left.

Driving home, Micah thought about Nora's comments. He knew it probably seemed odd to a lot of people that he and Alice got along so well after their divorce, but it also reflected on the fact that there wasn't any infidelity or abusive behavior involved in their breakup. He knew they could have stayed together, but it would have been a lifeless marriage that probably would have deteriorated into something they both would have regretted.

Twenty-eight

"The Reds are holding a news conference this morning," Spencer said on the phone to Micah, who was sitting at the kitchen table and reading the newspaper. "It's at 10:30. Presumably, they're going to name a new manager."

"I'll get on over there," Micah said. "Any idea on who the poor soul might be?"

"Frank believes it's one of three people. He's tried to nail it down the past couple of days but couldn't get anyone to say anything. *The Herald* said it was going to be Fran Thomas."

"Didn't Thomas manage the Brewers a few years ago? It seems like he got canned after a couple of losing seasons."

"That's the guy. But I still have my doubts about the Reds bringing him on board. I think they're looking for a manager who has had some success."

"I agree," Micah said. "I'll get dressed and be over there in about a half an hour. I'll give you a call if I hear anything."

Wearing his standard khakis, white shirt and blue blazer, Micah headed over to Riverfront Stadium. Several television trucks were parked outside, with cable stretching inside the room where the news conference was being held. Frank was seated in the front row, next to writers from AP, the *Herald*, and some smaller newspapers from the area.

Micah noticed Joey Marsh of the Reds' public relations office outside in the hallway, and waved for him to wait for a second.

"You guys have kept this under wraps pretty well," Micah said as he shook his hand.

"*The Herald* is going to think so," he said with a laugh.

"Thomas isn't the guy?"

"Shoot no. I have no idea where they came up with his name. They've been bugging the hell out of us the past few weeks but we've never given them any indication who it was going to be."

"Can you tell me now? I'd like to give the office a call so they can start putting together some photos and stats on the guy."

"I shouldn't do this but your paper has always been above board with us, unlike your competition. It's going to be Billy Rivers."

"Rivers," Micah said. "Good choice. He did a heckuva job with the Twins a few years back. It seems like he got out because of some back problems."

"That's right. He's had surgery, lots of rest and is supposed to be good as new."

"I appreciate you letting me know."

"I need to go now and finish getting everything set up," Marsh said, patting Micah once on the shoulder as he walked away. "See you a little later."

Micah headed toward a pay telephone when he was stopped by Dirk.

"I saw you talking to Marsh," Dirk said with a haughty look. "I guess you weren't surprised."

"What do you mean?" Micah said with furrowed eyebrows.

"If you read my column this morning, you know that Thomas is the new skipper."

"Oh," Micah said, trying to hold back a smile. "I guess I'm not going to be surprised. I need to make a call. I'll see you a little later."

As Micah went to the phone, he knew that Dirk would certainly be surprised by the announcement.

"It's going to Billy Rivers," Micah told Spencer. "*The Herald* was way off. Thomas wasn't even in the running."

"Thanks for the call, Micah. We'll start putting some stuff together here. I think we'll come out with another early edition. You and Frank try to file your stories by noon from your laptops. We'll put together some kind of reaction piece here."

"Sounds good," Micah said. "I'll be talking to you a little later."

Micah went back to the room where the news conference was being held. Several employees had placed a large Reds' banner behind the podium. A few minutes later, several Reds officials walked in. Micah was sitting down a few seats from Dirk. He couldn't help but grin when he saw Dirk's mouth drop open at the sight of Rivers.

The news conference lasted thirty minutes, giving Micah and Frank an hour to get their stories together. Rivers was carted around to the various TV reporters for interviews. Dirk glanced quickly at Micah and quickly walked away. Micah knew he was embarrassed and that his credibility would take a beating after predicting that Thomas was going to manage the team.

Micah's column focused on Rivers' winning record and the need for the Reds to bring in someone with a proven track record to turn the franchise around. Frank did a nuts-and-bolts story about Rivers' career, including comments from the new manager and Reds officials. They both sent their stories in from Marsh's office with ten minutes to spare.

After filing his story, Micah spent another thirty minutes interviewing several of the players who dropped by to attend the news conference for a follow-up column the next day. By the time he reached the *Register* building, the late edition was coming off the presses, proclaiming, *Rivers on Reds Alert* with his column down the left side of page one.

"Great job," Spencer said as Micah walked into the sports department.

"Thanks," Micah said as a big smile crossed his face. "I think they hired the right person."

"It looks that way," Spencer said. "Of course, you've got to have the players to win. Let's see what they do in the offseason."

After checking his mail, Micah strolled over to the city desk to see if Cora was working. One of the editors told him that she had the day off and could probably be reached at her home.

Micah went back to the sports department, and picked up a phone and called her. It rang several times before she answered. She was a little out of breath.

"Hi," Micah said. "Are you all right?"

"I'm fine," she said. "I was back on my exercise bike."

"Did I catch you at the wrong time? I can call back later."

"No, that's okay. I had just finished twenty-five minutes on it."

"They told me you're off today. Want to go out tonight?"

"Sure. I have a few errands to take care off but I should be back here around six. Is that okay?"

"How about if I pick you up around seven? Perhaps we could go to Big Shots. It's been awhile since we've been there."

"See you at seven then."

Micah went to a computer terminal and began writing his column about how the players felt about the new manager. He finished it in two hours, and decided to go visit Alice since the children would be coming home from school.

Alice met him at the door, wearing a blue floral house dress. She was getting around much better on the crutches and was able to drive. Ben and Annie were in their rooms, finishing homework. When Annie heard his voice, she darted out of the room and gave him a big hug. Ben came out a minute later with a sad look on his face. He said he had more homework and returned to his room.

"What's his problem?" Micah said.

"I haven't a clue," Alice said. "He's been acting this way for several days now. I don't know if it's something at school or sports. He won't tell me. I called the school today and his teachers said he's doing fine in his classwork but they all noticed that he seemed to be depressed about something."

"I'll talk to him a little later," Micah said. "You're looking good."

"I feel a lot better. The doctor said I should be able to get the cast off in another month. That will be wonderful. I'm so tired of lugging it around"

"Where's Nora?"

"Didn't I tell you? She went back home with Dad the other day. I think she was really getting homesick."

"I'm sure she was," Micah said. "But it was really sweet of her to stay with you this long."

"I don't know what I would have done without her," Alice said, smiling softly. "She told me about visiting you."

"Hmm," Micah said with a grin. "And what did she tell you?"

"She told me about asking you to get back with me and the kids. I'm sorry she did that."

"That's okay. That's what mothers do for their daughters, always looking out of them."

"I told her that we're very good friends and we want to keep it that way. She told me that you said the same thing so I think she's feeling better about it now."

"How is everything else?" Micah said. "Are you doing more work?"

"Actually, I've lined up a few people to show houses to this weekend. So that's progress."

"Good for you. I know you'll enjoy getting back out and doing that."

Ben stepped out of the doorway to his room and looked solemnly at Micah.

"Dad, can I talk to you for a few minutes? I need to tell you something."

"Go ahead, Ben."

"I'd rather tell you in my room."

Micah gave a perplexing expression to Alice before getting up from the couch and going to Ben's room. He closed the door behind him.

"What is it, son?"

"Uh, you're going to be really mad at me," Ben said, looking down at the floor.

"I'm not going to be mad at you. What do you want to tell me?"

"Well, uh, I've been calling your apartment and that woman that you know and hanging up."

Micah was momentarily at a loss for words.

"I must admit that I'm surprised," he said finally. "Why in the world would you do something like that?"

"I want you and Mom to get back together," Ben said, his eyes welling up with tears as he began to sniffle. "I thought it would help."

"Ben, you shouldn't have done that. This woman I've been seeing is very nice. She's never done anything to you or Annie or Mom."

"I know that, Dad. After I heard Mom tell Nanny about everything, I felt bad about everything I did."

Micah sat down next to Ben on the bed and put his arm around him. He knew that it hadn't been easy for Ben to make the confession.

"I'm glad you told me what you did," Micah said. "From now on, whenever something is bothering you, I want you to tell mom or me. Okay?"

"I will, Dad. Forgive me?

"Of course," Micah said. "I love you, son."

Micah ran his hand through Ben's hair, then got up from the bed and returned to the living room. He explained to Alice what had been going on the past few weeks with the phone calls.

"I guess we should have figured out something when you called me after seeing our number on your caller ID," Alice said.

"It never occurred to me that it could have been Ben."

"Or me?"

"Of course not," Micah said with a laugh. "Seeing your telephone number really threw me off."

"Can you stay for supper?"

"I really need to be going," he said. "I've already made some plans for the evening. But would it be okay if I came back this weekend and took you and the kids out for dinner?"

"I'll check my schedule on showing the houses and send you an e-mail. I think the children would love it."

"I'll check back later," Micah said as he got up and went to the front door. "I'm looking forward to it."

Twenty-nine

The waitress at the entrance to Big Shots told Micah and Cora they would have a fifteen-minute wait before they could get a table. They took a seat in the small waiting area to the side of the dining room.

"Another busy day for you," Cora said. "How did things go?"

"It was a piece of cake this time," he said while admiring how lovely she looked in her blue pants and beige top. "A news conference and then cranking out the stories. By the way, I thought the piece you did last Sunday in the corruption series was top-notch."

"Thanks," she said with a smile. "It was a lot of work but I enjoy sinking my teeth into stories like that. I hope there's some good will come from it."

"You never know. Sometimes politicians give stories like that lip service, then after awhile just let it die. I think it's going to be up to the paper to keep it in the news with editorials and follow-up stories."

"That's what we plan to do," she said. "In fact, that's all I'll be doing over the next few weeks."

The waitress called Micah's name to let them know his table was ready. As they made their way through the crowd Micah gazed over at the bar and saw Vanetta looking their way. He smiled but she turned her head as if she hadn't seen them.

After they were seated, Troy McDonald, a radio talk-show host, came over to their table.

"Did you hear about Dirk?" Troy asked in his deep baritone voice.

"I haven't heard anything," Micah said. "I saw him this morning at the news conference. What happened?"

"He was taken over to University Hospital shortly after noon after complaining of chest pains. I think he must have gotten a little stressed out by the announcement today."

"Oh, I'm sorry to hear that," Micah said with a concerned look on his face. "Is he going to be all right?"

"I think so," Troy said. "I heard they were going to run some tests on him and keep him overnight. I guess he probably shouldn't have stuck his neck out on the naming of a new manager."

"That's a hazard of the business. When you're right, you're on top of the world. When you miss, you want to crawl into a hole and hide."

"Did you have any idea it would be Billy Rivers?"

"Quite frankly, no. The Reds did a good job in not leaking it out."

"Well, I just wanted to tell you about Dirk."

Micah realized he hadn't introduced Cora to Troy. He glanced at both of them.

"Troy, I'd like you to meet Cora," he said. "Cora, this is Troy. Cora works at the newspaper. Troy is a big-time radio personality." They all laughed.

"Hello," Troy said while reaching back and flipping his short, red ponytail. "It's a pleasure to meet you. I need to get back now. I'll see you around."

"Take care, Troy," Micah said. "See you at the ballpark."

Troy smiled at both of them and returned to the bar where he was drinking with several other media friends.

"He seems like a nice guy," Cora said. "Have you known him long?"

"A couple of years," Micah said. "He's moved around from town to town. He keeps things stirred up once in awhile but I must admit that he keeps on top of things. He has a good show if you like to listen to those kinds of programs."

"Don't you?"

"Not really. I prefer spending my spare time doing things more worthwhile," Micah said.

"And what is that?"

"Hmm, reading, tennis, writing, and spending time with a special woman in town."

Cora blushed lightly.

"I hope it's time well spent," she said.

"Very well spent," Micah said, smiling.

They placed their orders and had light conversation about work while they waited for their dinners to arrive.

"That's a shame about Dirk," she said. "He isn't that old, is he?"

"I'd say he's in his early forties. That's another thing about this business. It drives you nuts," Micah said. "I don't know what the statistics are, but I bet we have a lot of folks with heart problems."

"You're probably right," she said. "I've know quite a few people who have had heart attacks."

"And I don't want to join the club."

"So what are you going to do about it?"

"To be honest, I don't plan to stay in this very much longer."

"Really? What do you plan to do?"

"I wouldn't mind working for a magazine. I wish I had the talent to be a novelist and support myself that way. There aren't many things we can do."

"I wouldn't say that," Cora said. "Corporate communications. PR. Newsletters. There are lots of jobs out there for people who can write and communicate."

"Probably so, but I'm not going the PR route."

"That's what a lot of us say but we end up doing it."

Micah sighed and looked at her with pursed lips.

"Let's change the subject. This is getting me depressed," he said.

"I know what you mean. Are you about ready to go?"

"Sure," he said. "It's still early. Do you want to stop anywhere and get some ice cream or something?"

"I have some ice cream and cake at home. Would you like to come over for a while?"

"Well, don't twist my arm too tightly," he said with a warm smile.

After arriving at her apartment, Micah followed her into the kitchen, watching her as she pulled a container of ice cream out of the freezer and a couple of plates from the cabinet.

"I only have vanilla," she said. "Is that okay?"

"Beggars can't be choosy," he said with a chuckle.

"I hope you like red velvet cake," she said while taking cover off the cake plate.

"Red velvet cake? I love red velvet cake. I haven't had red velvet cake since my mother baked it years ago. I could never get Alice to try it."

Cora smiled brightly and began slicing the cake. She put two dips of ice cream on his cake.

"This is going to make me fat but I don't care," he said before taking a bite from the cake. "Hmm, delicious!"

They took their desserts into the living room and sat down next to each other on the couch. For no particular reason, Micah leaned over and kissed her lightly on the cheek.

"What was that for?" she asked.

"I don't know," he said. "The cake?"

"I guess that's a good enough reason."

After finishing their desserts, Cora picked up the dishes and took them back and placed them in the sink. Micah waited on the couch. She came back and sat close to him as he put his left arm around her. She kissed him softly on the lips.

"What was that for?" he asked.

"Hmm, for liking my cake?"

They both lightly laughed as he pulled her a little closer. They kissed again, this time longer and with more passion. She gazed at him with a starry gaze and smiled.

"Do you want to get more comfortable?" Cora said quietly.

"I guess."

Cora stood up and took his hand and led him to her bedroom. He had never ventured past her living room and kitchen. An antique four-poster bed dominated the room. There was a cedar chest at the foot of the bed and an old vanity and chair in the corner. Light filtered dimly through the blinds and opaque curtains.

As they stood next to the bed, Micah put his arms around her and kissed her hard and passionately. He hadn't felt this way in a long time. He took a step back and began to unbutton her blouse. She arched her back as he removed it. He unsnapped her bra as she leaned against his chest for another warm kiss. Cora let the bra slide off of her, revealing firm breasts that Micah cupped with his hands. She shivered from his touch.

Cora slowly unbuttoned Micah's shirt. She ran her fingers through the hairs on his chest and kissed him on the neck. They both slipped out of their pants and got on the bed, as the kissing become more intense. After removing the remainder of their clothes, they slid under the soft, silk sheets and embraced each other. They made love several times before finally falling asleep with Cora's head resting gently on Micah's shoulder.

Thirty

Micah slowly rolled over in bed the next morning and put his arm around Cora. It was still early, the sun was just coming up and a faint light shone through the curtains. He gazed over to the clock radio. Six-fifteen. About the only time he was ever up this early was when he was on the road and had to catch a plane to another city or he was working on some non-fiction writing.

Cora moaned lightly and squirmed a little while tucking the pillow under her head. Her left leg poked out from under the sheet. Micah reached over to pull the sheet up when he noticed something on the side of her left buttock. Unsure what it was, he arose, rubbed his eyes, and there it was—a tiny rose tattoo, about an inch in size with red petals and a green stem.

"What's the matter?" Cora asked drowsily.

"Just noticing the rose on your butt," Micah said with a quiet chuckle.

Startled for a moment, Cora quickly pulled the sheet down over her leg and turned to face him. She frowned.

"You weren't supposed to see that!"

"I think it's kind of cute." Micah said with a warm smile.

"That happened a long time ago, back when I was in college. I've been thinking about having it removed."

"Why do that? It doesn't look bad."

"Really?" she said, looking back at it while holding up the sheet.

"Tell me the story behind it."

"I'm really embarrassed. Do you really want to know?"

"Of course."

"I think I was twenty-one at the time. I was down at Daytona Beach for spring break with some of my girlfriends. Well, one night we went out bar-hopping. One thing led to another, and after a few drinks, we started daring each other about getting tattoos. We walked out of one bar and there was a tattoo parlor next door. So three of us went in and went under the needle. Hurt like the dickens. I got the little rose on my butt. One of my friends got a cupid on her breast and the other got a little dolphin on her shoulder blade."

"You sound like you were a wild one in college."

"Really, I wasn't. I had a reputation as a goody-goody girl. I think I got the tattoo just to prove to people that I wasn't."

"So you showed it to a lot of folks?"

"Funny, funny," she said with a smile. "Only some of the girls back in the dorm. They couldn't believe it."

"How about your parents?"

"Mom didn't seem to mind. She thought it was kind of neat. We never told Dad. He would have gone through the roof."

"Most dads are that way when it comes to their daughters. I know I would be with Annie."

"Didn't you ever do anything wild and crazy in college?"

"Of course, but nothing as extreme as what you did."

Cora hit him playfully on the arm.

"About the wildest thing I ever did was go skinny-dipping at the campus pool one night. About twenty of us sneaked in to the pool about midnight. It was on a dare. It was a lot of fun."

"Boys and girls?"

"Of course. Do you think I'd want to go skinny-dipping with a bunch of guys?" he said with a laugh.

"So all of you all were running around naked in front of each other?"

"I wouldn't say that. We were in the water and it was dark. It wasn't like we got in there and turned on the lights. My, you're a little on the conservative side."

Cora giggled.

"I guess I am," she said. "I've never done anything like that."

"Would you like to do it sometime?"

"I'd be afraid I'd get caught. I could just imagine the newspaper headline — Local *Reporters Nabbed for Skinny-Dipping*. Wouldn't that be embarrassing?"

"It certainly would. I guess we'd have to be especially careful."

"We? I don't think so. You would have to be careful," she said. "I'm not going to do it."

"We'll see," he said with a devilish grin. "Perhaps I'll ask Vanetta."

"I don't think so," Cora said with a playful look.

Cora nudged up a little closer, kissed him on the cheek, and put her head on his shoulder.

"This is nice," Micah whispered. "It's been a long time since I've been in a position like this."

"I'm glad you like it," she said softly. "Not to change the subject but I haven't been getting anymore prank phone calls."

"I didn't tell you?"

"Tell me what?"

"I found out who was doing it."

"It wasn't Vanetta?"

"No. It was Ben."

"Ben?"

"My son, Ben."

"Why did he do that?"

"Apparently, he was trying to get Alice and me back together and he thought he could do it that way. He took me into his room and told me about it when I was at the house yesterday. He apologized."

"That's kind of sweet of him doing something like that for you and Alice," Cora said. "I can understand why he would try something like that."

"I can, too. I guess I just need to spend more time with the kids. I hadn't realized how much they missed me. This was a wake-up call. I haven't been the most attentive dad in the world."

Cora touched his cheek and kissed him lightly on the lips. Micah pulled her closer and gently rubbed her back.

"It's not easy being a parent, especially in this profession," Cora said. "I hear that from men and women all the time. I'm sure your kids understand that you try to do your best."

"It's hard for a twelve-year-old to see those things, especially when they see other boys with their fathers."

"Then you should try to make more time for him and Annie," Cora said.

"That's easier said than done. There's too much going on."

"You need to talk to Mr. Duggins about it. I'm sure he would try to work with you on it. A lot of editors are trying to be more family-oriented."

"I've mentioned it to him in the past," Micah said while rubbing his hand through his hair. "Perhaps I should talk to him again. He has been real good about things like that. He even told me to take the week off when Alice was in the accident."

"See? All you need to do is ask."

"I know what I'd like to ask."

"What's that?"

"Can I make love to you again?"

"Hmm, I thought you'd never ask," Cora said in a sultry voice. Micah took a hold of the sheet and pulled it over their heads.

"Oh, I like that," she cooed.

They spent the next thirty minutes making passionate love and cuddling. Afterward Cora got up and put on some coffee while Micah went to the bathroom and turned on the shower. Shortly after he got in, Cora opened the shower curtain and stepped under the steady stream of water with him.

"I try to conserve around here," she said with a laugh.

After taking the hot shower, they got dressed and sat down in the kitchen for a cup of coffee, and toast and jelly. Cora was dressed for work in a skirt and blouse while Micah would have to go to his apartment and change clothes.

"Thank you for last night," Micah said. "I don't normally spend nights away from home unless I'm on the road."

"Don't you think it was about time for us?" she said, smiling softly over her cup.

"It was probably the right time."

Thirty-one

Annie slipped past a defender and kicked the ball into the net in the soccer match on Saturday morning. Micah jumped up from sitting in a lawn chair while Alice eased up with her crutches and they cheered. Annie glanced over at them and smiled proudly.

"I had no idea she would be this athletic," Micah said to Alice. "She's never shown that much of an interest in sports."

"A few of her friends at school talked her into going out for the league," Alice said. "She flipped-flopped on whether to tryout. I think in the end she did it because of a dare from Ben."

"So Ben encouraged her?"

"I wouldn't call it that. I think it was simply him giving her a challenge. It surprised him, too, when she decided to come out here."

"I've really missed way too many of these activities with the children," Micah said. "I know I've said it before but I'm going to do something about it now. These kids are going to be grown before you know it and where will I be then?"

"What do you plan to do? Quit the newspaper?"

"I'm not sure. If I have to leave the paper, then I will. I would like to work something out with Spence and see if I can perhaps work out a contract for three columns a week or whatever. I'd prefer to stay if possible."

"Micah, you've got to do what's best for you and the kids," Alice said warmly. "I think they understand why you have to be away at times. It's been so much a part of your life that I don't want you to do something you're going to regret down the road."

"This is something I've been thinking about for a long time. And with Ben making those calls a few weeks ago, it made me realize even more that I haven't been around enough for them. I want to make things better now before they could get worse."

"How does your girlfriend feel about it?"

"I really haven't discussed it much with her. This really doesn't involve her."

"You're not that close?"

"Well, we're getting closer but not to the point where I feel I should consult her on personal matters. I've discussed some things with her, but that's about it."

A whistle blew, signaling the end of the match. Annie ran over to them, and they gave her a quick hug. Other players, most of them with grass stains on their shorts and soil smudges on their faces, flocked to their parents as two other teams were getting prepared to play.

"Did you see my goal?" she said with a toothy smile. "I've got a team meeting but I'll be back in a minute."

"Okay, sweetie," Alice said. "We'll meet you by the car."

Micah folded up the lawn chairs and carried them to Annie's car as she moved along briskly on the crutches. She didn't have any problem keeping pace. She unlocked the trunk and Micah stacked the chairs inside and closed it.

"It's still early," Micah said. "Would you and Annie like to go over to Denny's for breakfast?"

"I'm sorry, but I've got to show a house at noon and Annie has a birthday party to attend," Alice said. "And Ben probably won't be home from his friend's house until the afternoon."

"Those things happen. We'll do it some other time. Does Annie have another soccer match next Saturday?"

"They're every Saturday for the next six weeks. I'll call you and give you the times."

Annie ran up to the car and threw her arms around Micah's waist. He reached down and picked her up and kissed her on the cheek.

"Great game!" he said while hugging her.

"Thanks, Daddy," she said. "I can't believe I scored a goal. That was my first one."

"I'm proud of you," he said. "I'm glad I was here to see it."

"Me, too." she said gleefully. "Can you come again next week?"

"I'll try to. Will you score another goal?"

"I don't know," she said. "It's hard to score a goal."

"I know, sweetie," he said with a laugh. "I was just kidding. I'll do what I can to be here."

"We need to go now," Alice said. "I'll let you know about those times."

Micah kneeled down and gave Annie another hug and kiss on the cheek.

"You have a good time at the birthday party," he said, and then glanced at Alice. "Good luck with the house. Tell Ben to give me a call."

"I'll do that," Alice said as she opened the rear door and put in her crutches. "We'll see you."

"Bye, Daddy," Annie said, flashing a smile while getting in the car.

"Bye, sweetie."

Micah didn't like walking away from his children after spending time with them. It still seemed so unnatural. He was in the delivery room in the hospital when they were born, and had watched them through various stages of growing up. While he knew that Alice had her hands full in raising the children, he was still envious that she was able to spend so much time with them. Since the accident, when she was confined to the house for so long, he was wary about taking the children to his apartment for weekends because he didn't want to leave her alone for an extended period of time. He hoped that would change after she had the cast removed from her leg.

Micah stopped at Denny's for breakfast, and was seated at a booth in the non-smoking section. He placed his order and the waitress brought over a pot of coffee. Picking up a *Register* left by another customer, he turned to the sports pages. He was about to take a sip of coffee when he noticed at the bottom of the page that Dirk Rogers underwent triple-bypass heart surgery two days earlier. The story said the operation was successful and that he would be in University Hospital for a few more days.

"My, my," Micah said softly to himself while shaking his head.

"Disturbing news?"

The voice startled Micah for a moment. Vanetta stood next to his table. She was wearing a red dress and black heels, attracting attention from other men in the otherwise drab surroundings.

"Mind if I join you?" she asked.

"Please, have a seat," Micah said while removing the other sections of the newspaper on her side of the table. "I was just reading about a friend at the *Register* who had bypass heart surgery."

"My brother had it several years ago," Vanetta said. "I think he was forty-six. He says he's never felt better."

"I've heard that from others, too," Micah said. "I still wouldn't want to go through it. It's a mean operation."

"What are you doing here this morning?"

"I went to see my daughter in a soccer match a little earlier and decided to stop here for breakfast. How about you?"

"We had a little promotion involving the literacy program over at one of the malls," Vanetta said. "I didn't have time for breakfast at home either."

The waitress came over and took Vanetta's order. Micah poured some coffee in her cup, spilling a little on the side.

"Oops, sorry about that," he said as Vanetta took a napkin and wiped up the coffee.

"I want to apologize to you for my behavior," Vanetta said, brushing back her hair with her hand. "I don't know why I acted like I did. It was uncalled for."

"That's okay," Micah said. "I'm sorry if I led you on in any way because it wasn't my intention. I was just trying to be friendly."

"The more I thought about it, I realized you were," Vanetta said. "I was just coming out of a relationship about that time and was looking to get into another one. People can do strange things at times like that."

"I think we all do at times," Micah said. "Let's just put that behind us."

"I hope we can be friends."

"Of course," Micah said with a smile.

"Can I ask you something?"

"What is it?"

"Whatever happened to your friend that you brought over to my apartment that evening? I think his name was George, Gerald, Josh or something like that."

"It was Josh," Micah said with a light laugh. "Well, I hate to tell you this but he's dating someone pretty heavy right now."

"That's my luck," Vanetta said, shaking her head in mock disgust. "I can't do anything right. Well then, how are things with you and Cora?"

"Great."

"I figured that," she said with a smile. "I'm glad. I don't know Cora that well but I do know she's a great gal."

They finished breakfast as the conversation turned to the newspaper. Because of her contacts throughout the newspaper, she was interested in inter-office gossip. Micah listened but with little interest since he didn't know many of the people. They left the restaurant together.

"It was nice seeing you," Micah said as they went to their cars in the parking lot. "Take care."

"Toodles," Vanetta said with a smile as she turned and walked to her car.

Micah returned to his apartment. He picked up his mail, a few bills he put away in a drawer and the rest junk flyers that he tossed in the trash can without reading. Cora was on assignment and wouldn't be getting off until late in the evening. He picked up the phone and called Josh, but there wasn't an answer. He figured that Josh was out with Tammy since he seldom worked weekends.

Micah hated to waste the day. The sun was shining brightly and it was a warm afternoon for early October, with temperatures in the mid-seventies. He hoped that Ben would be home but all he got was the answering machine. Micah turned on the television and flipped around the channels with the remote but didn't come across anything he wanted to watch so he turned it off.

He thumbed through the newspaper again, and came across the story about Dirk's operation. With Cora working, his children busy, and unable to reach Josh, he drove over to the hospital to visit his newspaper rival. Walking through the corridors and smelling the antiseptic air reminded him of Alice's accident.

Dirk was in a private room. It was relatively dark, with some light filtering through the closed blinds. A heart monitor hooked up to Dirk was beeping and blinking in a rhythmic fashion. He had his eyes closed. Micah knocked softly on door.

"Yes?" Dirk said groggily.

Micah stepped inside, paused for a few seconds, and then walked over to Dirk's bedside. There were several flower arrangements sitting in the corner. Dirk half-opened his eyes and gazed at Micah.

"How are you?" Micah said with his hands on the bed rail.

"I could be better," Dirk said with a half-smile. His chest was wrapped tightly with bandages.

"I'm sure you could. I didn't even know about this until I read it in the paper this morning."

"It came about real quick. After I had the tests, they found some blockages. The doctor didn't waste any time in opening me up."

"How much longer will you be here?"

"I should be getting out Monday or Tuesday. They've already had me up and walking. They don't keep you in the hospital too long anymore."

A nurse came in and spent several minutes checking Dirk's vital signs. She raised him up in the bed and told him that he would have to be getting up in about five minutes to walk. Dirk groaned.

"I just wanted to drop by and check on you," Micah said. "Let me know if there's anything I can do."

"I appreciate you stopping by. It gets lonely around here at times."

Micah left when the nurse returned.

Thirty-two

Miles Jackson was keeping play-by-play notes and trying to write a game story while the Bengals were taking on the Jets. Micah sat next to him, almost in a daze, as the game was turning into a marathon contest with television timeouts, team timeouts, and a rash of penalties. Although the Bengals were ahead 26-18 early in the fourth quarter, some of the fans were already heading for the exits.

"Is this game ever going to end?" Micah said to no one in particular. "It seems like I've been here all day."

"It's been going on for nearly four hours," Miles said while typing on a laptop. "It seems like all the games are getting to be this way."

"It used to be baseball, but now it seems like football and basketball take forever to play," Micah said. "I can understand why some of these people are leaving. If I wasn't paid to be here, I'd be on my way home, too."

Miles grinned.

"You're really getting tired of this, aren't you?"

"How could you guess," Micah said dryly.

"What are you going to do about it?"

"I told my ex-wife the other day that I was going to talk to Spence. I still haven't done it. I may just have to go into the office tomorrow and have a heart-to-heart with him."

"Are you thinking about quitting?"

"I don't know if I can do that," he said. "I've got child-support payments to make and some other responsibilities. But I would like to cut back on all of this. I think I've been doing it too long."

The game finally came to an end, with the Bengals winning 34-28, and lasting nearly 4 1/2 hours. The stadium was half-empty by the time it was over although the Bengals needed a drive in the final three minutes to win the game. Micah and Miles went down to the locker room and talked to the players and coaches. Micah ended up writing about what the NFL should do to shorten the length of games.

Micah stopped by Big Shots after leaving the stadium. It was packed with many of the patrons wearing black-and-orange colors from the Bengals. Micah went to the bar and ordered a mug of light beer. After taking a sip, he turned around and surveyed the place to see if he could spot anyone he knew. His heart nearly stopped beating. Near the end of the pub, in the dining room section, was Cora. She was sitting with a dark-tanned man with thick wavy dark hair and movie-star good looks. Their smiles turned to laughs. Micah quickly turned around, not wanting her to see him. He left money on the counter for his beer and left quickly.

Numbness came over him while walking out to the parking lot. He couldn't believe what he had just seen. Cora with another man? He thought she was working. He drove over to O'Malley's. Tommy noticed him as he walked in and was pouring him a beer by the time he took a seat at the bar.

"Great game, huh?" Tommy asked as he placed the icy mug on a napkin.

"It had an exciting finish," Micah said. "But it took forever to get to that point."

"Probably so," Tommy said. "I guess that's why people pay big bucks for their tickets, to get their money's worth."

"I don't know about that," Micah said with a frown.

"What's the matter? You don't seem like you're feeling too well."

"I don't know. I guess I'm a little tired."

"Is that all?"

"There's something else but I really don't feel like talking about it now."

"Okay," Tommy said. "That's fine. You know where to find an ear when you need one."

"I appreciate that. Right now, I'm just a little down in the dumps."

"Josh and Tammy have been here a few times. He's really getting into the karaoke. He's up on the stage all the time."

"Josh is a big ham," Micah said with a smile. "I haven't seen him in a few days."

"Well, looking at his face, I think the boy's in love," Tommy said with a laugh. "He walks around with a perpetual smile. Tammy is the same way."

"I'm happy for both of them. They make a nice couple," Micah said. "Can I have another beer?"

Tommy took an icy mug from the refrigerator and poured him another beer.

"So how are things going with you and your gal?" Tommy asked.

Micah hesitated, and then cleared his throat. He still had the mental image of her in Big Shots.

"Oh, just fine," he said. "We work crazy hours so we don't see each other that often."

"That's bad. I can see where that wouldn't work too well for a couple. Quite frankly, I don't see why a spouse would put up with it."

Micah took a couple of big swallows from the mug and got off the bar stool.

"I need to run, big guy," Micah said as he put $5 on the counter. "Catch you later."

"See ya," Tommy said. "Don't be a stranger."

Micah drove on to his apartment. It was 10 o'clock. He wanted to call Ben but knew he would already be in bed. The answering machine light was blinking. There were calls from Josh, Ben, and Cora.

Josh wanted him to call back while Ben told him about an upcoming activity at school. Cora's message was from the afternoon said, "Hi, Micah. I'm sure you're at the football game. I'm on general assignment today. Give me a call when you get a chance. I've been thinking about you."

"Right," Micah said while slowly shaking his head. "I'm sure I've really been on your mind all day."

Micah then picked up the phone and called Josh. It rang three times before it was answered by Tammy.

"This is Micah. I sure didn't expect to hear your voice," he said with a chuckle.

"Oh, hi Micah," she said. "Josh is taking out the trash. He'll be back in a minute. How are you doing?"

"Oh, about the same. I was at the Bengals' game today. I had a message on the answering machine from Josh."

"Hold on a second, he just came through the back door. It's nice talking to you."

"Same here, Tammy. Take care."

"What's up?" Josh asked, slightly out of breath.

"Nothing much. Just returning your call."

"Hmm, I forgot what I called about. Oh, yeah, I remember now. I've got some tickets to an oldies music show next weekend.

I was wondering if you and Cora would like to go on a double date."

"I don't think so," Micah said. "I've got to work next weekend."

"Really? You couldn't get off?"

"No," Micah said while looking at his pocket datebook that was blank on those days. "I've already made a commitment for something."

"That's too bad. The Turtles, Grass Roots and a few other groups are going to be there. I think we would have had a great time. If you can get off, let me know."

"I will," Micah said. "Thanks for the offer. I need to be getting off here now."

"Is everything else all right?" Josh said. "You sound a little distant."

"I'm fine. I'm just a little tired. That was a long game today. It's going to take a day or so to recover from it," Micah said.

"Well, then, I'd better let you go. Tell Cora I asked about her. Give me a call this week."

"Will do," Micah said. "Bye."

After hanging up the phone, Micah walked back to his bedroom and changed his clothes, putting on gray workout shorts and University of Kentucky T-shirt. He went to the kitchen and took a can of beer out of the refrigerator, but when he pulled off the pop-top, the beer sprayed all over the cabinets and curtains.

"This isn't my day," Micah said to himself while tearing off paper towels to clean up the mess. The phone rang. It was Cora. He continued to wipe off the beer as she left a message.

"Hi, Micah," she said. "I thought I would have heard from you by now. I got home a little while ago. It wasn't very busy at work today. How was your day? Give me a call when you get a chance. I'll be up a little later than usual tonight, so if you get home late, go ahead and call me. Bye."

"I bet work wasn't too busy," Micah said under his breath. After wiping everything off, he took another beer from the refrigerator. He cautiously opened it over the sink, making sure he wouldn't have more beer to clean up.

He sat down on the couch and turned on the TV. A football game on ESPN.

"I don't think I want to sit through another game," he said and began to surf around to other channels, stopping on an old black-and-white movie from the 1940s. He watched it for about fifteen minutes, and then turned off the television.

Micah glanced over at the phone and the light blinking on the answering machine. He hit the replay button, listening to her message again. He put his hand on the receiver, then took it off. He took a couple of swallows to finish the beer, and then crushed the can with his hand.

He walked over to the front window and stared at the dark night for a few seconds. Shaking his head slowly, he reached over and closed the curtains and went to bed as silence enveloped apartment.

Thirty-three

"What are you doing in here so early?" Spencer asked as Micah stood at the doorway to his office.

"I was wondering if you had a few minutes?" Micah said in his usual relaxed manner. "If not, I could get back with you a little later."

"Well, I have the morning news meeting in about forty-five minutes. Will that be enough time?"

"I think so," Micah said as he took a seat in front of Spencer's desk. "There are a few things I want to discuss with you."

"Do we need to shut the door?"

"I don't think so."

"I hope it has nothing to do with Alice and the kids. I hope everything is fine with them."

"Indirectly, I guess. It's about work."

"I know this isn't the easiest place to work. The deadlines. The crazy hours. The travel. It's not easy."

"Spence, we've been together for a long time. You're the only sports editor I've ever known here. You've always been more than fair with me. You've always supported me, even when I was green rookie."

"I've tried to be that way with everyone on my staff," he said. "In fact, I've tried to treat people as I would want to be treated."

"I'd like to know if I could rearrange my schedule," Micah said. "I really need to be spending more time with my kids. And I hate to admit it, but there are times I really feel burned out. It's hard to get motivated at times."

"I'm not surprised about being somewhat burned out because we all go through that," Spencer said. "I experience that every few months but I always snap out of it. Would you like to take some time off, perhaps take a leave of absence?"

"No, I don't want that. I just need to get my priorities in order. I need to know that when I have a day off, that I actually have a day off. I need to be able to make plans to do things, not only with my kids but also for myself. I feel like I'm always on-call. It's like I never have a day off."

"I think we can arrange that," Spencer said with a reassuring smile. "I feel bad that you haven't felt that you could get away from the office. Of course, you know that I'm always on-call. I get calls from the office all the time, even when I'm 2,000 miles away on vacation. But that's part of my job. I knew that going in."

"And I understand that I need to be around on the big stories," Micah said. "I don't mind that. I enjoy being at the middle of the action. But it's those other times when it hardly matters one way or the other if I'm there. There seems to be a knee-jerk reaction from some of the staff that I need to be called for any story."

"Micah, in defense of the staff, I think they do that because of the respect they have for your ability," Spencer said. "The sports columnist is generally perceived as the voice of the sports department. I simply think they want you to be informed on what is going on. Furthermore, I think they'd rather be safe than sorry on breaking news."

"You're right, Spence," Micah said. "So what's the solution? What do I need to do?"

"Be firm. If they call you and you don't feel that it's something you need to do, then tell them. You know you've got my support. And when you're having a day off, get out and do something and quit worrying about what is going on at the newspaper. I think you may be part of the problem, just thinking about the newspaper when you're off. We're not indispensable. The paper will get published, whether we're here or not. I learned that a long time ago."

"I'm glad we had this talk" Micah said with a half-smile. "I feel somewhat better already. I just needed to get these things off my mind."

"Micah, you're a valuable member of this team," Spencer said. "Whenever anything is troubling you, I want you to come and see me about it."

"Thanks, Spence," Micah said as he stood up. "I'll try to do that."

After shaking hands, Micah went and checked his mailbox. He glanced over at the city room and didn't see Cora. He figured that she was probably out on a story or that she would be coming in later in the day. That was fine with him because after seeing her at Big Shots, he wasn't in the mood to see her.

Micah tossed most of the mail into the trash, keeping only The *Sporting News* and *Basketball Times* magazines to take home with him. He waved at Spencer as he left the department and headed to the elevator. As he stepped inside, he heard someone yell, "Micah!" but the door closed. It was Cora's voice but he didn't hit the open-door button.

When the elevator reached the first floor, Micah hurried out and went directly to his car. If he had met anyone he knew, he wouldn't have seen them because he kept his eyes straight ahead. He didn't want anyone catching up with him.

On the way to his apartment, Micah felt better for meeting with Spencer but there also was an emptiness because of the brief encounter with Cora. He wanted to talk to her but was still smarting over seeing her with the other man at Big Shots. He wasn't sure what feelings he had for her after that encounter.

Micah saw Tammy walking to her car after getting to the apartment complex and parking. She was wearing her hospital uniform and carrying a green tote bag.

"Off to work?" Micah asked.

"Hi, Micah," she said, turning and walking toward him. "Yes, I'm working days for the next few weeks. What are you doing out this time of day?"

"I've been to the office. Actually, this is my day off."

"Any plans?"

"Not really," he said. "All work and little play for this guy."

"Well, you need to get out and do something," she said with bright smile. "Josh and I went to the zoo a couple weeks ago. It was really nice."

"I bet it was," Micah said. "I may have to do that one of these weeks. Perhaps take the kids. That'd be relaxing."

"Well, I need to be going," she said. "It was nice seeing you. Have a nice day."

"Same here," Micah said. "Take care."

Micah went up to his apartment and laid the magazines on the end table. The answering machine light was blinking. He pushed the message button. It was Cora.

"Hi, Micah. I hollered as you were getting on the elevator at the paper this morning but I guess you didn't hear me. If you get a chance, call me tonight at home. I should be there around seven or so. Bye."

Micah walked back to the bedroom and took the sheets and pillow cases off his bed and put them in the washer. While the washer was running, he put clean linen on the bed and went through the apartment with a dust rag and tidied the place up. He washed two more loads of clothes and folded them. It was 1 o'clock when he finished.

For the second week in October, it was unseasonably warm. The temperature was in the upper sixties along with partially cloudy skies. Micah put on a sweater and started out walking. He hadn't really gotten to know the neighborhood since he moved into the apartment. After a few blocks, there were several used-book stores and antique shops that he browsed through for a couple of hours.

He enjoyed whiling away the hours looking at antiques or going through flea markets. That was something that he and Alice didn't have in common during their marriage. She preferred buying new furniture while Micah wanted to furnish the house with things that he said had "character and history." But he didn't argue with her over what went in the house because he figured he wasn't there as much as her to enjoy it. But when he moved to the apartment, he found several old lamps, a nice oak kitchen table and a few other pieces. He did buy a new bed, couch and easy chair but made sure they were traditional pieces that fit with everything else.

He bought a sack full of paperbacks, mostly works by Hemingway, Faulkner, and Grisham and found a few knickknacks at one of the antique stores, including an old 8 x 10 picture frame, a figurine of a wild horse on its two hind legs, and a magazine rack. His arms were full after stepping out of the last antique shop. He spied a coffee shop on the corner and walked in for a sandwich.

Bob Dylan music from the 1960s was playing softly in the background as he sat down at a table near the front entrance. There were some vintage posters lining the walls, everything from the Fillmore East to Jimi Hendrix to the Doors. Micah felt totally relaxed in the surroundings. He ordered a vegetarian sandwich, bowl of bean soup, and a cup of coffee from a waiter who had stringy blond hair down to his shoulders and a friendly disposition. He looked to be a generation past the hippie era, not quite old enough to be around during the psychedelic years or during Vietnam.

Micah took his time eating. He perused the free alternative newspaper provided for customers. It contained stories about new music, a few movie reviews and several stories about corrupt politics at city hall. Nothing profound but enough to keep his mind off more unsettling topics. When finished he paid his bill paid his bill and then called a taxi since he had too much to carry back to his apartment. He was surprised to see that it was nearly six o'clock when he got home. He put his new belongings away and turned on the television. After watching the sports, and seeing that nothing unusual happened, he turned off the TV.

He picked up *The Sporting News* and went back to the bathroom. While sitting on the commode, the phone rang. A few moments later, he could hear the answering machine click on and a voice come on. It was Cora.

"Hi, Micah. I got home a little earlier than I thought I would. Give me a call if you get a chance. I'll be home all evening. Bye."

Micah finished using the bathroom, went back into the living room and erased the message. He picked up the phone and called Josh. He tried his home first, and then got him at the office.

"I was wondering if you wanted to go out a little later and have a couple of beers?" Micah said.

"Tammy and I already have plans to go to O'Malley's for karaoke," Josh said. "You're welcome to join us. Hey, you might even give Cora a call and invite her."

"That's okay," Micah said. "I'm not in the mood for karaoke. Thanks for the invite."

"Anything been going on?"

"Hmm, not really. I walked over to a couple of neat shops this afternoon."

"Buy anything?"

"Some books and a few odds and ends."

"Ah, sorry Micah, I need to be going now," Josh said. "I told Tammy I'd be picking her up in about nine or so. I've got to wrap up a few things here at the office, then get home and change my clothes."

"I hope you have a good time," Micah said. "See ya."

After hanging up the phone, Micah picked it back up and called his children. Alice answered.

"Hello, Alice," Micah said. "How are you and the kids?"

"About the same," she said cheerfully. "How about you?"

"Same here," he said with a chuckle.

"The doctor said I may be able to get the cast off late next week."

"That's wonderful news," Micah said. "I know you must be excited about that."

"Oh, I am. I almost feel as though this cast is permanently attached to me."

They both laughed.

"Are the kids around?" Micah said.

"They're both at practice. They won't be home for another hour or so."

"Really?" Micah said, sounding downcast. "I just wanted to see how they were doing."

"You can call back later if you would like," Alice said. "I know they'd love to hear from you. Is everything all right?"

"Oh, I'm all right. It just seems like I can never catch them on the phone."

"Micah, you know what I'm talking about. You seem somewhat distracted. Is there something you want to tell me?"

"Really, Alice, there's nothing wrong. I'd tell you if there were."

"Promise?"

"Yes, I promise. I can't hide anything from you. Will you tell the kids I called?"

"Of course, Micah."

"I'll try to call again tomorrow night."

"Just remember they have practice about every day of the week. The best time to call is around 8:30 or so."

"I'll try to remember that. Bye, now."

"Bye, Micah."

Micah walked back to the refrigerator and took out a can of beer. He opened it warily, holding it in the sink. He took a swallow while staring out the kitchen window. It was already getting dark outside. The phone rang but he continued to stare aimlessly out the window.

"I guess I just missed you," Cora said in her message on the answering machine. "I tried calling a couple of times but your line was busy. I've missed not talking to you the past few days. Please call when you get a chance. Bye."

Micah took a couple more swallows from the can and walked back to the answering machine. He pressed the button to erase the message.

Thirty-four

The weather turned cooler the first two weeks of November, with even a few days of snow flurries. Weather was always unpredictable this time of year in Cincinnati. While it would be cold for the most part, there would be days when the temperatures would shoot up into the sixties. And on other days, it would be bitterly cold with a biting wind from the west.

Ben and Annie completed their fall sports seasons. Annie earned "Most Improved Player" award for the progress she made during the soccer season. Micah attended the team banquet at a local pizza establishment. He beamed when she picked up her small trophy and flashed a big smile toward him and Alice. Ben was already involved in basketball. He asked Micah to be one of the assistant coaches. Micah promised to help out on Saturday mornings although he couldn't make most of the weekday practices.

Alice had the cast removed from her leg, and although she walked with a slight limp, the doctor assured her that everything would be normal after she was able to build up strength through exercise. She didn't waste any time in plugging in the treadmill that had been gathering dust in the basement and going through a daily regimen to get the leg back in shape.

"You're looking great," Micah said after dropping by the house following Ben's practice on a Saturday morning. "How do you feel?"

"It's taking time but I feel I'm getting stronger and stronger all the time," Alice said. "I didn't realize my leg would be so weak. It's going to take some time to firm up the muscles."

"It won't take you anytime at all."

Alice, sitting on the couch, stretched out her leg and laughed.

"Probably not," she said. "I'm tired of being an invalid."

"Don't you think you're exaggerating that a bit?" Micah said with a chuckle. "I think you've done pretty well, considering what you've gone through. And in the past couple of months, you were getting around pretty darn good."

"I know," she said, shrugging her shoulders. "It just feels like I've had chains removed. I feel like a new person."

After taking a shower, Ben came back into the living room and sat on the arm of the chair next to Micah. He put his arm around the back of the chair.

"How do you think the team looks?" he asked.

"I think it's got potential," he said. "We need to handle the ball a little better."

"I'm glad you're an assistant coach," Ben said with a smile.

"Thanks, son," Micah said. "It's been a lot of fun."

"Do you think you'll be able to go to more practices during the week?"

"I'll try."

"We practice again on Tuesday night."

"I know. I'll see if I can be there."

"Mom, Jack invited me over to play this new video game. Is it all right if I go?"

"Just be back before dark," Alice said.

Ben hopped off the chair and put on his jacket.

"I'll see you Tuesday, Dad," he said as he opened the front door. "See you, Mom!" He scampered out the door before they could reply.

"Ben really appreciates you coaching the team," Alice said. "I think it has really settled him down somewhat. He was getting a little hyper at times."

"That's just being a kid," Micah said. "But it's been fun coaching. I wish I had done it a long time ago. Perhaps I can even help out during baseball next summer."

"Annie says she's going to play softball in the spring. I'm sure she'd like to have you coach her team."

"Sure," Micah said. "I'll just see how I can work it into my schedule."

"Micah, there is something wrong and you won't tell me about it," Alice said, turning serious and looking directly into his eyes.

"I don't know what you're talking about," he said, clearing his throat. "Everything is the same with me."

"I don't think so."

"I don't know what you're talking about," he said with a light laugh.

"There is something missing. You don't have that usual spark about you. Did you break up with the woman you've been dating?"

"I wouldn't call it a breakup," Micah said. "We weren't seeing each other exclusively or anything like that."

"But I sensed that you liked her a lot. Is there something you want to tell me?"

"Alice," Micah said, putting his hand under his chin, "there's really nothing to say. I haven't seen her in three or four weeks."

"Three or four weeks! Then there is a problem. You don't have to fill me in on the details but you need to call her. That's not like you to be that way."

Micah blushed lightly. Alice had always been able to read him, knowing when there was something troubling him at work. He knew it didn't take her any time to sense that he was drifting away in their marriage.

"I need to be going," he said. "The Bengals play tomorrow and I need to do some homework before I go to the stadium."

"Go ahead. Run away from your problems. They won't get solved that way."

"I'm not running away from anything," he said while getting up from the chair. "I'll call her when I please. Okay?"

"I wouldn't ask you these things if I didn't care for you," Alice said with a soft smile. "You know that?"

"Yes," he said. "I just need some time and space."

"Don't let it drag on for too much longer. You don't need to make yourself unhappy."

Micah touched her lightly on the shoulder and walked to the front door. He turned around and gave her a sad smile.

"I'll be all right," he said as he opened the door and left. "You don't have to worry about me."

Micah stopped by a shopping mall on the way home. He didn't have anything else to do so he did some window shopping. He went into a book store and couple of record shops but didn't buy anything. He stopped at the food court and ordered a veggie sandwich and a glass of water from Subway. He sat down at one of the tables and watched the shoppers scurry about as he slowly ate his lunch.

After finishing his meal, he went to the cinema located at the end of the mall. There wasn't anything playing that he really cared to see, but he decided on a suspense movie starring Harrison Ford. He purchased a box of popcorn and diet drink and found a seat on the left aisle of the auditorium. After the movie, he glanced at his watch and saw that it was only 3:30. He drove to his apartment.

Magazines and newspapers were scattered about on the coffee table and living room floor. In his bedroom, there were dirty clothes tossed in the corner or draped over a chair. The hamper in the bathroom was overflowing.

Micah grabbed a beer out of the refrigerator and then sat down on the couch. He put his feet up on the coffee table and turned on the television with the remote. There was a knock at the front door.

"Come on in," Micah said loudly. "The door's unlocked."

A second later, Josh peeked inside and gazed around slowly at the untidiness that wasn't typical of Micah.

"It's just me," he said with a smile. "Is this a war zone?"

"Funny," Micah said with a smirk. "Wanna beer?"

"Nah. Too early."

"So what's up?"

"Nothing really. I haven't heard from you in awhile and was wondering what was going on. Busy at work?"

"About the same. I've also been helping out on Ben's basketball team for the past couple of weeks."

"I bet you enjoy that."

"I do. It's fun to work with kids. I wish I had started it a long time ago."

"Well, it's better late than never."

"I guess so," Micah said before taking a sip of beer. "So how's everything with you these days?"

"Busy as always," he said. "I'm trying to line up several authors for autograph parties at several bookstores. I've also got a few manuscripts that I'm going over."

"And how's Tammy."

"She's just great," Josh said with a big smile. "I think I found the right woman."

"Good for you."

"We're going out a little later and I was wondering if you wanted to join us. We'll probably get a bite to eat and then go over to O'Malley's for karaoke."

"Thanks, but I don't think so," Micah said with a shrug.

"So what do you have planned that's so important."

"I just got some plans."

"With Cora?"

"No."

"Okay, I'm not going to quiz you about it. If you change your mind, I'll be down at Tammy's apartment for a little while," Josh said while getting up from the chair.

"I'll do that. Thanks for dropping by."

"Let's do lunch next week," Josh said while standing at the front door.

"I'll have to check my schedule first but I'll let you know."

"Good deal," Josh said with a smile. "See ya later, friend."

Micah finished the beer and went to the refrigerator to get another one. He frowned when he saw that he was out. He put on his coat and drove down to a convenience store and bought a case of beer and some potato chips and onion dip. He was back in his apartment within fifteen minutes, but during that time there was a message on his answering machine.

"Micah, this is Cora. Why aren't you speaking to me? Why are you avoiding me? I don't know what I've said or done. Let's talk. Please call me. Good bye."

Micah popped open a can of beer, then erased the message before sitting down on the couch. He skimmed over the TV channels with the remote, stopping at a football game between Ohio State and Indiana.

"Damn, I should have been there," he said to himself. "I don't know what I was thinking."

Micah quickly finished the beer and went back to the kitchen. He opened another can of beer and tore open the package of chips. He poured chips into a bowl, some of them falling onto the floor, and took off the lid to the dip. He carried it back to the living room, and settled back on the couch and watched the rest of the game.

Thirty-five

Vanetta was standing in the elevator when Cora entered on her way out to an assignment at city hall. They exchanged curt smiles and looked away from each other as the door closed and the elevator descended slowly to the first floor.

"How are you Cora?" Vanetta asked. "I haven't seen you around the apartments lately."

"I've been busy with some assignments," she said. "How about you?"

"About the same. We get busy once Christmas starts drawing closer."

After stepping off the elevator, they took a few steps toward the front foyer and stopped.

"Have you seen Micah lately?" Cora asked.

"Hmm, not in awhile. I did have breakfast with him several weeks ago but that's been it. I know he's been on the road quite a bit with the Bengals and a few college teams. Haven't you heard from him?"

"Uh, no I haven't," Cora said. "I've been so busy that I haven't been able to connect with him."

"That's surprising," Vanetta said, raising her eyebrows. "I would have thought if anyone had been in touch with him that it would have been you."

"Why do you say that?"

"Oh, come on, Cora, you know the answer to that."

"Micah and I are just friends."

"I think there's more to it than that."

"Believe what you must," Cora said in an irritated tone. "I've got to be going. I'll see you later."

As Cora turned and walked out the front door, a sly smile crossed Vanetta's face. She walked down the hallway with a little bounce in her steps from Cora's revelation.

Micah was sleeping in on Monday, having covered the Bengals game against the Colts the previous night. He didn't get home until nearly two a.m., and finally crawled out of bed at ten. Wearing a T-shirt and purple boxer shorts, he sauntered into the kitchen and made a pot of coffee. He opened the front door, peeked around for a moment, then took one quick step, reached for his newspaper and returned, closing the door promptly behind him.

Turning to the sports section, he glanced over his column to see if it read as well in the morning as he thought it did while composing it. He skimmed over Jackson's game story and glanced through the NFL roundup while sipping on his coffee. He poured another cup and flipped through the other sections when the phone rang.

He hesitated a second, not knowing if he should answer it or let the caller leave a message on the answering machine. He was off and didn't want to be called by the office. But he was always leery that a call could be an emergency, so he picked up the receiver.

"Hello," he said.

"Good morning, Micah. This is Vanetta. I haven't heard from you in awhile so I thought I'd call. I hope you don't mind."

Micah cleared his throat while returning to the kitchen table.

"No, that's okay," he said. "I'm just sitting here drinking coffee."

"Has everything been all right with you?"

"Sure. Everything is the same."

"I thought something was wrong. You've been kind of a stranger around here."

"To be honest, I seldom go into the office," he said, matter-of-factly. "It's a rare occasion when I do go in."

"I guess I always saw you on those rare occasions then," she said.

"I guess so."

Micah's eyes were focused on the editorial page and he wasn't paying much attention to what she was saying.

"Well, I'd better go now," she said. "Call me if you want to do something."

"I'll see you later," Micah said. "Bye."

"Toodles."

Micah shook his head as he placed the receiver on the table. Vanetta was the last person he thought he'd be hearing from. He went back to reading the editorials and news columns.

After finishing with the paper, Micah put his empty cup in the sink that was nearly full with plates, cups, glasses and silverware. He stared at it more a moment, then walked back to the bathroom and took a steamy, hot shower. He then put on a pair of jeans and white shirt but remained barefoot.

After pulling the covers up over the bed, Micah went back out to the living room and turned on the television. He lay down on the couch and stared at the screen during a game show. The clock on the wall chimed twelve times. A few seconds later, there was a knock on the door.

Micah remained on the couch, not sure if he should answer it or not. He wasn't in the mood for Jehovah's Witnesses and certainly didn't want Vanetta to be paying a surprise visit. It could be Josh but he usually called before dropping by. There were two more knocks as he lay still. He then realized the TV was on and the person outside could hear it.

"Micah! Would you please answer the door?"

Micah rose quickly from the couch and sat up. He shook his head a few times to clear out the grogginess. He knew the voice. It was Cora.

"Micah, please open the door. I know you're in there. I saw your car in the parking lot and I can hear the television. So please don't ignore me."

Micah walked slowly to the front door and opened it. Cora stood outside the storm door, staring directly at him. She didn't smile.

"May I come in?" Cora said in a business-like way.

"Uh, sure," Micah said sheepishly, unable to look directly at her as he opened the storm door. "Come on in."

Cora went to the sofa and sat down. She sat her purse down firmly on the coffee table, causing an empty beer can to rattle on the surface. She looked at the magazines and newspapers strewn about the apartment as Micah sat down in the easy chair.

"We need to talk," she said. "Can you tell me what's going on? I haven't heard from you in weeks and I don't have a clue as to why you're acting this way. You spend the night at my place, and then you treat me like this. Do you have any idea how it makes me feel?"

"I'm sorry," Micah said. "I didn't mean anything by it."

"Bullshit, Micah. There's something wrong and I want you to tell me. I thought we had something special between us. Be honest with me."

"Well, uh," Micah said clearing his throat. "I saw you at Big Shots with another guy."

"When was that? I haven't been there in a month."

"It was about a month ago. I stopped in there after a game for a beer and saw you in a booth with a guy."

Cora started laughing and raised her arms.

"Do you know who that guy was? He was my brother, James. He was on his way to San Antonio and decided to spend several hours here. I took him to Big Shots. I was hoping you would show up so I could introduce you to him."

"Your brother?" Micah said, his face turning red in embarrassment.

"Why didn't you come up and say something instead of running off?"

"I don't know," Micah said, lowering his head. "I guess I was just shocked to see you there with another man. I didn't know what to think."

"Then why didn't you call me at home? I've called you I don't know how many times and you never called back."

"I don't know what to say. You're the first woman I've cared about since my divorce. I just couldn't handle it when I saw you sitting there that evening having a good time."

"Come over here," she said, motioning him to sit down next to her. Micah got up and went over to her, sitting with his hands in his lap. She took his hand and squeezed it, then kissed him on the cheek.

"I really don't know what to say," Micah said. "I should have called you or done something. I don't have any excuse."

"Yes, you do," she said with a bright smile.

"I do?"

"You just told me in a round-about way that you care for me."

"I do care for you, Cora. A lot." He stretched his right arm around her and pulled her close, kissing her softly on the lips. Cora cuddled into him, and they held each other tightly for a few seconds before putting their mouths together in a long, passionate kiss, and their kisses become more intense.

"Is everything all right now?" she asked softly.

"Yes, I think so," he said before kissing her again.

"This is my lunch break so I've got to be going in a few minutes," she said.

"Can I fix you a sandwich or something?"

"No thanks. I'll pick up something at a drive thru."

"What are you doing tonight?"

"I don't have any plans."

"Would you like to go to Big Shots for dinner?"

"That sounds good to me," she said with a warm smile.

"About 7:30?"

"I'll be ready," she said.

Before they got up from the couch, he kissed her again long and passionately, savoring the moment. Cora picked up her purse and they walked to the front door. Before saying good bye, she pecked him on the lips.

"I'll see you a little later," Cora said with a smile.

After closing the door, Micah turned around and surveyed his apartment.

"What a mess!" he said out loud. He started tidying up the apartment, washing dishes, and taking out the trash that had been accumulating for the past few weeks. An hour later the apartment appeared tidy, and he was beginning to feel a lot better.

Thirty-six

"I'm glad you came to practice tonight," Ben said as Micah was driving him home on a cold Tuesday night.

"I enjoyed it, Ben," Micah said, looking over at him and smiling. "It's a lot of fun for me, too."

"Do ya think we're gonna be a pretty good team?"

"I think we're getting better all the time. I think it's important that everyone listens to Coach Blair and tries to play as a team."

"I like Coach Blair. Did you know he used to play college ball?"

"I saw him in college several years ago," Micah said. "He was a good point guard."

Micah pulled into the driveway and they both got out and went into the house. The smell of pizza hit them as they opened the front door. Alice and Annie were in the kitchen, setting the table. Annie dropped a few pieces of silverware on the table and ran over to Micah as he was taking off his heavy gray coat.

"Mommy ordered pizza," she said. "Can you stay and eat with us."

"Hmm, I think I can," Micah said, lifting her up and giving her a hug. "You know, I'm not going to be able to do this much more because you're getting awfully heavy."

"I'm not fat!"

Micah laughed.

"You're not getting fat," he said. "I didn't mean that. You're just getting taller and bigger. You're almost as tall as your mother."

Alice walked into the living room. She was using a cane to give her mended leg a little more support. She had been to the salon, her hair cut short around her ears. She was wearing loose-fitting slacks, a red pullover sweater, and a red-and-white checkered apron. She had a radiant look about her that didn't go unnoticed by Micah, who gazed at her from top to bottom.

"You look very nice," he said with a warm smile.

"Thank you," Alice said, blushing slightly. "So you can stay and eat pizza with us?"

"I don't have any other plans," he said. "Thanks for inviting me."

"Come on back to the kitchen table. I've just got to pour soft drinks and we'll be ready."

Micah held Annie's hand while following Alice into the kitchen. Ben went back to his bedroom to change out of his sweats into a pair of jeans and Bengals T-shirt. They sat down at the table, Micah and Alice at both ends and the children in the middle chairs. Ben and Annie reached in and took out their slices first. It seemed like old times for Micah.

"So how is work?" Micah asked Alice.

"It's a little slow this time of year but that's okay with me," Alice said. "I need a little transition period. And how are things with you?"

"About the same."

Alice gave Micah a worried look. His short reply was a signal to her that he still wasn't satisfied with work. But with the kids present, she didn't pursue the subject.

"You guys enjoying school?" Micah said to the children.

"I guess it's okay," Ben said. "I've got a couple of neat teachers. It's a little harder than last year."

"I like my teachers," Annie said. "We're going on a field trip to the Kentucky Horse Park on Friday."

"That should be fun," Micah said. "I've been there a few times. Do you remember when mom and I took you and Ben there several years ago?"

"I don't think she's going to remember that," Alice said with a chuckle. "She was in a stroller back then."

"Did I get to pet the horses?" Annie said.

"Yes, there were several ponies that you got to touch," Micah said.

"I'm finished eating," Ben said to Alice. "Is it okay if I get up and do my homework?"

"Of course," she said. "I thought you finished it before I took you to practice."

"I got about ninety percent of it finished. There're still a couple of math problems I have to do."

"I'll see you on Saturday morning," Micah said to Ben.

"Okay, Dad," Ben said while pushing his chair to the table. "Don't forget that the game starts at ten. Coach Blair wants us there by nine."

"I'll be there," Micah said.

"Can I go watch some television?" Annie asked. "I've already finished my homework."

"Go ahead," Alice said. "You can stay up for another hour. It's already 8:30. Why don't you go ahead and brush your teeth and put your nightgown on?"

"Okay, Mommy," she said, then skipped to her bedroom.

Alice picked up a breadstick and took a small bite. Micah leaned back in his chair and stretched his arms.

"I need to be going soon," he said.

"What's wrong, Micah?" Alice asked.

"What do you mean?"

"There's something not right. Is it work? Is there something in your personal life? You just don't seem to be your old self."

"Everything is fine. I'm just a little tired, I guess."

"I know you're not being straight with me."

"Yes, I am," he said sheepishly.

"I can even look at you and tell something is wrong."

"What are you talking about?"

"Look at your beard. You've always kept it neatly groomed. Now it's getting scraggily looking."

"I never noticed," he said, running his hand over his beard. "I guess I'd better get the beard trimmer out."

"And you're going to hate me for saying this, but look at your belly. You've put on ten extra pounds or more in the past two months."

Micah started laughing as he placed his hands on his stomach.

"You're getting personal now," he said. "But you're right. I need to get more exercise."

"And drink less beer!"

"OK," he said with a laugh. "Less beer."

"How are things at work?"

"Alice, things are improving somewhat," Micah said as his tone turned serious. "I've had a talk with Spence and he has been very understanding about the job. I'm writing three columns a week, and that is all that's expected of me. When I'm off, they don't bother me at home."

"That's good to hear," she said. "You should have done that a long time ago. And how are things with your girlfriend?"

"I hate to use the word 'girlfriend' around you," Micah said. "But Cora and I are doing well. We had sort of a misunderstanding but we've worked things out."

Alice got up and began clearing off the table. Micah picked up the pizza container and crunched it up and put it in the trash can. She started running water in the sink to wash the dishes.

"So how is your love life?" Micah said while standing next to her.

"I haven't had one since the accident," she said while working the suds in the water. "There's this guy at work who has been awfully friendly with me the past few weeks but I have no interest in him."

"Why not?"

"Because he's married."

"That's a good reason," Micah said with a laugh. "You don't want to get tangled up in something like that."

"I never have and never will. I've heard too many horror stories about those relationships."

"Would you like to start going out again?"

"Is that an offer?"

"Uh, I didn't mean me," Micah said while coughing.

"I was just kidding," she said, looking over at him with a grin. "I wanted to see your reaction. But yes, I do want to start dating again."

"You need to get out."

"I know but it's going to be difficult. There aren't many men interested in a woman with two kids. That's why Graham was so special. He treated the children like they were his own."

"Graham was a very good man," Micah said. "I'm sure you miss him a lot."

"And it's so hard to find someone that the kids will accept. You know that Ben wants us to get back together."

"I'm not surprised," Micah said. "I hope he understands why we haven't."

"It's hard for a child to grasp why parents divorce. Ben has taken it a lot harder than Annie. But with you showing him this attention in basketball makes it a lot easier for him."

"I'm still their father and I always will be," Micah said. "That's one part of my life that I will always treasure."

Alice wiped off the counter and flicked off the overhead light at the sink. They went to the living room and sat down on the couch. They could faintly hear music coming from Ben's room while Annie was watching TV in the den.

"I need to be going," Micah said. "Thanks for inviting me for dinner."

"You know you're always welcome here," Alice said, smiling. "Just consider this your second home."

"Thanks, Alice," he said. "I'm glad we have this relationship. So many other couples are at each other's throats when they divorce. We're very fortunate."

"Let's try to keep it that way."

"I will if you will," he said. "What are you and the kids doing for Thanksgiving?

"We're driving up to Cleveland and spend a couple of days with Mom and Dad."

"I bet you're looking forward to getting away for a few days."

"I am. I've been cooped up here for months. Although I don't like that long drive, it will still be refreshing to do something different."

Micah glanced at his watch and shuffled a little.

"I need to be going," he said. "It's almost 9:30. Let me peek in on the kids for a minute."

Micah got up and said good bye the children and returned a few minutes later. He retrieved his coat from the closet.

"If you need me to look after the kids or anything, just let me know," Micah said to Alice as he opened the front door. "It won't be any problem."

"I may have a few things coming up after Thanksgiving, especially with Christmas shopping."

"I'll see you, Alice," he said while taking a step outside into the dark coldness of the night.

"Take care of yourself," she said before closing the door and locking it.

Thirty-seven

Micah wiped off the steamy mirror with his wet towel after taking a long hot shower. He studied himself intently for a few seconds, and then rubbed his fingers through his beard. It had been two months since he had trimmed it. It was getting longer, but hardly out of control. He didn't exactly look like a mountain man. He took out a small pair of scissors and trimmed his mustache that was hanging too far over his upper lip.

He dressed in khakis, blue denim shirt and a tie that was covered with tiny brown footballs over blue. He almost always wore a tie, unless he was called unexpectedly into a breaking news story. He had been told by a journalist he respected when he first got into the business that a reporter should dress like he should be respected and that meant wearing a tie.

He stopped by football practice at the University of Cincinnati. The Bearcats had been invited to the Liberty Bowl after finishing the season with a 10-1 record. He spent an hour talking with several of the position coaches about why the team had been so successful after many publications had predicted the team to have a mediocre season. After the interviews, he drove over to the newspaper and began writing a column about the team.

While sitting at the computer terminal, focused on what he was writing, he was startled by a soft tap on his shoulder. He turned his head around and there was Spencer standing next to him.

"Can I see you for a few minutes after you finish writing?" Spencer asked in his raspy voice.

"Sure," Micah said. "I shouldn't be much longer."

"I'll be in my office."

Micah finished writing the column, spending most of the time working on the lead, and then went over to see Spencer. It was getting late in the afternoon, and reporters were beginning to show up to work on stories. Some copy editors had been in there for several hours, laying out pages and taking care of photo assignments and other art for the various sections.

"Whatcha need?" Micah said as he took a seat in Spencer's office.

"Nothing important. I just wanted to see how everything is going. Are you less stressed now."

"I'm getting there," Micah said. "I've been helping out with Ben's basketball team and doing a few other things."

"That's good to hear."

"Has it caused any problems around here?"

"Not at all," Spencer said with an assuring smile. "We're still putting out a sports section."

"How about my columns? Are they reading all right?"

"I don't see any problems with them."

"Will you let me know if you think I'm slipping?"

"Micah, you're too much of a professional for that to happen. That's the least of my worries. You're a helluva writer and I don't expect that to change."

"Thanks," Micah said with a smile.

"By the way, what's with the beard?"

Micah grinned and patted his beard gently.

"I think I'm going for a more mature look," Micah said with a laugh. "Plus, it's warmer in the winter."

They chatted for a few minutes about what was going on with the various teams and discussed several of Micah's column ideas. It was nearly 6:30 when they finished and dark outside when Micah left the building. A cold wind whipped through the streets, causing him to tuck his hands into his coat pockets and walk briskly to his car. After getting inside, he remembered that he had planned to stop by the city desk and see if Cora was working. Looking out at the shivering coldness, Micah turned the ignition and drove off. He ended up a Big Shots a few minutes later to get dinner before going home.

Standing in the front entrance, Micah noticed someone at the end of the bar trying to get his attention. He took a few steps to his right to see who it was. After a few seconds, he realized it was Dirk. His looks had drastically changed. He had lost weight since the heart surgery, giving him a gaunt appearance, and shaved his head. Micah approached him slowly as if unsure this was the same person.

"Dirk?"

"It's me, Micah," Dirk said while extending his hand for a handshake. "It's the new me." He patted the top of his head.

Micah shook his hand and smiled.

"Well, you've certainly done that. What brought this on?"

"I've changed my whole lifestyle. I'm a vegetarian like you. And I've quit my job."

"Quit?"

"Well, I've given them notice that I'll be around until the end of the year," Dirk said with a bright smile. "I'm getting out of the business for good. It's unhealthy."

"Damn," Micah said shaking his head. "Let me buy you a beer."

"No beer for me," Dirk said, holding up a bottle of Perrier. "No meats, no alcohol, no drugs in this body."

"Do you mind if I get a beer?" Micah said with a laugh.

"Good ahead friend, but I must tell you it's not good for you."

"Now doctors say that one or two drinks a day is good for the heart."

"They only say that because they like to drink. It's a rationalization."

Micah laughed.

"Well, perhaps so, but it's one I like," he said as the bartender took his order for a large draft beer.

"So what are you going to do after you leave the newspaper?" Micah said. "Anything lined up?"

"I'm thinking about becoming a nurse."

"A nurse?" Micah said, crinkling his nose.

"I was really impressed by the way they took care of me while I was in the hospital."

"Well, it's certainly a noble profession," Micah said. "More so than a journalist."

Dirk took a sip from the bottle of Perrier, seeming to savor every drop that trickled down his throat.

"Have you had dinner?" Micah asked.

"No. Want to get a table?"

"Sure. I just stopped by to grab a bite to eat before going home."

Micah went over to a waitress and put his name on the waiting list. When he returned to the bar, Vanetta was in his seat talking to Dirk. She had put her coat over the back of the bar stool and was wearing a dark blue pant suit and off-white blouse that highlighted her full figure.

"I think you two have met," Micah said.

"Hi, Micah," Vanetta said cheerfully. "Dirk says we met last summer but I don't remember it."

"It's Dirk but in a reincarnation," Micah said with a friendly smile. They all laughed. "Do you care to join us for dinner?"

"Sure," she said, moving her head as her long, red hair bounced lightly on her shoulders. "Why not?"

Before the waitress took them to their table, Micah ordered a margarita for Vanetta, another bottle of Perrier for Dirk and a draft for himself. Vanetta and Dirk sat next to each other in the booth across from Micah.

"So Micah, have you heard from Cora lately?" Vanetta asked.

"Why actually, just a couple of days ago," he said. "She's doing fine."

A look of surprise momentarily crossed Vanetta's face.

"I'm so glad," she said with a tight smile. "I've worried about you two."

"Who's this Cora?" Dirk asked.

"Oh, Micah and Cora are an item at the paper," Vanetta said.

"An item?" Micah said, nearly choking on some beer. "I hardly think so."

"I never knew you had a lady friend," Dirk said.

"Cora is a friend of mine from the newspaper," Micah said. "She's a reporter on cityside. We've dated for a few months."

"Have I met her?" Dirk asked.

"Probably," Micah said. "She's been in here before. You probably met her in your other body."

Dirk laughed while Vanetta appeared flustered by their exchange. The waitress came up and took their orders, with Micah and Dirk ordering vegetable soup and dinner salads and Vanetta going with a filet mignon, baked potato, and salad.

"Looks like I'm dining with a couple of rabbits," Vanetta said.

"Rabbits?" Dirk asked.

"She means vegetarians," Micah said. "You'll get used to that after awhile."

"Oh, I see," Dirk said, laughing.

After they finished their meals, Dirk left to go to the *Herald* and check on a story he had been writing. Micah ordered another beer while Vanetta got a glass of red wine.

"How well do you know Dirk?" Vanetta asked. "He's such an interesting man!"

"Dirk?"

"Yes. He's so fascinating."

"I've known him for quite a few years. We've covered a lot of the same stories together."

"Do you think you could arrange for him to give me a call?"

"Are you serious?"

"I'm dead serious," she said, arching her eyebrows slightly.

"I'll give him a call and see what I can do. I really don't like playing matchmaker but I'll make an exception this time."

"I'd appreciate it," Vanetta said, a slow smile oozing on her face. "It's hard to find a good man nowadays."

They paid their tab for the dinner and Micah walked her to her car in the parking lot.

"Will you promise me you'll call him?" Vanetta asked as she opened the door.

"I promise."

"And will you tell me what he says?"

"I'll think about that one."

"Please?"

"Okay. I'll let you know what he says. I need to be going now. It's cold out here."

Vanetta flashed a mouthy smile, waved and said, "Toodles."

Thirty-eight

"What are you doing for Thanksgiving?" Micah asked Cora during lunch at Wendy's. "Any plans?"

"I'm flying to my parents' home in Virginia on Wednesday afternoon," she said. "I'll be coming back on Friday evening. How about you?"

"I'm not sure yet. I'll think of something."

"Thanksgiving is only four days away. Can't you go eat with your ex-wife and kids?"

"They're going to Cleveland."

"How about Josh? Can you get together with him?"

"He's going to his girlfriend's parents' home for dinner. They live somewhere in northern Kentucky."

"So you'll be staying home for Thanksgiving?"

"It's no big deal. I can go to some restaurant."

"Why don't you go with me to Virginia?"

"I've got to work," he said, then took a sip of tea from a straw.

"Work?"

"Yeah," he said, nonchalantly. "I've got a column to write for the holiday edition."

"And you can't do it now between now and Wednesday?"

"Listen," he said. "It's okay. Thanksgiving isn't that big of a deal. I was only asking you because I wasn't sure if you'd be around or not. I'll be all right."

"Well, I hate the thought of you sitting around all day Thursday by yourself."

"There's lot of football games on. I'll stay occupied. I'm used to being at home by myself on holidays. It's kind of nice. Real quiet."

"Give me a break, Micah," she said with a laugh. "People don't like being alone during the holidays. You can act macho all you want but I can see right through it."

"If that's what you want to think." he said before taking a bite from his salad.

"I've been alone at holidays and I know it's no fun," she said. "So don't try to feed me that line of bull."

"Can we talk about something else?"

"Fine with me," she said tersely.

"Now don't start getting mad at me."

"I'm not mad."

"Well, upset then."

"I'm not upset," she said, then took a big bite from her hamburger.

"Do you want to do something this weekend?"

"I don't know. I'm on general assignment Saturday. I won't be getting off until eight. Is that too late?"

"That's okay. We'll go see a late movie or get something to eat. Josh has been trying to get me to take you to O'Malley's for karaoke."

"That would be fun. I like Josh."

"I think you'd like Tammy. She's a nurse over at University Hospital. They're getting somewhat serious."

"Let's do that then. I'd like to meet her."

They finished their lunch and Micah dropped her off in front of the newspaper building. She bent over and pecked him on the lips before getting out of the car.

"See ya," she said, smiling broadly.

"I'll call you tonight."

"Okay," she said, quickly closing the door and dashing into the building.

Micah drove to Turfway Park for interviews he'd set up with the track's general manager and several horse trainers about the riverboat gambling on the Ohio River. He wanted to get their perspective on how the gambling boats affected the future of horse racing for a column he was writing for the weekend. He set up interviews the next day with officials from the gambling boat.

While driving back from Turfway Park, he turned on the radio to an all-news station, tuning in during the middle of a breaking news story. He turned up the volume. All he could gather was that a gunman had entered a Cincinnati building and killed four people and wounded two, then there was a commercial break that seemed to last ten minutes although it was no longer than two.

"...All we have now is that a man forced his way into the newsroom of the *Cincinnati Register* and opened fire about 2:15 this afternoon. Police say that four people were killed and two were injured. The names of the victims or the gunman have not been released..."

A sense of panic came over Micah. He dropped Cora off at the newspaper about 1:30. He knew she didn't have any news assignments that afternoon. He stepped on the gas but it didn't help much being in heavy traffic heading toward the Brent Spence Bridge. He blew his horn but it was lost in other vehicles doing the same in the logjam.

When he reached the newspaper, the police had lined the entrance to building with yellow tape. He ran to the front door but was stopped by a policeman.

"I'm Micah Stewart," he said. "I work here."

"I'm sorry, sir," said the policeman, peering at him through dark sunglasses. "We can't let anyone in at this time."

"Damnit. I have friends in there. You have to let me in."

"We can't let anyone in while we're investigating the crime scene."

At that time, Perry Loggins, an assistant city editor, came out the front door. Micah vaguely knew him and grabbed his arm.

"Will you tell this officer to let me in?"

"You don't want to. It's horrible. It's awful. They're taking out bodies right now."

"Can you tell me if Cora is all right?"

"Cora?"

"Yes, Cora Miller. Is she all right?"

"I'm sorry Micah, but she's dead," Loggins said with a blank expression. "The man just walked up to her and shot her for no reason at all."

"You've got to be wrong. She can't be dead."

"I'm sorry, Micah. I didn't know that you were friends."

Micah turned an ashen color as he stood in front of the building. Loggins put his head down and slowly walked away.

"Are you all right, sir?" the officer asked.

"No," Micah mumbled. "I'm not all right."

Micah stared at the officer for a few seconds with a glazed look in his eyes. He walked back to his car. A television news crew spotted him and tried to get an interview but he walked past them without acknowledging their presence. After getting inside the car, he sat there until he heard someone tapping on his window.

"Micah! Micah!"

Micah looked up and saw Spencer trying to get his attention.

"Open up!" Spencer said.

Micah rolled down the window. He didn't say a word.

"Are you all right?" Spencer asked. "The lot attendant told me you've been sitting here for forty-five minutes."

"I knew Cora Miller. We had lunch today."

"I'm sorry, Micah." Spencer said. "I knew two of the editors."

"Why?"

"Apparently it was a disgruntled politician who was mentioned in that investigative piece the paper did a few weeks ago. He just came in without any warning and started shooting at people. He finally turned the gun on himself."

"It all seems so unreal, like a nightmare or something."

"I know Micah," Spencer said while patting him on arm. "Can I take you home?"

"No. I'll be all right. Thanks anyway."

Micah rolled up the window and turned on the ignition. The radio station was giving another account of the shooting, but Micah turned it off. It was too painful to hear the details.

He drove to his apartment. It was pitch dark as he fumbled around to find the light switch. He didn't want to see or talk to anyone. The answering machine was blinking but he didn't check the incoming messages. He went to the refrigerator and took out a beer and went back to the living room and turned off the light. He sat quietly in the darkness.

The phone rang twice and there was a knock on the door, but Micah didn't budge from the recliner except to get another beer. He drank four in less than an hour, intentionally trying to numb his mind and body. But they couldn't mask the hurt he was feeling inside as he finally broke down and sobbed uncontrollably.

Micah dozed off but was awakened by the sound of a key in the front door. He sat motionless in the chair as the door creaked open. A lamp flicked on. The apartment superintendent stood inside the door, and behind him was Josh.

"Uh, Mr. Stewart," the superintendent said. "This fella said it was okay to unlock the door. He says he was worried about cha."

"That's fine. Come on in Josh."

The superintendent stepped out and slowly closed the door as Josh took a few steps over to Micah.

"I've tried to call several times but no one would answer," Josh said. "I'm so sorry. Is there anything I can do?"

Micah wiped tears from his eyes and turned his head away.

"I don't know. I've never felt so empty in all my life. We had just finished lunch and I had dropped her off in front of the building. She kissed me before getting out of the car."

Josh sat down on the couch quietly.

"Did you know I didn't speak to her for about a month because I saw her talking to another guy?" Micah said, shaking his head. "It was her brother, of all people."

"Those things happen. You got upset because you cared for her so much."

"She wanted me to go home with her to Virginia for Thanksgiving. She didn't want me to spend the holiday by myself."

"Listen, pal, I can't imagine what you're going through but I know it must be painful. Is there anything I can do? Just tell me."

"There's nothing anybody can do right now, Josh," Micah said, wiping his eyes and sniffing. "It's all over. I can't bring her back."

"Do you want me to spend the night?"

"That's okay, Josh. I'll appreciate the offer but I'll be all right. I just need some time alone."

Josh stood up and patted Micah on the shoulder.

"I'll call again in the morning. All right? You let me know if I can do anything."

"Thanks, friend."

As Josh opened the front door, a cold breeze whisked through the living room, ruffling the newspaper on the coffee table.

Josh looked at Micah with pursed lips, and then closed the door. Micah sat in the chair for the remainder of the night.

Thirty-nine

Micah awoke the next morning tired and emotionally drained. He stumbled into kitchen and put on a pot of coffee before going to take a shower. He stood under the hard, steady stream of water, sobbing intermittently while trying to grasp what had happened to Cora. After stepping out of the shower, he put on a white T-shirt and jeans and poured a cup of coffee before sitting down at the kitchen table.

Micah knew the newspaper was at the front door but didn't want to read the horrifying news about Cora's death. It was too early and too painful. He glanced over at the answering machine and saw the blinking light but stayed in the kitchen. He wanted to be left alone. The voices on the answering machine would be an intrusion on his privacy.

A knock on the front door brought him out of his thoughts. He waited a few seconds, hoping the person would leave, but there was another knock. He figured it was Josh checking up on him.

He got up and opened the door and Tammy was standing there, teary-eyed and long faced that revealed the hurt she had for him.

"Oh, Micah, I'm so sorry," she said as she stepped inside and hugged him. Micah put his arms around her, resting his head on her shoulder. After a few seconds, he guided her to the couch and they sat down. She reached over and took his hand, clasping it tenderly between hers.

"It's all seems so unreal," Micah said, breaking the silence. "It all seems like a dream. I should say a nightmare. I keep thinking I will snap out of it and everything will be all right. But that's not going to happen."

"Josh told me that you had lunch with her yesterday. You should be glad that you were able to spend some time with her."

"I don't know what to think anymore," Micah said. "I feel so empty today."

"It's going to take awhile to get over this. One of these days you'll have the pleasant memories of her. But there's going to be a grieving process that will take some time for you. What you're feeling now is normal."

"I know it's going to take time. It's going to take a long time."

Another knock came on the door and Tammy got up to see who it was. Josh, his eyes puffy, came in carrying a box of pastries and a newspaper. He kissed Tammy on the cheek and went over to Micah.

"I don't know if you've eaten anything or not so I picked up this up at the bakery," Josh said. "There's a little bit of everything."

"Thanks," Micah said with a half-smile. "I'm not hungry. I've made some coffee if either of you care to have any."

Tammy went back to the kitchen and poured each of them a cup and brought it back. Micah always drank his coffee with creamer, but didn't complain about it being black.

"I don't want to upset you, Micah, but I looked into funeral arrangements for Cora," Josh said. "I thought you'd want to know."

"I appreciate that. My mind isn't functioning too well right now. What did you find out?"

"The services are going to be on noon Friday in Charlottesville, Virginia. There won't be any visitation except for two hours before the funeral."

Josh took out a piece of paper.

"Let's see, it's going to be at St. Andrew Episcopal Church," Josh said while perusing his notes. "I guess they'll have other details later in the day. I hope you don't mind but I booked you on a flight to Charlottesville on Friday morning. You'll be leaving at six from Cincinnati International with a couple of changes. You should get there by nine."

Micah smiled warmly at Josh, and then at Tammy.

"You've been true friends," Micah said. "Thanks for everything you've done."

"I wish I could do more," Josh said. "And if there's anything else I can do, just let me know. Do you want me to order flowers?"

"I guess I can do that this afternoon," Micah said. "Do you know if there's any kind of scholarship fund in her name?"

"I think there will be but I'll have to let you know later," Josh said. "Let me make a few calls."

Micah opened the box of pastries and held it open for them.

"I won't be able to eat all of these," he said. "Go ahead and take a couple."

Tammy reached in and took out a glazed donut, and Josh, looking over the assortment for a few seconds, finally pulled out a creamed long john. Micah put the box back down without taking any.

Josh and Tammy ate their pastries quickly and finished their coffee. After a couple of minutes, they got up to leave.

"I'll be at the office if you need me for anything," Josh said.

"And I'll be in my apartment for most of the day," Tammy said. "I don't have to go in until seven p.m."

Micah saw them to the door and they each gave him a hug.

"Hang in there friend," Josh said. "Everything will be all right."

After they left, Micah picked up the pastries and carried them to the kitchen table. He turned off the coffee maker and sat down on a chair. He glanced up at the kitchen clock. It was 10:15. He closed his eyes and put his head in his hands. When he looked at the clock again, it was 10:40. The phone rang. Micah picked up the receiver after the third ring.

"Good morning, Mr. Stewart! This is your lucky day," the voice said. "We're going to have representatives in your neighborhood today giving free demonstrations on a new carpet-cleaning process..."

Micah slammed down the receiver.

"Go to hell!" he said.

A few seconds later, the phone rang again. Micah picked it up and was ready to lay into the caller when he realized it was Alice.

"Where have you been?" she said. "I tried calling last night but all I ever got was the answering machine. Are you okay?"

"I'm getting by," he said in a tired voice.

"Micah, is there anything I can do? This is so tragic. I ache inside."

"I'll be fine, Alice," he said slowly. "It's beginning to sink in what has happened but I'll get through it. I appreciate your concern."

"Do you want me to come over?"

"No, Alice, I'll be okay. Josh has been over a couple of times. I'm okay."

"Micah, don't try to go through this by yourself. I know you haven't been feeling well lately."

"Everything is under control. I'm going to the funeral on Friday. Everything has been taken care of."

"Please call me if there is anything I can do," Alice said pleadingly.

"I will, Alice. Everything is under control. Bye."

"Bye, Micah."

A few second after hanging up, the phone rang again. Micah was getting weary from the calls but went ahead and answered.

"How are you doing, Micah?" Spencer asked.

"I'm hanging in there, Spence."

Spencer paused a second and cleared his throat.

"Micah, I want you to take some time off. Do what you need to do. Come back to work when you feel you're ready."

"I'm okay," Micah said. "I'll be back on Monday."

"No you won't," Spencer said in a fatherly tone. "You'll come back when you get over this. I hadn't realized how close you were to this woman. I was talking to a woman in promotions this morning and she told me that you and Cora had been dating for quite awhile. No one here had a clue about that. So you just take your time and get your head on straight. We'll get the newspaper out without you, so don't worry about that. I just want you to get over this."

"If you insist," Micah said, dryly.

"I insist."

"Okay, Spence," Micah said. "I don't know what to say. You're right. I do need some time."

"If I can help in any other way, just let me know."

"Thanks, again. Bye."

"Take care of yourself. Good bye."

Micah fought back tears after putting back the receiver. He sat on the arm of the couch, running his hands through his hair while trying to regain his composure. Without thinking, he clicked the message button on the answering machine.

"Hi, Micah. This is me. I saw you only five minutes ago but I've decided that I won't be going to Virginia on Thanksgiving. I want to spend it with you so don't you go and make any plans. I'll try to fix up a big vegetarian feast for us although I may get a few slices of turkey for myself. Got work to do now. I hope you can call tonight. I love you!"

Micah sat dazed after listening to the message. Others followed from Josh, Alice, Tammy and Vanetta, but he didn't hear them. He dropped his head and began crying.

Micah glanced down at the newspaper on the coffee table and the headline that screamed, *Gunman Kills Four in News Room*, across the top of the front page. He picked it up and stared at the small photos of Cora and the three other victims. Then he noticed the photo of the gunman. He stared at it for a few seconds before realizing he had seen the man before. He thought about where he knew the face, then his thoughts went back to the evening at O'Malley's when he was accosted by the drunk. It was the same person.

Forty

Cora's funeral was simple yet elegant. St. Andrews was a small church that seated about two hundred people, and every pew was full of mourners. Her mother and step-father and her brother sat on the front row, their arms around each other during the closed-casket service. Micah sat near the back, taking in each word during the eulogy as he found out more about Cora's short life.

Cora had never told him that she had been involved in a horse-riding accident as a child that left her in the hospital for nearly four months. She had never mentioned about joining a group that volunteered in poverty-stricken areas of the country. He never knew that she was once engaged, only to have her fiancée die in an automobile accident just days before the wedding. There was mentioned of various journalism awards. But most of all, Micah was moved by the compassion that she showed others. Tears streamed down his cheeks as the service came to a close. He followed others as they went up to the casket to pay final respects. He took a single rose that he had purchased before going to the church and placed it on the casket.

Micah followed the funeral procession to the cemetery in the country. The sun shined brightly although there was a cold breeze sweeping through the site that caused the funeral tent to shake. After her coffin was lowered into the ground, Micah solemnly walked up to her grave and whispered, "I love you," then turned and walked away.

"Mr. Stewart?" a woman's voice called on his way to the parking area. "Mr. Stewart?"

Micah turned around and a woman dressed in black and wearing a veil approached him. She pulled the veil back from her face, and Micah knew it was Cora's mother. She had the same gentle features of her daughter. Her smile brought him to tears.

"Yes, ma'am," Micah said. "I'm Micah Stewart."

"I saw you put the rose on her casket at the church and thought you would be Micah," she said warmly and taking his hand. "I'm Lois Hampton, Cora's mother."

Micah gently squeezed her hand and returned the smile.

"I wish there was something I could have done," Micah said softly. "I don't need to tell you that she was a wonderful woman."

"She spoke so highly of you Micah. She wanted us so much to meet you in person."

A man in a dark suit came up to them, putting his arm around Mrs. Miller's waist. He was distinguished-looking, with gray streaks through his hair and chiseled facial features that sent a signal of strength. He appeared to be in his early sixties, about four or five years old than her.

"William, this is Micah," Lois said. "This is Cora's step-father."

Micah shook his hand.

"It's a pleasure to meet you, Mr. Stewart. Cora spoke very highly of you."

"Thank you, sir. She was quite a woman. I'm going to miss her terribly. We're all going to miss her."

"It all seems so senseless," Mr. Hampton said somberly. He shook his head and wiped his eyes.

"Now, William," Mrs. Miller said while patting him gently on the back. "We've all been through that. It's not going to help rehashing it again right now."

"If there's anything I can do, please let me know," Micah said. "I know this is a very difficult time but if there's anything..."

"We will, Mr. Stewart," Mrs. Hampton said abruptly. "Thank you for your kindness."

Mr. and Mrs. Hampton smiled and walked away slowly. Others came up to them and offered their condolences. Micah glanced up at Cora's grave site one more time as workers had already began to fill in the hole.

~ * ~

Micah took off his suit coat before getting into the rental car he picked up at the airport. He turned right out of the cemetery and headed south. He lost track of time, and before he knew it, he had crossed the state line into North Carolina. He stopped in Greensboro for gasoline, drove three more hours to Charlotte, where he pulled into a Motel 6 for the night. After checking in, he walked across a busy street to a Shoney's Restaurant for dinner. He ordered the salad bar and iced water. He took his time eating while reflecting on the day's events. He wasn't sure why he was in Charlotte and didn't know where he would end up. He only knew that he was in no hurry to get back to Cincinnati.

Asleep almost the moment he put his head on the pillow but it wasn't a restful sleep as he tossed and turned throughout the night. Several times he woke up as images of the funeral flashed through his mind, and then he would drift back off to sleep. He woke before the sun came up and took a shower, pulling on a pair of jeans, pullover sweater and tennis shoes. After paying his bill, he drove down the road and filled up his gas tank at a self-

A LONG HIGHWAY

serve station. The air was chilly as he pumped the gas, but it helped clear his senses before hitting the long highway, destination undermined. He stopped at a McDonald's drive-thru for a large coffee and cinnamon roll, and then drove south on Interstate 77 in the red Ford Probe.

When he stopped in Columbia, South Carolina, for more gas and a map, he studied the map for a few minutes while drinking a Pepsi and eating snack crackers. He fooled with the radio for a few minutes, finding a country station that was playing Garth Brooks' *Longneck Bottle* and turned up the volume, then pulled away from the station, traveling southeast on I-26 to Charleston. He had never been there before, and he wasn't going anywhere in particular, so it didn't make any difference.

He cruised into Charleston late afternoon and found a HoJo's motel. He checked in, went up to his second-floor room and sat down in one of the plastic-backed orange chairs. He glanced at the clock radio. It was only 5:45. He wasn't hungry but didn't want to stay in the motel room.

Micah went back to the check-in desk and asked the clerk where there the nearest shopping mall was located. He didn't bring along enough clothes with him and wanted to buy a few pair of jeans and shirts to wear along the way. It was only a fifteen-minute drive to the mall. He bought two pairs of jeans, two pullover shirts, six pairs of boxer shorts, and six pairs of socks. On the way out, he saw a Western wear store and peeked in the window at a pair of suede boots. He eyed them for about a minute, then went inside and bought a pair along with a gray, wool hat. He walked out of the store adjusting the hat on his head with one hand while trying to carry the other packages with his other.

Near sundown he drove by the ocean-front walk and parked his car, got out and strolled along the sidewalk. There were a few others sitting along the way, watching the Atlantic waves beat harshly against the shoreline.

Micah walked to the restored downtown area and found a small café where he perused the menu on the door, noted the few vegetarian items, and went in. The waiter went over the specials of the day, including what he called the establishment's "succulent" seafood. But his bright smile faded when Micah ordered pinto beans, corn on the cob and broccoli along with a hush puppy and iced tea. Sitting undisturbed at a table next to a window, he glanced around at the decor, an odd combination of Civil War and fishing, while waiting for his food.

Micah took his time eating, and when the waiter returned to refill his glass with tea, he ordered a key lime pie and a cup of coffee to top off the meal. He left a twenty-five percent gratuity to make up for the waiter's disappointment in not ordering the house specials.

The wind off the ocean picked up when Micah left the cafe and he bundled his jacket around his neck. There was no one to be seen along the sidewalk as he hurried to his car.

Momentarily lost returning to HoJo's, he located a landmark that refreshed his sense of direction. It was nearly nine o'clock when he got back to his room. He looked at himself in the mirror while wearing the hat and grinned, then turned on the television, turned down the volume, and sat down on the bed. He leaned over and picked up the telephone and called Josh.

"How did everything go?" Josh asked. "I thought you'd be home sooner."

"It was a beautiful service," Micah said. "I met Cora's parents. They're really sweet people."

"When did you get home?"

"Uh, I'm not home. I decided to take a little trip."

"Where are you?"

"Charleston, South Carolina."

"Are you kidding me? Charleston, South Carolina!"

"I needed to get away so I started driving after I left Charlottesville."

"When are you coming home?"

"I don't know. The newspaper told me to take as much time as I needed."

"I can understand that."

"If anyone asks about me, would you tell them that I'm all right?"

"Sure. Could you keep me posted on your whereabouts?"

"I'll try to. I'll either call or send a postcard."

"You sound like you may be gone for a while."

"I'm in no hurry to get back."

"Just be careful."

"I will. I'll see you. Bye."

Forty-one

Micah donned his western hat and boots, jeans and gray flannel shirt the next morning, ready to hit the road for southern points. He was behind the wheel at six, stopping only for coffee at a fast-food restaurant and gas. There was little traffic on Charleston streets as he drove on Highway 17 to I-95, with Savannah, Georgia, his next destination as the sun was rising radiantly above the Atlantic.

He glanced into the rearview mirror, admiring his new look with the hat, and ran his fingers through his beard that was getting longer and fuller. He looked more like a cowboy about to go out on a roundup rather than a sports writer trying to find himself. He set the cruise control on seventy and listened to an oldies station as made his way out of South Carolina and into Georgia. He was in Savannah by eleven.

Micah always wanted to visit Savannah and see its antebellum architecture. He parked his car near Bull Street and began walking. He went into some of the shops in the downtown historic district, and then strolled through several neighborhoods, viewing the stately mansions and genteel courtyards that graced the city. The hours passed by quickly as he tried to absorb much of the rich history. When the sun began to set, he started back to his car. It was already dark by the time he drove in search of a motel. An hour later, in one of the busy arteries into the city, he found a small mom-and-pop operation called Pearl's.

Pearl, a short, stocky black woman in her seventies, sat behind the desk when he walked through the front door. She gave him a suspicious look after examining the clean-cut look on his driver's license.

"You can never be sure who's using someone else's credit card," she said in a slow drawl as he filled out the registration form. "And you don't know how much trouble it can be for small businesses when we take a stolen credit card. That's why I always check. It's just too much trouble. You know what I mean?"

"I'm sure it is," Micah said, giving her a quick smile. "I'd probably do the same thing if I were you."

"Some people really get offended when I ask for their driver's license with their credit card," she said, keeping her eyes fixed on the form. "I don't mean to offend anybody but it's something I've got to do. You know what I mean?"

"I think I do," Micah said, handing the pen to her as she studied the form.

"So you're staying here three nights?"

"Yes, ma'am."

"What are you here for?"

"Pleasure," Micah said with an easy smile. "I've never been to Savannah so I thought I would see a few of the sites."

"I see you're from Cincinnati. I've got a cousin who used to live there. Ever hear of any Powers? Her name is Edna Powers."

"Don't believe I have," Micah said. "Cincinnati's a big city."

"I know it's a big town but you just never know. A couple years ago I mentioned a cousin's name to this gal from Fort Worth, and would you believe it that they lived on the same block. So you just never know."

"You're right," Micah said as he backed away from the counter. "Well, if you don't mind, I need to go to my room and rest. My feet are killing me."

"Okay, Mr. Stewart," she said. "I hope you have a nice stay."

Micah walked back to his car and parked it in front of his room. He opened the trunk and took out his suitcase.

The room had a slight musty order, but it was tidy with two double beds. An air-conditioner was propped up in the rear window while steam heat was used to keep the room warm in the winter. The thermostat had already been adjusted to a comfortable sixty-eight degrees.

Micah laid the suitcase on the red chenille bedspread and removed his toiletry case and took it to the bath room. He turned on the television, an old Zenith color model that carried only local stations. He turned it off and sat down on a green chair that had torn plastic fixed with gray duct tape. He glanced around at the surroundings for a moment, and then realized he hadn't eaten since morning. He opened the curtains and saw a Chinese restaurant across the road.

Donning his coat, he scampered across the busy road. He was the only customer. An elderly Chinese woman took his carryout order of a vegetarian plate and egg roll and large cup of water. She wasn't friendly when he came in but was smiling and gracious when he left.

Micah set his food on a small table in front of the front window in his room, leaving the bright orange curtains open. He slipped off his boots gingerly, and then took off his socks. Large, pink blisters had formed with some of the skin rubbed off on his heels. He lifted his feet on the side of the bed, then opened the container of food and began eating. The food was good but the pain increased in his feet. He tiptoed to the bathroom and soaked two wash cloths with cold water and placed them around his heels. It gave him relief but the pain quickly returned.

Micah went through his toiletries but didn't find anything to put on the sores. He put on his tennis shoes, grimacing as he loosely tied the laces, and headed down to the motel office. Pearl was sitting behind the counter watching TV, and stood up when a bell sounded as he opened the door.

"Is something wrong with the room, Mr. Stewart? Is the shower not working? Something wrong with the TV set? I hope you're not wanting to run the air-conditioner this time of year."

Micah waited patiently for her to finish.

"I was wondering if you had a first-aid kit or some bandages."

"What for?"

"I did more walking than I expected to do and rubbed some blisters on my feet. I was hoping you'd have something I could put on them."

"Let me see what it looks like. Sit down on the couch over there."

Micah stepped over to an overstuffed couch, sat down and untied his shoes, slightly moaning as he slipped them off. Pearl bent down and looked at them.

"You're right," she said. "You've got blisters. Those are humdingers. You shouldn't have walked that much."

"I know," Micah said, nodding in agreement. "But I've done it. Do you have anything I can put on it?"

Pearl rose and put her right hand under her chin.

"Well let me go see," she said. "I'll have to go back into my apartment and see what I have in the medicine cabinet."

"That's okay," Micah said. "I don't want to put you to that much trouble. I'll just get in my car and find a Wal-Mart or something."

"It's no problem at all, Mr. Stewart," Pearl said as he disappeared behind curtains leading to her apartment. "I'll be gone only a minute. Would you watch the counter for me?"

"Yes, ma'am," Micah said, while lifting up a foot to examine it more closely.

Pearl returned a few minutes later with a bottle of iodine, a roll of gauze, and white tape. She got down on one knee in front of him.

"I think we can fix you up," she said, flashing a toothy grin. "Now you just put that foot on my leg."

Before Micah could move his leg, she already took hold of his foot and set it firmly across her leg and turned it over.

"My, my," she said. "That's really nasty. How long did you walk?"

"I guess about six hours. I kind of lost track of time."

"I would say so," she said. "Now this is going to sting a little." She dipped the applicator in and out of the iodine bottle and smoothed it gently on his heel.

"Ouch!" he yelled.

"I'm sorry," she said. "I didn't mean to hurt you."

"That's okay. It's not your fault."

"So don't you have any walking shoes?"

"I was wearing some new boots."

"New boots? You should have known better than that," she said while placing gauze on the blisters and wrapping it with tape.

"I know. I've learned my lesson."

"Now, put your other foot up here," she said.

Micah slowly lowered his one leg to the floor and raised the other, which she guided carefully.

"This is going to hurt again," she said while holding the bottle of iodine.

"I know," he said. "Let's hurry up and get it over with."

Micah felt a shot of pain but didn't yell out this time. His tightly-closed eyes and clenched teeth were an indication that it hurt.

"Now, that wasn't too bad, was it?" she said with a sweet smile while closing the bottle.

"That was much better," he said. "I really appreciate you doing this for me."

"It was no problem," Pearl said as she finished wrapping the gauze and tape on his heel. "I'm just happy that I was able to help you."

"You've been a lifesaver tonight," Micah said, slowly putting on his tennis shoes but leaving them untied.

"If you have any more problems, Mr. Stewart, just dial O on the telephone. I'm usually here at the counter until eleven or so, then I switch it to my bedroom. So it won't inconvenience me in the least bit if you need to call me."

"Yes, ma'am, I'll do that," Micah said as he opened the door. "Thanks again."

Micah walked on the balls of his feet back to his room, trying to keep the back of his tennis shoes from rubbing too much against his heels. When he got inside, he took them off, closed the curtain and lay down on the bed. After a few minutes the pain began to ease. He picked up the telephone and called Alice.

Ben answered the phone in an irritated tone.

"Where are you, Dad? Didn't you know we had ball practice tonight?"

"I'm sorry, Ben. I'm out of town right now."

"Are you going to be at the game on Saturday?"

"I won't be able to. I'm not sure when I'll be back."

Micah could hear Alice in the background asking Ben who he was talking to.

"That's great," Ben said. "It's just like old times."

"Now Ben, you know I had to go to a funeral. I'll be back when I can."

"The funeral was last week."

"Yes, Ben, I know that," Micah said, realizing it was no use to argue with him. "Let me speak to your Mom."

"Micah?" Alice asked. "Where are you?"

"I'm in Savannah, Georgia."

Alice started laughing.

"Seriously," she said. "Where are you?"

"Like I said," he said. "I decided to take some time off after the funeral. I guess it's kind of a mental-health trip."

"Are you okay?" she asked with concern in her voice.

"I'm fine except for blisters on my feet."

"Blisters?"

"It's okay," he said. "I just wanted to let you know that I won't be back home for a few days."

"When are you coming home?"

"I don't know. I guess when I feel like it."

"Okay, Micah. Just be careful and stay in touch."

"I will," he said. "Would you give the kids a hug for me?"

"I will," she said. "We miss you."

Micah eased off his jeans and shirt and draped them on the back of the chair. He reached over and took a pillow from the other bed and put it down at the foot off his bed to prop up his feet. He got up and turned off the overhead light and got back into bed. He closed his eyes and dozed off, waking up several hours later in a dream-like state as lights from the street filtered through the curtains and danced on the walls. He fell back asleep, but was awakened by a knocking on the door. He could see that it was already light outside.

"Mr. Stewart?"

Micah rubbed his eyes and stretched his arms.

"Yes," he groaned. "Who is it?"

"It's Mrs. Jones."

"Huh?"

"You know, Pearl," she said, sounding a little irritated. "The woman who fixed your feet."

"Oh," Micah said. "Wait a minute."

He reached over and slowly pulled on his jeans, slipped a T-shirt on and tip-toed to the door. Pearl was there with a cup of coffee and a plate of biscuits, scrambled eggs, and bacon.

"I didn't think you'd be out this morning for breakfast with your feet the way they are," she said while stepping into his room. "So I brought you a little something to eat. We don't usually have room service here."

She giggled and put the food on the table next to the Chinese leftovers.

"That's awfully nice of you," Micah said. "You shouldn't have gone to the trouble."

"It's no trouble at all," she said. "Now you better start eating before the food gets cold. There's nothing worse than cold bacon and eggs. Now I don't mind a cold biscuit once in awhile because you can put butter and jelly on it, but cold bacon and eggs don't cut it with me. But I do like cold bacon on a bacon and tomato sandwich. Have you ever had one of them?"

"A long time ago," Micah said as he sat down. He picked up a fork and took a couple bites of the eggs.

"Now I put a little milk in your coffee," she said. "I hope that's all right with you."

"Yes, ma'am. I always use a little cream."

"Now that's not cream. It's just regular milk."

"I use milk, too," he said with a smile.

"Aren't you going to eat that bacon?"

"Uh, I don't eat meat," he said. "I'm a vegetarian."

"You're kidding!" she said with her hands on her hips. "Oh well, cousin Fred was one of those. He died of a heart attack a few years ago. I think he was fifty-four years old. He thought that vegetables would make him live longer."

Micah was at a loss for words. He took another bite of eggs and sipped a little coffee.

"Mind if I have that bacon?" she said, raising her eyebrows. "There's no sense in letting it go to waste."

"Of course, Mrs. Jones," he said, turning the plate to where she could take the three slices.

"I best be off," she said. "I'll be back a little later to change your sheets and get this plate and cup."

"Thanks again," Micah said. "You've been very kind."

"The Lord says to do unto others and you'd want them to do unto you," she said. "So that's what I'm doing."

Pearl put a piece of bacon her mouth and opened the door.

"You call if you need anything, Mr. Stewart," she said, then closed the door and left.

Micah smiled as he took another swallow from his cup.

Forty-two

Every time Micah got out of bed, his feet throbbed. He wanted to take off the bandages and look at his sore heels, but it hurt too much to lift up his legs. He glanced around for a remote control to turn on the television, and then realized that the model was either too old to have a remote or it had been stolen. The only reading material was a Gideon's King James Bible he found inside the top drawer of the night stand.

"I can't believe I got myself into this mess," he said to himself. "This is unreal."

A soft pecking came on the window. Micah could tell by the outline of the person through the curtain that it was Pearl.

"Yes?" he said, raising his voice.

"Is it safe to come in?"

"Yes ma'am."

Pearl inserted the master key into the lock, then pushed the door open with her foot. She carried a cardboard box in both hands.

"Hi, Mr. Stewart," she said smiling. "How are you feeling?"

"My feet ache."

"I brought some dressing to put on the blisters. It's a salve that I've used for burns. It should clear it up in no time."

"I hope so. I don't know how longer I can stay in this bed."

"Is there something wrong with the bed?" she asked, her eyes expressing concern.

"No," he said. "The bed's fine. I'm just tired of lying in here. I want to get up and about."

"Oh, I see," she said. "I can't say that I don't blame. I hate being in bed all day. Even when I feel all out of sorts, I still like to get up. You know what I mean?"

"Yes, ma'am. Very much so."

Pearl lifted his left leg at the ankle and slowly pulled off the tape and gauze. She gently turned his foot to the side to get a better look at the blisters.

"Oh, my," she said, shaking her head slowly.

"Is something the matter?"

"No. It's about the same. Those blisters are really nasty. They look like they're ready to pop."

Pearl took some creamy, white salve out of the small jar with her fingers, and then spread it gently over the blisters.

"I'm not hurting you now, am I?" she asked.

"No. It feels kind of cool."

"That's good," she said while placing gauze on top of blisters and wrapping it with tape. She lifted the other leg and did the same without saying a word.

"Now, that should help you heal faster," she said, patting him on the knee.

"Could I ask a couple more favors?"

"What is it? I'll do whatever I can."

"Could you turn on the television? I couldn't seem to find the remote."

"There hasn't been a remote in the rooms for years," she said while reaching over and turning on the TV. "I got tired of replacing them. They don't cost that much but when you have to buy them all the time, that really adds up. I even had them fastened to the nightstands. See where those holes are?"

Micah nodded.

"Folks would even yank them out of holders. Can you believe that? It beats me why people do things like that. You know what I mean?"

"I think so," Micah said with a crooked smile.

"What station do you want?"

"I don't care. Anything."

"This time of day you won't find much but soaps."

"That'll be fine."

"Is there something else I can do for you?"

"I was wondering if you had a newspaper or some magazines to read."

"I have today's paper I'll let you see," she said. "I have a few old magazines in the lobby. Do you like *Reader's Digest*?"

"Yes ma'am. That would be nice."

"When I get back up there, I'll get that newspaper and look around for some *Reader's Digests* for you."

Pearl went back to the bathroom.

"It looks like you need a couple of wash cloths, too," she said. "Do you want me to make your bed?"

"I'm fine," Micah said. "I won't be getting up from here today."

Pearl walked over to the window and opened the curtains. Micah covered his eyes for a moment as he adjusted to the bright sunlight.

"It's a beautiful day," Pearl said. "You'd hardly know it's almost December. You want me to leave the curtains open."

"Could you close them about half way?"

Pearl took the frayed drawstrings and tugged the curtains midway over the windows.

"How's that?"

"That's great," Micah said, nodding approval.

"So you think you'll be staying here a little longer, being your feet are the way they are?"

"Probably so," he said. "Will that be a problem?"

"Goodness, no! I like the company."

"How long have you been in business here?"

"My husband, Frank, bought it around forty years ago," she said. "He died twelve years ago from cancer and left it to me. I've been running it ever since."

"Do you have any children?"

"I've got a daughter and a son. The girl lives up in New York. Her name is Dorothy. She's made me a grandmother four times," Pearl said with a bright smile. "My son Johnny is in prison in Kentucky. Some place called Eddyville. He killed some man in Louisville. They were fighting over some woman."

"When does he get out?"

"He's got another five years. He doesn't write that often but I guess he's doing okay."

"Do you miss him?"

"Shucks, no. That boy was in trouble from the time he started the first grade. He got kicked out of high school for drugs. He's been in and out of jails all his life. I just wished he'd finally grow up."

"Does your daughter visit you"?

"Oh, she comes down once in a blue moon. She married this guy who drives a taxi. She works in some restaurant. They make a good living but they seem to have to work all the time. I thought once about going up there, but I just don't like to get in airplanes. And I don't drive anymore."

"So you stay here all day?"

"That's about it," she said with a soft smile. "I got some kin that check in on me once in awhile and take me to the grocery so I'm not all that lonesome."

"Do you have anyone to help you with the motel?"

"I run it all by myself," she said proudly. "I had a young man working for me a few years back. I think his name was Jack. He seemed like a nice enough boy but one day he up and left and took all the money in the cash register. I didn't trust anyone after that."

"But isn't it a lot of work for you?"

"Goodness, no," she said with a hearty laugh. "Look down that highway and you see all sorts of places to stay. That's where people go. I about had a heart attack when you pulled in here and said you wanted to spend several nights. That's the first time someone has done that in the longest time."

"I think you have a nice inn, Pearl."

"Why, thank you, Mr. Stewart. I try to keep it clean and everything. The buildings are getting kind of old. I need to put some new roofing on and some of the air conditioners don't work. But it's all I have. My kin want me to sell it and move in with them or find some nice senior citizens home. I just don't know if I'm ready for that."

"If you're happy with what you're doing, that's all that matters."

"And I am happy to be doing this," she said. "I'll be seventy-four next spring. I think if I didn't have something to do, that I'd just drop dead. You know what I mean?"

"I guess so."

"What do you do, Mr. Stewart?"

"First of all, please call me Micah," he said pleasantly.

"I'll do that, Micah." she said smiling. "I like that name. Micah. Micah. Now, Micah, what do you do for a living?"

"I'm a sports writer," he said, almost apologetically.

"A sports writer? My, my, that sounds so interesting. You ever saw Michael Jordan?"

"Yes, ma'am," Micah said warmly. "I saw him play in college and a few times in Chicago."

"That boy can sure play basketball," she said, shaking her head. "How about the Braves? Do you ever see the Braves?"

"I've seen them quite a few times. I've seen them play the Cincinnati Reds a couple times a year. I've also covered them in the World Series?"

"The World Series!"

"Yes, I go to the World Series about every year."

"Oh, my, my," she said. "Oh, do I envy you. The World Series. I always wanted to go to a World Series."

"I take it that you like sports," Micah said with a laugh.

"Well, sometimes," she said abruptly. "I like my game shows, too. And I like to travel when I can."

"Where do you like to travel?"

"Frank used to take me to the ocean about every Sunday after church," she said. "That was back when we had some help here and we could get away for a few hours. I just loved sitting there on the beach and watching those waves just roll in. It was so peaceful."

"Do you still go?"

"I haven't been back since my husband passed away."

"But it's not that far?"

"Didn't I tell you I don't drive?"

"Oh, I'm sorry. I forgot."

"Well, Mr. Stewart, I mean Micah, I need to do a few things," she said. "I'll bring back those reading materials a little later. Is that okay?"

"I'm in no hurry."

Pearl pushed herself up from the bed and stood. She peeked down at his bandages quickly, and then touched him on the leg.

"Looking good," she said. "You'll be up and about before you know it."

Micah smiled as she went to the door. She reached down and picked up the plate and cup from breakfast and the Chinese containers, and then opened the door.

"I'll check back on you a little later," she said before closing the door.

Micah tried watching television but couldn't get interested in the soap opera. He wanted to turn down the volume but didn't feel like scooting off the bed and maneuvering to the controls.

He dozed off to sleep but woke up when he realized he had to go to the bathroom. He inched himself to the side of the bed, swung his legs around to the side, pushed himself up with his hands and stood. He could feel the throbbing begin in his feet, but he forced himself to the bathroom, taking small steps until he got to the toilet. After he finished, he trudged slowly back to the bed, turning off the TV along the way. He fell back into the bed, and positioned his aching feet back on the pillow.

A few seconds later, Pearl unlocked the door and peeked in.

"I've got something for you to read," she said with a grin.

"Come on in," Micah said.

"Did the TV go bad?"

"No, I turned it off."

"You? Now you shouldn't be trying to do those things, Micah. How are those feet ever going to get better if you're on them all the time?"

"I had to go to the bathroom."

"Well, I guess you need to get up once in awhile," she said. "You got to go to the bathroom when you've got to go. You know what I mean?"

"Exactly, Pearl. I know exactly what you mean."

Forty-three

Micah spent the afternoon skimming through several old magazines and the newspaper. The swelling began to decrease although his heels were still very tender. He managed to get up another time and go to the bathroom. He wanted to take a shower, an everyday habit, but sensed that the water and soap touching the blisters would cause unbearable pain. But he did brush his teeth for the first time in two days and combed his hair.

Pearl returned at 6:30, just after he finished watching the local news, with a tray containing a glass of milk, and bowls of kale, sweet potatoes, and pinto beans, and cornbread. There were two plates, and one contained a slice of beef liver sautéed with onions.

"I hope you don't mind a little company for supper," she said, setting the food on the table. "It gets a tad bit lonesome up there in the office at times. You know what I mean?"

"I think so," he said with a smile. "You really didn't have to do all of this. I could have ordered a pizza or something to be delivered."

"You need to eat a balanced meal. And this is no trouble for me at all. It's simply a matter of taking out another plate from the cupboard."

Pearl pushed the table to the side of the bed, and Micah sat up. She took a chair and sat across from him at the table, she spooned out even portions for each of the bowls on their plates.

"Now eat up," she said.

Micah sprinkled some vinegar on the kale and took a bite. He stuck his fork in the sweet potatoes and took another bite. She watched him for a few seconds.

"This is delicious, Pearl," Micah said. "I haven't had kale in years. My mom used to fix it all the time."

Pearl raised her head and smile.

"Thank you, Micah," she said. "I love to cook. I used to fix Frank a big meal every day at lunch and at supper. He appreciated a big meal. But since he died, I haven't cooked that much unless some relatives stopped by on a Sunday. It's kind of hard to fix a big meal for just one person. Sometimes when I do it, I have leftovers for the next two or three days. And that gets a little boring eating the same thing. You know what I mean?"

"I think so," Micah said. "I usually eat out quite a bit at restaurants because I don't want to cook just for myself."

"Don't you get tired of that restaurant food?" she asked.

"I must admit that I do," he said.

"Sometimes I go across the road and get a few pieces of chicken at Kentucky Fried Chicken but I take care of all the fixins that go with it. I don't suppose you like chicken."

"I used to," Micah said.

"So you've been a single man all your life?" Pearl said while slicing the liver into small pieces.

"I've been divorced for a couple of years," he said. "I've got a son and daughter."

Micah stretched around and took his wallet off the top of the nightstand. He opened it and took out a family portrait that was taken a few months before the divorce and handed it to Pearl.

"Here's my family," he said proudly. "The kids are Ben and Annie. Ben just turned thirteen and Annie will soon be eleven. My ex-wife is Alice."

"Oh, you've got good-looking children. And your wife is so pretty," Pearl said while examining the photograph.

"Thanks," Micah said.

"So why did you leave them?"

Micah nearly choked on his cornbread with her question.

"Uh, I didn't really leave them," he said, clearing his throat. "We see each other all the time. I even coach my son's basketball team. We're still close."

"Oh, I see," Pearl said, then scooped up some beans on her fork and put them in her mouth.

"Really," Micah said, defensively. "My ex-wife and I are still friends. She was in an automobile accident last summer and I visited her all the time. And I attend my children's activities when I can. We've got a real good relationship."

"So what are you doing here in Savannah?"

"I just needed some time to get away from everything."

"Even your kids?"

"Not my children although it seems that way," Micah said. "I had to get away from work and other things and look at my life."

"So you just got in your car and drove down here?"

"Not actually. I attended the funeral of a friend in Virginia, and then decided to get away from it all for a few days. So I ended up here in Savannah. I had always wanted to visit Savannah because I had heard so much about it."

"I'm sorry to hear about your friend. How did he die?"

"It was a woman," Micah said. "She was shot at the newspaper building."

"I remember reading about that a week or so ago. That was just terrible. Was she a good friend of yours?"

"Yes, very much so," Micah said as a look of sadness came over his face.

"Do you want some more beans?" Pearl asked with her hand on the spoon.

"No, thanks," Micah said. "You've filled me up. Everything was delicious."

"I've got some apple pie back in my refrigerator. Would you like to have a slice of it?"

"I think I'll pass," Micah said, patting his stomach. "I'm stuffed."

"You don't seem like you should be so unhappy," Pearl said all of the sudden. "You get to go to the World Series and do things like that. You've got a lovely family."

Micah hesitated for a few seconds before answering. He glanced at the old woman who had spent many years tending to the motel. He thought if anyone should be unhappy with their station in life, it was Pearl.

"It's hard to explain," Micah said. "There comes a time in a person's life when they start examining everything and try to figure everything out. I guess I'm at that point. Some people call it a mid-life crisis. We get burned-out with our jobs and most everything else so we try to find ways to justify our lives. Does any of that make sense?"

"No."

Micah chuckled.

"Well, it doesn't make sense to me either," he said. "That's part of the whole problem. Life just doesn't make sense anymore."

Pearl gathered the dirty dishes and stacked them on the tray. Micah used his hands to push himself back on his pillow and swing his feet back on the other pillow.

"I think you may have too much time on your hands, Micah," Pearl said. "I've been too busy all my life to think if I'm happy or sad. Oh, there have been some bad times like when my boy went off to prison or when Frank died. That was a lonesome time. But I just tried to pick myself up and stay busy."

"Maybe my life is a little more complicated."

Pearl flashed him a scornful look.

"Do you work seven days a week?" she asked. "Do you have a daughter and grandchildren a long ways off? Do you have a boy in prison? Did your wife die? Do you have to worry about running a business?"

"I'm sorry," Micah said. "I didn't mean it that way."

"We all have our burdens to bear," she said, still with a tinge of anger. "I'm not saying mine are worse than yours. I wish I could have driven off after Frank died and spent time by myself but I had to open up this place the next day."

"I'm sorry, Pearl, I know we all have obstacles in our lives that we must deal with. I didn't mean to offend you. We all approach them differently."

"You don't have to apologize," she said, her eyes welling up with tears. "It's none of my business what you do. I shouldn't have said anything. I was just being nosy."

"That's okay. I don't mind talking about it. It's good to get things out in the open rather than keep them bottled up inside. It's good to hear another opinion."

"Well, then, how do your feet feel?" she said with a gentle smile. "I see that you made it back to the bathroom."

"They're much better," he said. "I may be able to hit the road in a day or so. I know I won't be able to wear my boots for a while."

"After I take these dishes back to the apartment, I'll come back a little later and put some new dressing on you. I need to go now because *Wheel of Fortune* and *Jeopardy* are about to come on. Do you remember that *Let's Make A Deal* show? I loved that show. I don't know why they ever took it off the TV. Me and Frank watched it all the time. There's not that many good shows on anymore. Do you know what I mean?"

Micah laughed and nodded in agreement.

"You're right about that, Pearl," he said. "They ain't what they used to be."

After Pearl left, Micah picked up the telephone and called Josh, reaching him at the office.

"What's going on?" Micah asked.

"Hey!" Josh said. "I've been thinking about you. Where are you?"

"Would you believe Savannah?"

"What in the world are you doing in Savannah?"

"I was doing a little sightseeing but hurt my feet."

"Hurt your feet?"

"I'll explain it when I get back."

"So when do you think you'll be coming home?"

"In a few days," Micah said. "There's a few things I want to do here before I leave."

"Remember Vanetta?"

"How in the world could I forget her?"

"I saw her the other evening at Big Shots with Dirk. Can you believe it? They seemed a bit more than friends."

"I had dinner with them a few weeks ago. She had her eyes on him then. So how's Tammy?"

"Great. We're getting along famously. She's the best thing that ever happened to me."

"I'm happy to hear that. She's a sweet woman."

"I was wondering if you'd like to start another book?"

"What are you talking about?"

"It would be a complete history of professional sports in Cincinnati. It would include the Reds and Bengals of course, but also basketball, hockey, soccer and anything else in the past one hundred years. I think I can come up with a decent advance for you."

"How much?"

"Would $50,000 be enough?"

"Let me give that a lot of thought," Micah said. "I'll let you know when I get back to town. Is that too late?"

"Just take your time. You're the person my boss wants to do the book."

"I'm flattered," Micah said. "Is anything else going on?"

"That's about it. It's been relatively quiet around here."

"Well, I'd better get off here," Micah said. "I'll get back in touch with you when I get home."

"Drive safely."

Micah watched *Wheel of Fortune* and *Jeopardy* and a few minutes later, Pearl knocked on the door and came in carrying the cardboard box with the medical supplies.

"I watched the two shows," Micah said.

"Aren't they good?" Pearl said while she unwrapped the bandages. "I just love Alex Trebek. He's so clever."

Micah rose a little and glanced down at his heels. They were still raw but not nearly as red.

"You should have been a nurse," Micah said as she lightly touched the sores with a damp wash cloth.

"I wanted to be a nurse when I was younger," Pearl said while continuing to wipe off his foot. "But then I got married and had babies. We couldn't afford for me to go into any nurses' training back then. We were just able to make ends meet. You know what I mean?"

"It's kind of hard starting out," Micah said.

"It sure is," Pearl said. "Then Frank's mama got sick and I had to take care of her. She died from breast cancer. Poor woman. It was so pitiful seeing her lying in that bed, just wasting away to nothing. It broke my heart."

"I can imagine."

"Then his daddy had a stroke and came to live with us. He could hardly talk and get around. Then he died."

"How about your parents?"

"Oh, they were killed in a fire when I was about six years old."

"Oh, my God. I'm sorry."

"That's all right. That was a long time ago. We lived in this little house, me and my two brothers and three sisters and mom and dad. Me and my sisters slept downstairs and we got out but my parents and brothers slept upstairs and they didn't make it. The firemen thought something was wrong with the wood stove. I had to go live with my aunt. I stayed with her until Frank and me got married when I was fifteen."

"That was awfully young."

"I know it was but people got married young back then. I think we were more mature back then, more grown up. You know what I mean?"

"You're probably right," Micah said. "People don't grow up very fast these days."

Micah looked down at his feet again, and Pearl had already finished taping over the gauze.

"That sure was quick," he said with a warm smile.

"That's because they're looking better," she said. "I bet they don't hurt like they did yesterday."

"No, they don't."

"So are your parents alive."

"They were killed in a plane crash about twenty years ago."

"You poor boy," she said, pursing her lips. "We all have our burdens to carry."

Forty-four

Micah awoke early the following morning and ventured into the bathroom. He was determined to take a shower. After staying in bed for two days, his skin felt oily and his hair was going in every direction. Turning on the shower to a pleasant lukewarm temperature, he took off his boxers and stepped under the water. The pelting drops felt good against his skin as he closed his eyes and put his face under the water for a few seconds. He removed a small package of soap and began washing all over. He left the bandages on his heels, unsure how they would feel against water. He shampooed his hair and then rinsed off his body for nearly five minutes.

After getting out, he trimmed his beard, noticing that some gray was beginning to show through on his chin. He combed his hair back, and brushed his teeth and smiled as he gazed in the mirror, pleased with his appearance. He walked gingerly back to the bed, opened the suitcase and took out a new pair of boxers. He wanted to put on a new pair of jeans and shirt, but they were in the trunk of the car. Instead, he wore the jeans he'd been wearing and took his last clean T-shirt out of the suitcase.

He turned on the television and sat on the side of the bed. A local news program was reporting on the weather, saying it was going to be gray and gloomy with temperatures in the low fifties. The sports followed and there was nothing about any major news in Cincinnati, which pleased him, and he turned off the set.

Moments later, Pearl knocked at the door. She waited a few seconds, and then let herself in as she had been doing all along. She carried a tray with a pot of coffee, two cups, milk and sugar, and blueberry muffins.

"Good morning, Micah," she said cheerfully. "My, don't you look nice this morning."

"Good morning, Pearl. How did you know I was up already? It's only 6:30."

"I saw the light shining through the curtain. Do you like blueberry muffins?" she asked as she poured coffee into their cups.

"Yes, ma'am," he said. "They look delicious."

"How did you sleep last night? Did your feet cause you any problems?"

"I slept like a kitten. I don't think I moved the entire night. My feet are much better, thank you."

"I'll change that dressing a little later this morning."

"How was your evening?"

"There wasn't much on TV so I did a little reading. I also had a couple of people check in so I stayed a little busy."

"That's good to hear. How many units do you have?"

"I've got twelve. If I can get three or four rooms checked out a night, I'm doing really good."

"Have you ever had all the rooms occupied?"

"Not a whole lot but sometimes during the middle of the summer when all the visitors come to town. It's hard on me to keep all the rooms ready when it's like that because you can't get good help. Did I tell you about that young man I had?"

"Yes, the guy who stole from the cash register?"

"Can you believe someone would do something like that?"

"It happens a lot."

"Sometimes I can get one of my cousins to come over and help me change the linen after a busy night. They really don't want to but they like to have the extra money."

"I bet they do," Micah said before taking a bite out of a muffin. "These are really good."

"Thank you," she said with a satisfied smile. "I make them from scratch from a family recipe."

She picked up the coffee pot and poured some more in their cups.

"Do you ever have any trouble around here?" Micah asked.

"Oh, sometimes it gets a little noisy when someone plays music too loud. I just tell them that if they don't turn it down that I'll call the police. That usually does the trick. I remember when we would get a lot of families staying here. That doesn't happen too much anymore. I get single men like you just passing through or couples. I don't think they're married though because they don't stay too long. Would you believe that sometimes they check in at nine and leave by midnight? Can you imagine paying for a night and staying only three hours? I remember a long time ago when Frank would make sure the man and woman were married. He didn't want any shenanigans going on. He was a religious man and he didn't believe it was right. But things have changed since then. It seems like everybody lives with each other and they have children without being married. They talk about it on those talk shows and never give it a thought. Can you believe that?"

"I know, Pearl," Micah said, shaking his head. "These are different times we live in."

"I don't want to be personal, but did you ever live with another woman?"

"No. My ex-wife and I spent some time together before we got married but we never lived with each other."

"I shouldn't be telling you this but I was a virgin when I got married. I was just fifteen. Me and Frank decided that we should get married before having sex. Oh, we came close at times but we didn't do it. We didn't want to fornicate and sin. So we talked to my folks and they said we should get married."

Micah smiled warmly and took a sip from his coffee. "That was a wise thing to do," he said. "More people should wait until they're married before having sex."

"Well, it's not easy," she said, shaking her head.

"Can I ask you a personal question?"

"I hope it's not too personal," she said with a laugh.

"Have you gone out with any men since Frank died?"

"Goodness, no!" she said, lifting her arms and laughing. Her leg brushed against the table, causing the coffee to nearly spill over the side of the cups.

"How come?" Micah asked, amused by her reaction.

"I'm an old woman, that's how come," she said. "Men don't ask out old women. They want those young ones."

"I'm sure there've been some men who've given you some attention."

"Ain't no man going to give me the eye," she said, wiping tears from her eyes from laughing.

"Well, would you like to get married again?"

"Shucks, no. I like my freedom. I don't want no man telling me where I can and can't go. Now I didn't mind Frank doing it once in awhile but I don't want to be taking orders from someone else. It's nice to be able to come and go as I please. You know what I mean?"

"Come to think of it, I guess you're right," Micah said. "I've had my freedom, so to speak, for more than two years. I miss my children but I'm not complaining about some of the other things."

"Now I bet your wife wasn't a bad person."

"Seriously," Micah said, "she was more than what I deserved. She's an excellent mother."

"Then why did you leave her?"

"We just didn't love each other anymore."

"Just didn't love each other anymore?" Pearl said, shaking her head in disbelief. "Now how can you love someone for all those years and suddenly not love them anymore? That doesn't make any sense, Micah."

"You ask me the hardest questions," Micah said with a chuckle. "I don't know if I can answer it."

"You know there's all different kinds of love," Pearl said. "You got that physical love when you get married, then it changes all through your life. Now I'm not saying Frank and me didn't have some of that physical love before he died, but I could tell by the way he looked at me that he loved me."

"That's very touching," Micah said. "I'm sure you shared a wonderful life with him."

"We had some hard times but we stuck together through it all. We got a lot of bills, then raising that boy of ours really put a strain, then when he got sick with that cancer. But he worked every day, trying to make a good living for me and the kids. There wasn't a lazy bone in his body. He was a good provider."

"I still care for my wife."

"Then why don't you go back to her?"

"It's really complicated, Pearl. We've gone our separate ways. We're still good friends."

"It's none of my business anyway," she said. "I didn't mean to pry."

"You weren't doing that. We were just sharing thoughts on our marriages. I appreciate you telling me about you and Frank. I wish Alice and I could have had the same kind of relationship. Some things aren't meant to be."

"At least you're speaking to each other. My cousin Berniece divorced her husband and they haven't talked to each other in twenty years. She still bad mouths him. I told her to let bygones be bygones, but she still goes on and on about him. And you know, I didn't think Charlie was such a bad fellow. He was friendly to me and Frank, and even helped us out a time or two here at the motel. He left after they divorced and no one has seen or heard from him since. They didn't have children. That was good. Divorce isn't good on children. You know what I mean?"

"Unfortunately, I do," Micah said with a sigh. "My son Ben is upset with me now because I can't attend all his sports activities. He just doesn't understand."

"Maybe you don't understand, Micah. That boy needs his daddy to be around for him."

"Was Frank around for your son?"

"Frank did all he could for Johnny but that boy got in the wrong crowd. He started smoking that dope when he was in junior high school. Frank did everything he could do to set that boy straight. Now Frank didn't care for sports like I do, but he would go to all those ball games and buy Johnny baseball gloves, footballs and basketballs. We even took Johnny to see the preacher but that didn't do any good."

"I'm sorry to hear that," Micah said. "It's not easy raising a child."

"I've been talking your ear off," she said while putting the cups back on the tray. "I bet you get tired of talking to this old woman."

"Hardly," Micah said with a smile. "I've enjoyed talking to you. You've been wonderful company. You've been a great nurse, too."

"Well, I'd better get back to the office. I may have some messages for me. I've also got some rooms to get cleaned," she said at the door. "I'll be back a little later to check on those feet."

"Thank you, Pearl."

Pearl opened the curtain halfway across the window, like she had done it the previous day, before leaving.

Micah opened the suitcase and took out a pair of socks and slowly tugged them over his feet. He slid his feet into the tennis shoes, tying them loosely, and took a few steps around the room. It brought a painful grin to his face.

Forty-five

Micah walked carefully to his car and opened the trunk and picked up the package of shirts that he had bought in Charleston. He glanced down toward the office but didn't see Pearl. There were no other cars in the parking lot.

He went back into his room and put on a gray flannel shirt. He bought it to go with a western look but the tennis shoes definitely detracted from the desired image. But he liked wearing something different than the T-shirts he wore the past few days. He was ready to go out and see more of the city, even if it was only going to be through the car window.

It was clear outside although the wind was getting up a little and causing a chill in the air. He pulled out of the motel and drove east toward the downtown area. He wasn't looking for anything in particular, simply wanting to get a flavor of the historic town. He drove on River Street, along the Savannah River, and then turned off to view some of the city's 18th century architecture.

He returned to the motel two hours later, pulling up in front of the office. He went inside and rang the bell on the counter. Pearl peeked out of the curtain a second later.

"I was wondering where you went," she said.

"You didn't think I was going to skip out of here without paying did you?" he said with a smile.

"Now you know better than that," she said with an elfish grin. "I knew you'd be back."

"So what are you doing tonight?"

"I'm working," she said. "What did you think?"

"Well, I was wondering if you could shut down for a couple of hours and let me take you out to dinner?"

A thoughtful look came over Pearl's face.

"You want to take me out for dinner?"

"Why not? It's the least I can do for taking care of me the past couple of days. I want to show my gratitude."

"Oh Micah, you don't have to do that."

"I know I don't have to," he said. "I want to. So are we going to have a date?"

"Hmm, well let me call one of my cousins," she said with a bright smile. "Can I let you know a little later?"

"You'll know where to reach me," he said. "Just call me and tell me the best time and where you want to go."

Micah gave her a playful wink and walked out the door. He went back to his room, where Pearl had already made up the bed and tidied up the area. He slowly took off the tennis shoes, then lay back on the bed, his head propped up on the pillow against the headboard. He picked up *a Reader's Digest* from the nightstand, but dozed off within fifteen minutes. He was awakened two hours later by the phone.

"Micah?"

"Yes."

"This is Pearl."

"I know it's you," he said with a chuckle. "So what time are we going out?"

"My cousin Sally said she could come over about seven or so and could stay here for a couple of hours. Is that okay?"

"That's fine. So where do you want to eat?"

"Would it be any trouble to drive to a restaurant near the ocean?"

"Pearl, you just name the place and that's where we'll go."

"Frank used to take me to this little seafood restaurant on the other side of Savannah. I haven't been there in years. It's the Old Cove Inn."

"You call me when cousin Sally arrives and we'll be on our way."

"Okay, Micah," she said with a lightness in her voice.

Micah got out of bed and turned on the television. He watched the end of a *Bonanza* episode, and then the local news. When it was over, he went to the bathroom and brushed his teeth and combed his hair. He then sat down on the chair, and picked up a two-day-old newspaper while awaiting Pearl's call.

The phone rang about 7:15. Pearl said she was ready to go. Micah put on the dark blue suit coat that he wore to Cora's funeral and a white dress shirt, jeans and tennis shoes. He drove down to the office and went inside for Pearl. She came out from behind the curtain wearing a dark red print dress, low heels and had her hair neatly pulled back in a bun.

"You very look very nice," Micah said warmly.

Sally came out after Pearl. She was a few years younger and slender. She barely made eye contact with Micah.

"I'd like you to meet Micah," Pearl said, turning to Sally. "He's stayed here for a few days because of sore feet."

"Hi," Sally said softly with a smile.

"It's a pleasure to meet you," Micah said. "Pearl has taken good care of me. I wouldn't be standing here right now if it wasn't for her. I'd probably still be in bed."

"Oh, Micah," Pearl said. "You give me too much credit."

"Not enough." he said. "Are you ready to go?"

"Yes," Pearl said. "Sally, we should be back in a couple of hours."

"Take your time, Pearl," Sally said. "You have a good time. It was nice to meet you, Micah."

"Bye, now" Micah said. "We'll be back a little later."

Micah opened the door for Pearl, and they walked out to the Probe, where he unlocked the passenger door and let her in.

"This is going to be fun," Micah said after he got in and turned the key to the ignition. Pearl gave him directions to the restaurant and it took them twenty-five minutes to get there. It was dark when they arrived, but they could hear the pounding of the waves on the shore. They walked about 100 yards past some small buildings and bushes, then the great expanse of the Atlantic Ocean was before them. A full moon cast a glimmering glow across the deep water.

"This is simply beautiful," Micah said, slowly looking up and down the shoreline. "I can see why you wanted to come here."

"Frank and I loved it here," Pearl said serenely. "We would come out here and just sit for hours. It was so peaceful. It hasn't changed a bit."

"And you haven't been here since he died?"

"At first, I didn't want to because I was afraid it would bring back memories that were too close to my heart because I missed him so. Then I guessed time just passed by and I couldn't get away from the motel to get here."

"I'm glad you asked me to bring you," Micah said. "It makes this a very special evening."

Pearl took a hold of Micah's forearm and started walking back toward the restaurant. Micah glanced down at her, noticing tears welling up her in eyes.

"Let's go eat now," she said. "I'm starving."

Micah ordered a bottle of white wine to go with their dinner. Pearl ordered a sampler plate, something she'd always done with Frank, while Micah had a dinner salad and baked potato. The dimly-lit restaurant was nearly full, mostly with couples talking quietly over candlelight. A small fire cackled in the fireplace.

"You're missing out on some good seafood," she teased.

"I'm sure I am but once a veggie, always a veggie," he said with a chuckle.

"You know something, Micah," Pearl said, "I may just sell that motel and do what you're doing."

"Are you serious?" he said, arching an eyebrow.

"I am," she said. "I'm not getting any younger. I'd like to get out and do a few things. I'd like to go see my daughter in New York. I really miss not seeing those grandkids. And I would even like to visit my boy in Kentucky. I know he must get lonesome up there."

"That's a good idea," Micah said. "Do you think you could sell the motel?"

"I've had some of those real-estate folks come around once in awhile asking me if I'd be willing to sell it. I think one of those big hotel outfits would like to come in and tear my little place down and build a new place."

"Would that bother you?"

"Micah, I'll tell you the honest truth. It used to bother me because Frank and me had put so much of our time here. But the more I think about it, those are all good memories. They can't take away those memories. You know what I mean?"

"That's a good way to look at it. Perhaps it's about time for you to spend some time on yourself rather than working seven days a week."

"They've got a new place for senior citizens to live. I could move in there. They've got everything you need in those apartments. Kitchen. Bathroom. Living room. Bedroom. They even got a nurse there when you get sick."

"That does sound nice," Micah said. "Do you think they have room for a forty-two-year-old?"

They laughed. Micah then picked up his glass of wine and motioned for her to do the same.

"Here's to Pearl and her future plans," he said. "May everything turn out right for her." They tapped their glasses together, then took a sip of wine.

The waitress brought their food. Pearl's plate was loaded with shrimp, scallops and whitefish along with coleslaw and hush puppies.

"Now Micah, if you get hungry, you eat some of my fish," she said.

"Thanks for the offer," Micah said, taking a knife and fork to cut up his salad.

"When are you leaving?"

"I think I'll be going in the morning. My feet feel a lot better. It's no problem for me to drive."

"Will you be going back to Cincinnati?"

"I will. When I first got to Savannah, I thought I'd end up driving all the way to Key West in Florida. Now I think it's time to go home. I've had a few good days to think about a lot of things."

"Are you going back to that ex-wife and kids?"

"Uh, yes and no. I'll be going back to see them, but not to get back with her."

"I guess you know better," Pearl said, unable to hide a look of disappointment. "I'm sure you've got your reasons."

"I want to be more of a father to the kids," he said. "I don't know if you can understand this or not, but my ex-wife and I don't love each other anymore. We like each other but not to the point where we want to spend the rest of our lives together. It wouldn't be fair to either of us to try to do something like that."

"You're probably right," she said. "You just take good care of those children. You can't give them too much love."

"I'll try to do that," he said.

Pearl ordered a slice of pecan pie with two dips of vanilla ice cream for dessert. Micah got a cup of coffee.

"Frank never wanted much dessert," she said. "He would always take a bite from the pie and a dip of ice cream."

After they finished, Micah drove down the coastline for several miles while Pearl sat quietly and gazed out the window. They returned to the motel at 9:30. Three cars were parked in front of units. Sally was sitting behind the counter listening to a radio program about relationships.

"I'm sorry we're a little late," Pearl said.

"It's no problem," Sally said. "It's been real quiet around here except for three customers. The telephone hasn't even rung. Did you have a nice time?"

"Oh, Sally, it was just the way it was when Frank used to take me," Pearl said almost breathlessly. "It was wonderful."

Pearl turned and looked at Micah, who was standing at the doorway.

"Thank you so much," she said with a gentle smile. "I'll never forget this evening."

"I'll never forget it either," he said. "You were the perfect date."

Pearl walked back to him and gave him a gentle hug. He put his arms around her and kissed her softly on the forehead.

"I need to go now and get to bed since I'll be leaving early," Micah said. "Thanks again for watching the place for Pearl."

"I'm glad I was able to," Sally said. "Good night."

"Good night, Micah," Pearl said. "I'll see you in the morning."

"Good night," he said, smiling at both of them as he stepped out the door and went to his car.

Forty-six

Micah woke up before sunrise the following morning. He removed the bandages from his heels and stepped into the shower. His heels tingled in the water. The swelling had gone down and he was able to move his ankle back and forth. After stepping out of the shower, he shaved, brushed his teeth and combed his damp hair straight back. He put on a pair of new jeans, shirt, socks, and tennis shoes. He was anxious to hit the road back to Ohio.

Gazing out the front door he noticed a light shining out of the motel office. The alarm clock showed 6:20. The three other cars were still parked in front of their units. He finished packing, then carried everything out and placed it in the trunk of his car. He got into the car and drove slowly to the front of the office. He got out and left the motor running.

Pearl was behind the curtain when he walked in. A few seconds later, she peeked out and frowned.

"What are you doing here so early?" she asked, wearing a pink housecoat and white slippers. "I was going to bring you some breakfast."

"I've got a long drive ahead of me and I need to get on the road early."

"Well, I've already fixed it. Can you stay for a few minutes and eat?"

Micah glanced up at the wall clock. It was 6:30.

"Okay, but I need to get out of here by seven," he said. "Let me go back out and turn off the engine."

When he returned, she motioned for him to come through the curtain to her compact apartment. The kitchen table only had room for two chairs. Although the kitchen was cramped, it was tidy and nothing was out of place. She took the scrambled eggs off the four-burner gas stove and divided them up on their plates on the counter. She also made two stripes of bacon for herself.

"Can I help?" Micah asked while sitting at the table.

"Well, you can pour the coffee," she said. "The cups are in the middle cabinet."

As Micah took care of the coffee, Pearl put their plates on the table and got out the silverware and margarine. Two pieces of toast popped up in the toaster, which she placed on Micah's plate, then put two more slices in for herself. She poured a small amount of milk into a cup for Micah's coffee.

"I'm really going to miss these breakfasts," Micah said as they sat down.

"You know you're always welcome down here," she said as she got up to get her toast.. "By the way, I'm going to miss your company."

"You'll have to come up and visit me in Cincinnati."

"You'd better watch what you say because this old lady may take you up on it."

"I'm serious, Pearl. I do hope that you will think about coming up. Didn't you say you were going to do some traveling?"

"Then I may just do that then. Would you take me to see the Reds?"

"Of course," Micah said with a smile. "And maybe they'll be playing the Braves. Wouldn't that be neat?"

"How are those feet of yours?" she asked.

"They're still a little tender but not nearly as bad as they were when I first got here. I can get around pretty well now."

"You better take care of them. Do you want me to wrap them up before you go?"

"I think they'll be all right. The main thing is not walking too much. I'll be driving most of the time."

Pearl got up and warmed their coffee, and took away their plates and put them in the sink. Micah glanced up at the kitchen clock above the stove and saw that it was almost seven.

"I need to be going," he said, taking a final sip of coffee. "I want to get on the road before the rush hour."

"You can't stay another day?" Pearl asked sadly.

"I really need to be going. Some people in Cincinnati are probably wondering what happened to me."

They got up and Micah followed her to the office. He went to the other side of the counter as she took out his bill.

"You owe $63," she said.

"Are you sure? I was here three nights. That can't be right."

"I know how to add," she said, giving him a mock glare.

Micah took a $100 bill from his billfold and handed it to her.

"Keep the change," he said.

"I don't think so, Mr. Stewart."

"That includes the medical care and food you brought to my room."

"I didn't expect to be paid for that."

"I know," Micah said. "That's why you're so special."

Pearl's face puckered up and tears began to well in her eyes dark brown eyes. Micah felt a lump began to form in his throat.

"I've got to go," he said. "Come around here and let me give you a hug."

Pearl walked slowly from around the counter with her arms out. They hugged for a few seconds before she reached up and kissed him on the cheek. Micah blinked his eyes a couple of times to keep the tears from coming, then headed for the front door.

"Bye, Pearl," he said as his voice slightly cracked with emotion.

"Good bye, Micah."

Micah wiped away a tear running down his cheek as he walked to his car. As he backed out, he waved at her as she hovered by the door. She stepped out outside and waved back, standing there until he had pulled out of the parking lot and was out of sight.

~ * ~

Micah got on I-16 and headed toward Macon. He stopped an hour down the road in Statesboro and filled up his gas tank. He reached Macon by 10:30, and then he took I-75 that would lead him to Cincinnati.

The weather was sunny through Georgia, although the traffic was congested around Atlanta. He drove until late afternoon, stopping at a Holiday Inn in Knoxville to spend the night.

After checking in, he ate supper in the hotel restaurant, then went back to his room and watched a pay-per-view movie. It was still too early to go to bed, so he picked up the phone and called Josh. This time he reached him in his apartment.

"So where are you now?" Josh asked.

"I'm in Knoxville. I should be back tomorrow afternoon. How's everything been going?"

"About the same. Cincinnati and Xavier have played a couple basketball games. The Bengals are still trying to get in the playoffs. That's about it."

"How's Tammy?"

"She's fine. She been working her butt off at the hospital but other than that she's doing well. Have you given much thought to the book proposal?"

"I have," Micah said. "It sounds awfully tempting. I want to give it a little more thought. Is that okay?"

"I'd like to know something in the next few weeks," Josh said. "I may even be able to come up with a little more advance money."

"That'd be nice."

"Just between us, my boss wants this to be a model book for some other cities with pro sports teams. If this goes over well, we'll look into Chicago, Cleveland, and Detroit and branch out to other cities."

"Would I have to live in Cincinnati or work at the newspaper?"

"You thinking about leaving?"

"I didn't say that," Micah said. "It was just a question."

"I don't think it would be a problem where you wrote it. The main thing would be able to keep the deadline."

"Well, Josh, I may as well tell you that I'm thinking about leaving the newspaper. That was one of the reasons behind this little trip. You know how unhappy I've been the past few years."

"I knew you were getting tired of the grind but I thought you'd snap out of it. But I can understand why you'd like to move on to something else."

"That's just between us," Micah said. "I may still remain at the paper. I need to talk to Spencer about a few things. I may even ask them to let me take a year's sabbatical. I'm still looking at different options right now."

"Well, give it a lot of thought," Josh said. "We'll discuss it more when you get back if you want to. All I can advise now is not to rush into anything that you might regret a little later on."

"Oh, don't worry about that friend. I've been thinking about these things for quite a while. I'm just getting near the end of the process where I need to make some definite decisions and get on with my life."

"Give me a call when you want to talk about the book."

"I will," Micah said. "It will probably be in a few days. I need to get off here now."

"Take care and drive safely," Josh said. "Bye."

Micah put down the receiver and lay back on the bed, his hands behind his head. He closed his tired eyes and drifted off into a light sleep. He was awakened a little later when a hotel guest banged a suitcase against his door.

Micah got up, took off his pants and shirt, and turned off the lights. He got under the cover and quickly fell back asleep.

Forty-seven

A cold rain greeted Micah about fifty miles south of Cincinnati and got heavier as he approached the city. He didn't have an umbrella when he pulled into his apartment parking lot. Instead he held his coat over his head as opened the trunk and took out the suitcase, then walked as fast as his sore heels would let him to the apartment. Newspapers were stacked inside the storm door and he kicked them inside as he stepped into the apartment.

Although he had been gone for only a week, and there had been times when he had been away for longer stretches of time, the apartment seemed different to him when he turned on the light switch. Everything was as he had left it, but it didn't seem like home. It felt more like another motel room.

The answering machine light was blinking but Micah ignored it and went to the mailbox outside the apartment. He brought back a handful of mail, but nothing that immediately caught his eye that he should open. He hadn't eaten since breakfast in

Knoxville, and it was only mid-afternoon, but he was getting hungry. There wasn't anything in the refrigerator that appealed to him. The milk had soured and the bread on the counter was moldy. He knew Ben and Annie would be getting home from school. He picked up the phone and called the house but there was no answer.

He went back to the bedroom and took off his clothes and got into the shower. His heels still felt the tingle from the water but he was able to put more motion into his ankles. After toweling off, he took out a small pair of scissors and trimmed his beard. He put some gel on his hair and slicked it back, then put on a blue shirt and khaki pants.

In the living room, he sat on the arm of the sofa and touched the message button on the answering machine. There was a message from Spencer wanting to see how he was doing, one from Ben apologizing for being upset with him about the practice, and from Josh about the book proposal.

It occurred to Micah that he should call Pearl and let her know that he made it safely to Cincinnati. He took her number out of his wallet and dialed. She answered on the second ring.

"Pearl's Motel," she said. "This is Pearl speaking. May I help you?"

"Do you provide medical care of folks with sore feet?"

"Micah! I've been worried sick about you. Are you home now?"

"Yes. I got back about an hour ago."

"That's good to hear."

"So how are you?"

"It's about the same as always. Nothing much ever changes around here."

"Are you still thinking about putting the place up for sale?"

"Believe it or not, but I called a real-estate man today. He's going to come out here in the morning and look the place over. I may just go through with it."

"Good for you, Pearl. I'm sure those grandkids would support you. Will you let me know what you plan to do?"

"I've got your number right here in front on me," she said. "I took it off your check-in form when you left. I was about ready to call you. I wasn't sure if you had forgotten about me."

"Pearl, how could I ever forget you?"

"You better not!" she said with a laugh.

"Well, I've got a few more calls to make to let folks know I'm back in town," he said. "I'll check back with you in a few days. Bye now."

"Bye, Micah."

A smile came over Micah's face after he put down the receiver and he felt warm all over. He couldn't ever recall making a close friend in such a short period of time. That was certainly a benefit of the trip.

Micah dialed Alice's number again, and this time Annie answered.

"How's my little sweetheart?"

"Daddy! Are you home?"

"I got back a little while ago. Where have you been?"

"Mom had to go talk to one of Ben's teachers after school. He's not doing too good in math."

"Is mom at home?"

"She's down in the basement doing some laundry. Do you want to talk to her?"

"Yes, sweetie."

Annie put the receiver down and walked to the top of the basement stairs. "Mom! Mom! Daddy's on the phone!" she yelled. "He wants to talk to you."

After a short pause, Annie picked up the phone, "She'll be here in a minute, Daddy."

"Thanks," he said with a chuckle.

Micah flipped through the mail while waiting for Alice, sorting the bills from the junk mail. Tucked in the middle of it all was a small envelope from Cora's parents.

"Hello" Alice said.

"I'm back," Micah said. "I just wanted to check on you and the kids."

"How was your trip?"

"Very relaxing, except for the feet but they're better now. So what's up with Ben?"

"He wasn't doing some of his math homework. He's been so busy with other things that he hasn't been putting in the effort at school. I think I got it straightened out today. He knows if his work doesn't improve then there'll be no more basketball."

"Let me know if I can help," Micah said. "I think you're doing the right thing. Any problems with Annie?"

"Nope. She's getting straight A's."

"Another reason I called was I was wondering if you and the kids had plans for tonight. I thought I could drop by and take all of you out for pizza or whatever."

"Hmm, would you mind just taking the kids?"

"That's fine. Are you feeling all right? Any problem?"

"Actually, Micah, I'm having dinner with a real-estate agent."

"It's not the married guy in the office is it?"

"No, it's not him," she said with a laugh. "I met this man at a meeting this week. I've known him for a couple of years. His wife died last year. He's a very nice man."

"That's good," he said. "Do I sound possessive?"

"Yes, but a good kind of possessive."

"Will it be all right to pick up the kids around 6:30?"

"That's good. I'll be going out at seven and should be back home at nine or so."

"I'll see you in a few hours then," Micah said. "Bye."

"Good bye."

Micah opened the card from Cora's parents. It was a thank-you note for the flowers and had a few words from Lois Hampton.

Dear Micah,

I want to thank you for attending Cora's funeral. The flowers were thoughtful and beautiful. It was nice to meet you. Now we know why Cora thought so much of you.

Sincerely,
Lois Hampton

Micah held the note for a few seconds, then put it back in the envelope. He brushed away a tear as he lay back on the sofa and closed his eyes. His thoughts raced back to Cora, those few special moments they spent together, and then the tragic news of her death and her funeral. So much had happened in so little time.

He drifted off to sleep, awakened by the ringing of the telephone.

"Hello," he said.

"Dad?"

"Yes, Ben. What is it?"

"It's 6:45. We thought you'd be here fifteen minutes ago."

"Oops!" Micah said, lifting himself off the sofa. "I'm sorry. I fell asleep. I'll be there in about twenty minutes."

Micah put down the receiver, put on his coat and headed out the door. He went to the Probe, and was on the highway before he realized that his other car was sitting in the lot. He figured the children would like the sportier car. Alice had already left when he got to their house. He left the car running in the driveway as he went to the front door. Ben and Annie were sitting in the living room, watching TV, but had their coats on.

"Mom had a date tonight," Ben said sarcastically on the way to the pizza restaurant.

"Now there's nothing wrong with that," Micah said. "Your mom deserves a life as much as you do. She just can't stay around the house all the time and take you kids all over the place."

"He seems real nice," Annie said.

"I'm sure he is," Micah said.

"Where did you get the car?" Ben asked.

"Do you like it" Micah said.

"It's kinda neat," Ben said.

"It's a rental car," Micah said. "I thought I'd give you kids a ride in it before I take it back tomorrow."

After they ordered the pizza, Micah talked with Ben about school work and the importance of balancing time. Although he couldn't tell him, Ben was following in Micah's footsteps as far as school was concerned. Micah had been an underachiever until he went to college, then being around Alice got him more focused on class work.

"Are you going to be able to come to the game in the morning?" Ben said with a hopeful look on his face. "It's at eleven."

"I'll be there," Micah said with a smile. "And I'll try to be at every practice and game from now on. But you have to promise to work hard in school? Deal?"

"It's a deal," Ben said, beaming a big smile as they shook hands.

Alice was already at home by the time Micah got back with the children. He let them out in the driveway, and waited until he could see her letting them through the front door.

Micah drove back to his apartment. He went straight to bed, falling asleep a few minutes after laying his head on the pillow.

Forty-eight

"Okay, what's the offer?" Micah asked Josh during lunch at Big Shots on Monday. "I'm ready to listen."

"Good," Josh said with a smile. "As I told you, we want to do a professional sports history of Cincinnati. It will be all-inclusive. We want something in the 70,000-word range with lots of photos. You'd have eighteen months to research and write it. That would give us time to get it out for the Christmas season two years from now."

"How much of an advance?"

"Would $75,000 be enough?"

"I could live with that," Micah said. "How come my other books were worth only $5,000 advances?"

"You should have bargained!" Josh said over the noisy lunchtime crowd. "Not that it would have gotten you any more money. But this is a big project. My boss wants it as a springboard to similar books in other major-league towns."

"And I wouldn't have to live in Cincinnati?"

"Well, I guess not, but I'd hate to see you leave. Are you thinking about moving?"

"It's a thought but nothing that I've acted on. I just wanted to clear it with you."

"So what do you think? Do you want to write it?"

"Yes," Micah said as a smile slowly came over his face. "I'm ready to do something a little different, and this appeals to me. I've given it a lot of thought and I'm excited about it."

"I know you've been restless the past few years. That's one reason I recommended you to my boss."

"I want to do other things and have time to do things for myself. After I got back from Savannah, I took the kids out for pizza. The next morning I helped out at Ben's basketball game. And tomorrow night, I'm going to his practice. Annie has a school play on Thursday that I'm going to attend. If I were working right now, I'd miss both activities. I'm tired of that."

"I understand," Josh said. "So when are you going to tell the newspaper?"

"After we're finished, I'm going to stop over at the paper and talk to Spencer. He's been good to me and I'm not going to keep him hanging over this. I really don't think he's going to be too surprised."

"You seem a lot more relaxed. That trip must have really done you a lot of good."

"It was great just to get out and clear my head. I was getting to a low point and then Cora died. I didn't know if I could go on anymore. But spending a few days away from here helped me get things in perspective. And I met the most delightful woman in Savannah."

"A woman?" Josh said, arching his eyebrows. "Anything serious?"

"Serious in the sense that I made a very dear friend," Micah said. "Her name is Pearl and she owns a motel there. She's in her seventies. She took care of me after I got the blisters on my heels.

Whether she realized it or not, she made me think about my life and what's important."

After they finished their meals, Josh told Micah that he would have the contract drawn up for him to sign in a few days. Josh picked up the tab. "It's a business expense for one of our authors," he said.

Micah drove to the newspaper office, his first time at the building since Cora was murdered. Much like his apartment, the place almost seemed foreign to him as he entered the front door. Although he noticed several familiar faces, the newspaper had set up a security booth for visitors to sign in. Micah was sent to personnel to get an identification card to wear on his clothing.

He took the elevator to the newsroom. When he stepped out, there was some activity as copy editors were beginning to show up to read copy and begin layout of the newspaper. Spencer was sitting in his office with one of his assistants, going over the placement of several stories. Micah caught his eye, and he silently mouthed that it would be a few more minutes before he could talk to him. Micah strolled over to the mailboxes, where he pulled out a stack of mail. He went through about twenty pieces, all press releases, and tossed them all in the trash before walking over and sitting down next to a computer terminal to check e-mail. There were sixty-seven emails, mostly from the company's human resources office about various benefits. He scrolled down the list, deleting every one until it was empty.

"It's good to see you!" Spencer said walking up to him. "I was beginning to worry about you. I called Alice last week and she told me about your foot problems while in Savannah. I can see you're getting around pretty good now."

"It's all healed now," Micah said while standing up. "Can we talk in your office?"

"Sure," Spencer said. "I've got a few minutes before the afternoon budget meeting."

"This shouldn't take too long."

"I hope it's nothing serious," he said with a half-hearted laugh. Spencer sat down behind his desk as Micah closed the door. The office had newspapers stacked in the corner and books placed haphazardly in a metal two-shelf bookcase. Paperwork was strewn across his desk, giving the impression of a very disorganized person, but Micah knew that Spencer was always on top of things.

"I guess this might be serious," Micah said, clearing his throat. "I've decided to leave the newspaper."

"What?" Spencer said, his eyes opening wide. "I don't know what to say."

"Spence, you've been more than fair to me. I've thought about what I want to do with my life, and I need to make some changes. I didn't want to become a half-assed sports columnist for the paper. That's what would happen if I stayed."

"To be honest, I sensed that you were getting a little tired of the routine, even getting into a little rut. But I thought that taking some time off would help you get refocused."

"It did. Now I know what I want to do."

"Can you tell me what that is?"

"I can't say too much right now except that I'll be writing a book. I'm also thinking about some business opportunity."

"Micah, I appreciate you being up front with me," Spencer said. "Do me a favor?"

"What's that?"

"Would you request a sabbatical, just in case things don't work out? If you do that, then I can bring you back in your old position. If you just resign, then there's no guarantee for you if things don't work out in your new venture."

"That's awfully generous of you, Spence. I'll do that."

One of the editors tapped on Spencer's door, pointing to his watch to let him know that it was time for the news budget meeting.

"They're calling me," Spencer said, pulling his chair away from the desk.

Micah stood up, and when Spencer walked up to him, they shook hands.

"You know I'm going to miss you," Spencer said.

"I'll miss you, too."

Spencer opened the door, and headed to the news meeting as if nothing had happened. He was a newspaperman, and had a newspaper to put out.

Micah felt emptiness inside as he walked out of the sports department. There were times in the past that he thought that he would spend his entire career at the newspaper. But he knew in his heart that it was time to move on.

Meet Michael Embry

Michael Embry is the author of three nonfiction sports books and four novels, including *A Confidential Man* for Wings ePress in 2008. His career includes more than 30 years in journalism as a reporter, sportswriter and editor. He lives in Frankfort, Ky., with his wife, Mary, and Yorkshire terriers, Baxter and Bucky.

Other Works From The Pen Of
Michael Embry

Shooting Star, Jesse Christopher finds out that it's not easy being the new kid in school, no matter how well you play basketball. When discovered shooting hoops at a school playground by a high school coach, Jesse seems to be the missing piece to the puzzle for a team that aspires to win the Kentucky state championship.

But Jesse faces an array of problems in his new environment as he tries to make friends in the classroom and become part of the school's close-knit basketball team. Can Jesse overcome the obstacles and lead his team to a state high school basketball title?

A Confidential Man, Sports columnist Chase Elliott has earned a reputation around the newsroom of being a person that others can confide their deepest problems. What happens when someone goes over the line? And what if a fellow worker dies from mysterious circumstances?

Elliott tries to deal with all the rumors and innuendos circulating around the newsroom while coming to terms with his own sense of trustworthiness and high ethical standards. Can he discover the truth without betraying confidences?

<u>Foolish Is The Heart</u>, Brandon Wilkes is a 45-year-old sports columnist who has never settled down to the point of marriage. At first it was his career that caused him to go the bachelor route. He became a respected and successful sportswriter. As he grew older, he seemed content to be single the remainder of his life. That's not to say that he didn't have relationships or that women didn't pursue him. He just didn't want to make a permanent commitment to a woman.

He was content with the way things had been in his life. Going to work, meeting friends at the local pub and covering various sports events for Kentucky Sports Weekly. His easy-going lifestyle undergoes changes as some big events happen in his personal and professional life. Brandon tries to come to terms with the direction his life is heading and trying to deal with those things he believes to be important.

<u>A Long Highway</u>, Micah Stewart is in the throes of a mid-life crisis. He's bored with his job as a sports writer. While he maintains a good relationship with his ex-wife and children, he feels unfulfilled in many areas of his life.

A random act of violence in the workplace forces Micah to hit the road in search of meaning to his life. Will he find enlightenment? Can he find happiness again? Can he find contentment at the end of the long highway?

The Touch, A woman in an abusive relationship finds strength and romance from a single dad.

The Bully List, Two boys get fed up being picked on and decide to come up with a list of things to get even with the bullies.

Old Ways and New Days, John Ross discovers there are many adjustments he has to make as he moves from the ranks of the employed to retirement, or as some refer to it, the pajama club.

Darkness Beyond the Light - Retirement plans are put on hold for empty-nesters John and Sally Ross when they discover a dark side about their son.

New Horizons - John and Sally Ross take a long-overdue vacation to Budapest to get away from it all but encounter headaches and heartaches on their journey that make them wish they were back home.

Make Room for Family - John Ross returns from vacation to a big surprise when he is greeted by his brother- and sister-in-law, who seem to have made it their home.

Reunion of Familiar Strangers - John and Sally Ross venture off to attend his 50th high school reunion, a gathering of former friends who seem more like strangers.

Cradle of Conflict - John and Sally Ross encounter joy, tragedy, and conflict after the arrival of their baby granddaughter.

A Message to Our Readers

Enjoy this book?

You can make a difference.

As an independent publisher, Wings ePress, Inc. does not have the financial clout of the large New York publishers. We can't afford large magazine spreads or subway posters to tell people about our quality books.

But we do have something much more effective and powerful than ads. We have a large base of loyal readers.

Honest reviews help bring the attention of new readers to our books.

If you enjoyed this book, we would appreciate it if you would spend a few minutes posting a review on the site where you purchased this book or on the Wings ePress, Inc. webpages at:

https://wingsepress.com/

Thank You

**VISIT OUR WEBSITE
FOR THE FULL INVENTORY
OF QUALITY BOOKS**:

http://www.wings-press.com

*Quality trade paperbacks and downloads
in multiple formats,
in genres ranging from light romantic
comedy to general fiction and horror.
Wings has something
for every reader's taste.
Visit the website, then bookmark it.
We add new titles each month!*

www.ingramcontent.com/pod-product-compliance
Lightning Source LLC
LaVergne TN
LVHW011801060526
838200LV00053B/3644